.

Balboa Press books may be ordered through booksellers or by contacting:

Balboa Press
A Division of Hay House
1663 Liberty Drive
Bloomington, IN 47403
www.balboapress.com.au
AU TFN: 1 800 844 925 (Toll Free inside Australia)
AU Local: 0283 107 086 (+61 2 8310 7086 from outside Australia)

Interior Graphics/Art Credit: John Wamsley

Print information available on the last page.

ISBN: 978-1-5043-2292-8 (sc)
ISBN: 978-1-5043-2295-9 (e)

Balboa Press rev. date: 10/26/2020

# CONTENTS

# PROLOGUE

Sometimes society forgets. Not that John Wamsley would lose sleep over this, for his aims go beyond personal elevation, but when we owe so much to one pioneering intellect, we ought to give due credit.

What started for John as a work of love has become the template for huge conservation projects all over Australia. His model of feral-proof sanctuaries is now the accepted way of saving wildlife and we owe the continued existence of more than one animal species to his work.

This authorised memoir aims to showcase his peculiar genius. Only a maverick personality could have achieved what he did in the often hostile climate of the mid twentieth century, when innovation aroused suspicion and envy.

We are enriched by those people who are different enough to see the lateral pathways and foolhardy enough to walk them.

Such are a vanishing kind.

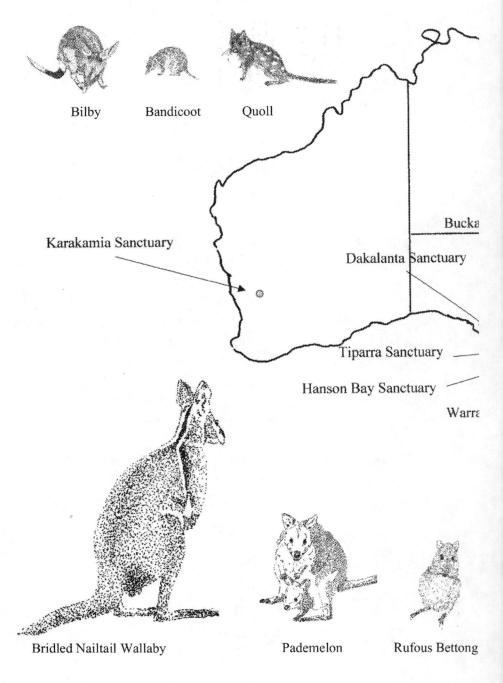

Bilby

Bandicoot

Quoll

Bucka

Karakamia Sanctuary

Dakalanta Sanctuary

Tiparra Sanctuary

Hanson Bay Sanctuary

Warra

Bridled Nailtail Wallaby

Pademelon

Rufous Bettong

*Earth Sanctuaries Projects*

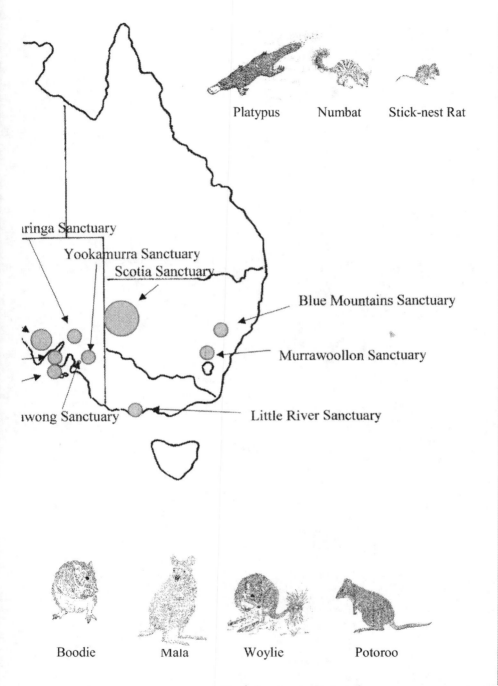

Platypus    Numbat    Stick-nest Rat

ringa Sanctuary
Yookamurra Sanctuary
Scotia Sanctuary

Blue Mountains Sanctuary

Murrawoollon Sanctuary

wong Sanctuary

Little River Sanctuary

Boodie    Mala    Woylie    Potoroo

*Earth Sanctuaries Projects*

CHAPTER ONE

# POLYMATH

LIKE MANY PEOPLE WHO KNEW John by reputation only, I was fascinated and a little intimidated to encounter him for the first time. *He* knows that *you* know who he is and there is almost a posture that he adopts to *be* that person. Perhaps this is all unconscious or imagined. John is accustomed to people reacting to him in a particular way. If they only see the cat-hat man, I'm sure it doesn't matter to him.

I heard an awe-struck bush care volunteer saying, 'Is this *the* John Wamsley?'

There is a sense of all that has gone before, as if he cannot be taken merely for the persona which exists in the present.

It didn't take long for the humour to manifest. This is the trademark of John Wamsley, the real person. The broad smile and the chance to make a quip or tell a tale. In the presence of such humour, frequently self-deprecating, I couldn't remain uncomfortable.

After a few meetings I thought it better to come clean. It had to be done some time, so out-of-the-blue I confessed to John that I owned a Persian cat.

He immediately came back with, 'Oh, I could make you a great hat out of *that* one!'

This broke any remaining ice for me. It didn't matter. What mattered was *doing something on the ground*. And we were there to take action in the most pedestrian of ways, by weeding (or, as John would say, 'gardening') in the bush.

Once we were among the trees and the understory he would not usually stop to talk for very long, unless someone had a plant to be identified. Botany may not be John's primary skill, but he knows more than most of us in the Friends group and often provides interesting background information.

I learnt why the parasitic native vine, Cassytha pubescens, is commonly called 'Snotty Gobbles' and how John used the fruit of this plant to great advantage when giving a talk to children. And then there is the interesting weed which resembles celery but one species is, in fact, the famous poison called Water Hemlock. This poison has killed more people than any other because it gets mistaken for its edible cousin.

Beneath the canopy of trees bearing Mistletoe, I learned, the litter is richer in nutrients because a parasite like Mistletoe can afford to shed its leaves with the nutrients intact, rather than withdrawing them as non-parasitic plants do. Hence there will be a more diverse micro-flora in evidence. The bush has infinite secrets.

Smoko time brings out the thermos, biscuits and nuts, along with the stories and banter. For someone who professes not to be a 'people person', John makes a good impersonator. Some of his personal revelations are remarkably frank. It was the extraordinary stories from his life that prompted me to canvas, half seriously, the idea of a book.

Perhaps a year later, I was still thinking it was a good idea and broached the subject again. John appeared receptive and I dared to elicit a commitment.

Some of the things I want to present as part of the story are unconnected to anything in the rest of the narrative, yet they reveal much and so I include them here as an introduction.

During the tenth taped interview I asked John if he had any creative pursuits outside of his involvement with recreating natural systems. He got up from the table where we sat outside and walked over to another table where he retrieved a bulky object from its hiding place among other miscellaneous objects.

When he set it down in front of me I saw it to be a perfectly carved wooden head, about eighteen inches high, emerging from a block of black wattle and astonishingly well made, its proportions faultless.

The heavily bearded, thick-lipped and snub-nosed face had a vague resemblance to John. 'This is how I remember my grandfather,' he said.

Decades old, it stood on the table, staring at me, for the rest of the interview.

Next John asked me to follow him inside to where another object lay hidden in a corner. Here I found a second artefact, carved from wood, and which represented the only other work of art John has ever made, its workmanship flawless. Before me stood a functional spinning wheel of substantial proportions, each part carved from red gum fence posts and beautifully polished. John once used it to spin yarn from which he made a pullover.

It dates from the days of his friendship with Keith Oliphant, brother of the former governor of SA, when they had what today would be called a 'men's shed' wherein they could undertake their respective creative pursuits.

The craftsmanship left me speechless. It takes innate skill to make such an object, as well as the carved head I had already seen. To find the three dimensional form inside a piece of wood is a skill which one must be born with, yet he saw it almost as a 'throwaway' skill, scarce regarded. Just one of the many practical abilities I couldn't fail to notice.

Ability comes in some strange forms. I include a story John gave me but which is, like the fact of his wood carving, unconnected to any particular set of events. It serves to illustrate, in a very graphic way, how John's thinking went to places you or I might never go.

Giving up smoking is an unspectacular and prosaic part of self-improvement for many of us, but John turned it into a fascinating study in self-discipline and the power of the subconscious mind.

He started smoking cigarettes at sixteen before leaving home. His mother and grandmother both smoked but his father and grandfather didn't. Perhaps quite unusual for the time. John was a very 'heavy' smoker, using the strongest tobacco possible and eventually adopting a pipe. Amusingly, his grandmother encouraged him in the habit.

At age thirty-seven he gave up smoking and didn't smoke for two years. 'And for all of that two years I was dying for a cigarette. *The whole bloody time*! At the end of that time I went to a party and someone offered me a smoke and "bang" it was all over. I was back smoking again. So it's not easy to give up smoking.'

'I decided on my thirty-ninth birthday that I would give up on my fortieth birthday. I did an interview for one of the radio stations. While I was waiting to be interviewed there was another person sitting next to me on the bench. We got to chatting and he was a hypnotist. He used to hypnotise people to stop them smoking. I was interested in that because I wanted to stop smoking very badly. I asked him what it cost and it was more than I wanted to pay.

'When I got home I thought about it a lot and I thought well, I don't understand hypnotism but I'd seen people hypnotised and some people are pretty hard to hypnotise. I thought that if he could hypnotise me then why couldn't I hypnotise myself? You see? So on my thirty-ninth birthday I decided I would give up smoking on my fortieth birthday and in between I would have a smoke whenever I wanted one but while I was having that smoke I would say to myself over and over again, "You're not enjoying this. You don't want a smoke. You don't want this." Over and over again while I was having a fag, you see?

'My birthday is on the tenth of July. I woke up on the tenth of June, a month before my fortieth birthday and I didn't feel like a smoke. I haven't had one since and I haven't felt like a smoke since. So that's how I did it. I reckon you could sell that as a method of giving up smoking and I carried a packet of fags in my pocket for probably twelve months because I knew what it was like to feel like a smoke and not have one. I get some tinglings sometimes but I say to myself, "All right, if you still feel like one in five minutes you can have one." In five minutes I will have forgotten all about it.

'It was absolutely easy. All you have to do is talk to a hypnotist. You don't have to get him to hypnotise you, *just ask him how he does it*. I didn't put myself under because I was a bit afraid I might not wake up.'

*Lateral, unique and disciplined.*

On another occasion John brought out a set of wooden blocks (called Cuisenaire Rods) in an attempt to teach me some real understanding of mathematical principles, as opposed to simply knowing, from having been told in the dim past, that one plus one equals two, and so forth.

These same wooden objects were what he used to enlighten his very young granddaughters, but it is easier to teach the young than to teach an old and rusty mind.

Recounting the time with one of his granddaughters, he says, 'Once she has handled the number one, I can proceed to number two. I then bring up the concept of addition or adding. I do this via the Cuisenaire rods by placing "one" (that's the uncoloured Cuisenaire rod) on the floor in front of her and placing another uncoloured Cuisenaire rod to the right of it and against the first. I then take the "two" Cuisenaire rod (the pink one) and demonstrate that it is the same length as the two number ones together. I tell her that we call the pink one "two". At this stage there is a bit of bedlam. She immediately begins to show me all sorts of things that can be done with Cuisenaire rods. Such as showing me two number twos make the number four, etcetera. I say, "Is 2+1 the same as 1+2?" She laughs and shows me that you just have to turn them around. They have discovered that addition is commutative (the same either way). I feel so proud. I know adults who do not understand that.'

*He then proceeded to teach them Pythagoras' theorem.*

'Of course all this happened over some time. I could only proceed after I was sure they understood so far. But after a few weeks they knew more than many university mathematics graduates. They can prove Pythagoras' theorem.'

*Pythagoras indeed*!

Finally, from his early years in New South Wales comes another example of self-diagnosis and treatment, this time to cure the extreme shyness which held him back in social situations. Notwithstanding his back-breaking regular job as a furnace-man at the Newcastle steelworks, this is what he did:

'I knew I had to do something about this. It was holding me back. So I thought, *what would be the hardest job for a shy person to do?* I decided that the thing that would terrify me the most was being a door-to-door salesman. I got a job selling encyclopaedias.

'I would get so nervous before approaching a house that I would literally vomit. But I forced myself do it. I would go up to the door and make my spiel. I became good at it, selling more encyclopaedias than anyone else. I could earn more money on a Sunday than I could in a month of shovelling in the furnace.'

The legacy of that experience lies in the way he will approach anyone without fear, even if it means confrontation.

John can build, repair and invent; he can write, do advanced mathematics, carve in wood, understand Botany and zoology, sell, run a multi-million dollar business or re-establish biodiversity in hopelessly degraded landscapes. Perhaps the word 'polymath' is not out of place.

All this from a man who grew up on a chicken farm and refused to pay attention at school.

CHAPTER TWO

# STRANGER IN A STRANGE LAND

SIZE MATTERS. THROUGHOUT JOHN'S ADULT life, no sensible person would physically challenge him. It is as much about a projection of authority as size, yet this inbuilt protection came from unlikely beginnings.

'I have a memory,' he says, 'though it may represent a memory of a memory rather than an actual event. I was standing up at the rail of a cot, looking at the door, wondering why no one was coming to see me. Why I had been abandoned.'

At length, his father arrived to visit him at the Camperdown Children's Hospital and overheard medical staff discussing the prognosis. *His two year old child would probably die.*

'My father decided to take me home. He thought that if I was going to die it may as well be at home. No one knew what was wrong, except that I wouldn't eat.'

A whole side of lamb regularly fed the family. His mother used *Weet-Bix* to crumb some of the meat. From the left-over crumbs on the table she saw him take a morsel of this cereal and place it in his mouth. Thereafter, she served these crumbs with every meal.

'So I gradually began to eat. But only *Weet-Bix*. I should have died, but I didn't. I survived. It's really interesting.'

His consumption of the cereal in early adult life is beyond legendary, although the Sanitarium Company didn't respond when he wrote to them about their life-saving product.

Maybe he was simply one of the lucky ones, marked for survival even if he remained thin and frail.

More than seventy years later, following a routine colonoscopy, the specialist commented on the old evidence of a twisted bowel. Here, at last, a possible explanation. Sometimes it takes that long for the penny to drop.

The condition left him truly stunted in his early years. 'I was tiny,' he says. 'At fifteen years of age I was under five feet and weighed six stone four pound. At the age of sixteen I had the minimum weight of a fourteen year old.'

*The weakling child. John at 11 years of age riding his horse Timmy.*

It is hard to believe that anyone the size of John Wamsley could ever have been small and weak, but photos from his childhood bear this out, showing a slightly built child, shorter than his younger sisters. That hidden kink in the body profoundly affected the rest of his life. Like a mathematical equation, small equals vulnerable and vulnerable equals being bullied. The memory of that treatment occurs time and again in our conversations, both on and off the taped record.

But there is another equation which, for some individuals, arises like a corollary from the first. It says that bullying begets self-reliance. Further, it engenders a hatred of bullies and, in John's case, a feeling that if people treated him that way, they could go to hell.

What others thought of him was never going to matter and there is evidence of this in so much he did. He determined not to conform and this, in the hands of a strong and intelligent person, becomes an asset. I suspect the mistrust, which the bullying generated, drove an already reclusive personality deeper into insularity, tinged with suspicion.

When John says, 'I don't like people in large numbers. I don't feel safe around people,' it seems to be at odds with his obvious social skills. He is assertive, occasionally inflexible and capable of being blunt, but at the same time generous with his attentions and always personable. When necessary, he will approach anyone, but his natural preference, freely admitted, is for his own company.

Introverts recharge from solitude. They will withdraw in order to regroup. Inability to withdraw had disastrous personal consequences for John much later, when he was thrust into the necessity of constantly being available in a professional capacity.

Now in his ninth decade, John is still a big man. Six foot two inches and solid. There is a quality of *immovability* in his features. Not in the sense of a lack of animation, for that is far from true, but more like the stolid features of a rock outcrop which has grown moss and lichen upon its surface as a reaction to the dynamic processes around it.

Certain of his physical faculties may be diminished; hearing and vision need a little help, but the mental processes are sharp, ready to break out into discourse, given the right cues. The voice is that of a born storyteller, inflected with humour and irony. The stories used to earn him free beers.

Half joking, John claims that as a child he retreated into the bush to escape his sisters. There were no less than six of them, and he was the only boy, although, as the third oldest child he knew some of his siblings only as young children. But there was something more to it. The word 'safe' entered the conversation. So slightly built, even his sisters 'beat up on' him and he wasn't allowed to hit back. Later there were other, more serious adversaries. He spoke a great deal about the bullying which dogged his school years. This became the first topic of our recorded interviews.

During the tough times between the wars, John remembers little or no affection, in common with many children of large families. Of his mother, he says, 'I don't think she had time. There were seven kids.' If not attentive, at least she was fair, and from John's older sister Marcia's account in her memoir, a resourceful, kind and wise parent.

*John's boyhood home at Niagara Park, NSW*

His father, on the other hand, treated him with complete indifference. 'I watch my son and his family today,' John says, 'and there was no way in the world I got anything like the affection he gives them. And I just assumed it was normal. That's the way it was. My old man, he just worked hard. He worked bloody hard, because it was the depression. Things were pretty tough. We were on different sides of the ball-park. He never abused me or anything, but I wasn't what my father wanted. *I was a cripple from his point of view.*

'What was the bloody good of me if I couldn't work hard? And he was very much that way. He didn't have time for anybody who wasn't "up to it". The daughters were a different matter. Each of them got a considerable inheritance while he was still alive. He bought them all a block of flats each. He never bought me anything.'

Early in the twentieth century, women were often immune to career expectations. A father scarcely had reason to be disappointed in his daughters.

A man who understands only hard work must have found it baffling that his son was off in the woods. The same woods represented to his father only a backbreaking obstacle to developing a farm and supporting a large family. The bush became the enemy and the world remained engulfed in a second 'Great War'.

*John, at twenty years of age, with his father.*

Nothing John achieved earned his father's approval, not even owning thirteen investment properties by his early twenties. This went hand-in-hand with back-breaking labour at the Newcastle Steelworks, where John developed from undersized boy to a veritable giant of a man.

John learned a lifelong lesson from a co-worker named Horrie, at the mill. Both John and Horrie lived on Lake Macquarie and both liked to fish. From Horrie, John learned the 'factor of ten' rule.

The story involves fish. Horrie's fish were always, in his estimation, 'two pounders', whereas John always described his catch, from the same source, as 'quarter pounders'. The fish were called 'Taylors'.

Men sometimes brought food to work and cooked it using the heat of the furnace. One day Horrie produced some fish for this purpose. John got the feeling 'something was up', but he knew he had to approach the subject carefully. This is how John remembers the conversation:

'What size would you call those fish, Horrie?'

'Why, these are two pounders.'

'You're a bloody liar, Horrie! All those fish together wouldn't make more than a pound and a half.'

Horrie was indignant. 'Yeah, that's if you *weigh* 'em. It doesn't matter what they weigh. *These fish are two pound Taylors.*'

John learned something about communication. What you call something isn't necessarily the same as what that thing actually is. It's not lying, but more a question of nomenclature. *The name defines the thing.* So it is about labels and perception, rather than hard reality.

Weekends selling encyclopaedias and the gruelling work of a furnace man took its toll. At 23 years of age John broke down from overwork, physically and mentally, unable to do anything except rest.

'One morning I was having my breakfast and I got these terrible pains in my chest which used to happen before I went to sell encyclopaedias and I was physically ill which happened before I went to knock on doors. I sort of said to myself, *you don't have to go and sell encyclopaedias.* I lived on the shores of Lake Macquarie. I looked out on the water and I thought, *why don't I go fishing instead of going to work?* As soon as I made that decision the pains went and I was fine. And the next morning I went fishing. And the next morning I went fishing. For six months I went fishing. I felt fantastic. I felt on top of the world again. I was ready to get into it again.

'I got sick of the taste of fish. I didn't always catch fish, I just sat in the boat. I prefer not to catch fish than to catch them because if you catch them you have to clean them! That six months changed my life completely. It taught me that I had a limit and I realized that the only thing I'd ever had in my life that I loved was the bush.'

But John felt puzzled by what had happened to him. It wasn't about depression or lack of motivation and even today a clear explanation is something he isn't able to articulate. Here presented the next mathematical problem to solve. What was going on in the human psyche?

Typically, he sought an occupation to give him an insight into the machinations of the brain.

'At the southern end of Lake Macquarie, where I used to go occasionally, was Morriset Mental Asylum. You could see it from the water. I could see people wandering around in the exercise yard and thought it was a different world. I didn't understand it. So I wandered in and asked for a job and I got one as a male nurse. And because I was a big bloke they thought that was good. I got measured up for a uniform and it suited me what they did because we used to work from 6 am to 6 pm seven days, then you'd have seven days off. It was a good job.'

What better way to get inside knowledge of the human mind than as a psychiatric nurse at the Morriset Mental Asylum. Simple. At least, if you are John Wamsley.

His first taste of nursing involved a man who, in his psychotic state, had bitten off his own tongue. During electro-convulsive therapy the resulting infection became obvious in a most gruesome way, causing John to faint. Not a good beginning, but he overcame the slight on his reputation and went on to enjoy the job.

John has intriguing things to say about the inmates of the Morriset asylum, the people who fell outside acceptable parameters.

'I got on very well with the inmates. Better than with the staff. In fact people I meet now remind me of different inmates I knew. One of the things I realized was that these people weren't really very different to the people outside. The reason they were there was because they had no one to support them. And there were two kinds of insane people there, those who were happy and those who were terrified. Most people are mad. There's no differentiation. They're all a lot of bloody lunatics. . .

'I thought they would know what was wrong with me (the hospital people) but I wasn't about to admit myself so that's why I went and got a job there instead. I learnt that there is nothing wrong with being different. *Normality is just the average of deviance'*

CHAPTER THREE

# MATHEMATICS

ONE VERY SIGNIFICANT EVENT AT Morriset sent John's life in an entirely different direction.

On night duty, while reading the Government Gazette, John realised he could earn money and have a job doing mathematics. The fact his prodigious talent had up to this time been overlooked is shameful in itself, but in those years no career guidance seems to have been forthcoming.

Echoing a modern-day self-help formula, John's approach to problem solving is to say, 'It's not *can this be done*, but *how do I do it*.' Mathematics gives him this coldly logical approach and the certainty there is a solution.

Nothing illustrates this better than the process by which he *became* a mathematician, following on from the time at Morriset. Somehow his phenomenal and innate mathematical ability counted for nothing in his family's eyes. Today he would be recognised as a prodigy and given a specially tailored education. This is how John relates the story of his approach to university:

'I called in at Newcastle University. It had just become a university. I told the man I wanted to do a mathematics degree. He said, "Oh yes, how old are you?"

'When I told him he said that as an adult I could get advanced standing and start basically where I wanted to in the course. If I passed everything

I could go on. At the end of the first year they would decide how I should proceed.

'So I thought, okay, I'd like to start in the second year of the honours degree in mathematics, and told him so.

'He laughed and said, "No, hang on, hang on, when did you last go to uni?" When I told him he said, "There's a whole gap there. You wouldn't know what you're doing."

'And I thought, *yeah, he doesn't know how good I am . . .*

'So I said, "Am I allowed to start in honours, second year?"

'He said, "Yeah, you could do that but I'm just advising you against it."

'So I said, "That's what I want to do."

'So, anyway, I went to my first lecture in mathematics. It was algebra and the lecturer was John Lambert. It was a third year algebra course because that's what you did in second year honours. And it was in abstract algebra, group theory, which I ended up getting my PhD in. And I sat there. And this was the first time I'd ever sat in a class and tried to absorb what was being said instead of trying to *not* absorb it.

'*I didn't understand a word he said, not a bloody word!*

'He could have been talking French and I would have been just as well off, so after the lecture I went to him and I said, "Look, I've got a bit of a problem. I didn't understand a word you were saying.

'And he said, "Of course you didn't, you silly bastard, you should be back in first year. That's where you start."

'I said that *I couldn't afford to waste my time. I had three kids, I needed to get on with my life.*

'I asked him to give me a list of books such that if I knew everything in them I could do this course. So he gave me the list and I bought them all at the book shop.

'I went home and I started to read them but I hate reading so I started doing the problems at the end of each chapter. I'd sit down when the kids had gone to bed and I'd start working at a desk and when the sun came up and the light started to break I'd go to bed for a couple of hours and then I'd go to uni again.

'So this went on for the whole of the first term. I thought, *I've got to give this a term and if I can't do it then I'll give up after that term.*

'But I topped all the third term exams and blew all their minds and suddenly they were saying, "Bloody hell, this bloke knows what he's doing." So after that I never had to work hard again, really, I just did it.'

John's mathematical acumen cannot be overstated. In his third year he took part in the university of NSW mathematics problem competition which was open to all students from first to fourth year. Students were given eight problems to solve. He solved seven of them and while he knew the solution to the eighth problem he couldn't easily articulate it. The problem had to do with how coins could be arranged on a surface to most efficiently cover that surface

'I couldn't prove it, but I could visualise the answer. So my answer was, "The bees solved this question many years ago."

'They ticked me as right. Bees worked out that the best way to get coverage is with a hexagon, so that's what they do. And why would they fuck up? Of course they'd know what they were doing. Evolution would have taught them to do it the most economical way. So I got all eight questions right, but that one I faked, you see. I won the competition and the person who came second only managed to answer three questions. Not only that, the person who came second was a fourth year student and I was a third year student. So from then on I was pretty hot stuff as far as they were concerned.'

The only hiccup came when he had to complete a couple of arts degree subjects in order to fulfil the technical requirements of his science degree. The first subject was economics one.

'I didn't realize that such trivialities were ever taught in a university. I was dumbfounded at how pissy it was. And of course I was a mathematician by then. I'd topped third year in mathematics.'

He recognised that all of the questions fell into one 'general case', which he wrote out, thereby demonstrating that he understood everything he needed to know. It was then just a matter of applying the 'general case' to answer all of the questions. This he did in fifteen minutes, before walking out of the exam.

'I went home and I got a call from the head of the maths department. He said, "What are you trying to prove? How the hell can you just leave after fifteen minutes? The discussion is whether you get a distinction or a fail." The problem was that passing me on my efforts would only have proven that the course was trivial.

'I told him to go back in and tell them that a pass would be okay, because I needed it, but if I got a fail they would have a court case on their hands. They gave me a pass.'

Another subject required him to read Shakespeare's 'Macbeth' and write an essay on it. Being completely averse to doing any such thing, John freely admits to getting his grade dishonestly, with help from his sister.

His doctoral thesis on Group Theory was completed at Brisbane university; he was then 30 years of age. His is the shortest thesis ever presented in the university's history and was completed in the shortest time. It took just a year, although he was obliged to remain at the university for another year due to the technical requirements.

Of his thesis, John says, 'I could have presented it as one page. I basically invented a new branch of mathematics in order to solve a problem.'

Professor Bernhard Neumann, the distinguished Professor of Mathematics at the Institute of Advanced Studies in the Australian National University, Canberra, said that John Wamsley was, *if not the best, then the second best mathematician of his generation.*

It was time to start earning a living from mathematics.

When looking into job offers, after completing the PhD, John investigated the rules in each state as they related to keeping native animals. Mathematics was never going to be the whole of his passion, although he believed it would be the whole of his career. Strange to think that without mathematics the conservation achievements might never have come about.

The vague idea of 'wanting a piece of bush in order to do something with it' became more specific. It had to do with the animals. The bush, for him, was about animals. An appreciation of the integrated role of plants in the system of life-forms came later. 'The bush for me was a place where you went to see animals.'

In this his experience differs markedly from that of most Australians, for whom the animal component is like a missing link. The animal experience is a zoo experience, not something which happens when you walk out into the bush.

Assuming sufficient numbers of animals exist in a given piece of landscape, their secretive and often nocturnal nature means they will be all but invisible. *They are active while we are asleep.* Patient, quiet observation is necessary and over huge areas it was already too late to find them, even during the years of John's boyhood.

If wildlife and mathematics was a strange or unlikely amalgam of passions it didn't seem so to John. Mathematics offered a career, but nature conservation had to be right there beside it. Sanity demanded it.

At that time, South Australia was the only state in Australia where it wasn't illegal to obtain and keep native animals.

'It wasn't exactly legal,' says John, 'but it wasn't *illegal*. When I got my PHD I got a job and I was very careful to get a job where I could do a sanctuary. I didn't have any idea of what it would be like, but that's why I came to SA. I had the intention of building it but I didn't have any intention of opening it to the public.'

Flinders University in South Australia offered a lecturing job in mathematics. Accordingly, he moved his whole family to Adelaide and pitched a tent in the campground at Belair National Park in the Adelaide Hills, while waiting for a promised house to become available as part of the job.

South Australia's climate, population size and culture were and remain very different from that of NSW. The remaining bushland close to the city is very limited, although the big advantage Adelaide has over the eastern cities is the ease and speed with which people can get out of the city into the hinterland. It is only fifteen minutes from the eastern side of the CBD to the edge of the Mount Lofty Ranges.

Settling in SA was but a short step from purchasing the land that became Warrawong, the place destined to put John's name at the forefront of the conservation movement in Australia.

However, if your name is John Wamsley, the way forward is never going to be anything but interesting, at best, and notoriously convoluted, at worst.

## CHAPTER FOUR

# THE MAKING OF AN ACTIVIST

I THOUGHT THE STORY OF WARRAWONG would be straightforward and follow a logical progression from idea to reality, but as the poet T.S. Eliot once said, 'Between the idea and the reality lies the shadow.'

Events in John's life at this time are complex, with many interlinked threads. Mathematics and nature, local government and notoriety are so jumbled together that it is hard to chronicle the events separately. Our conversations had to follow parallel lines. It is extraordinary to think that John managed to combine his role as lecturer at Flinders University with all the other major things that were going on in his life, not the least of which was being a father to three children.

The campground at Belair, where John was temporarily settled with his family, got flooded out in a rare rainfall event, but someone who knew of his plight told him of a house at Uraidla, in the Adelaide Hills.

'We had nothing. *We moved into the house with camping gear and three young kids.* The Italian neighbours used to bring us food. Bowls of spaghetti and such. I couldn't say no because obviously we needed it. They were good people. It was a good introduction to Adelaide. We were there for a month or two before the house became available near the university.'

The Wamsleys were no strangers to camping with a whole family in tow, having done this for a period of time in Canberra while John attended a mathematics seminar.

Just a few months later, in June of 1969, he purchased the 14 hectare property he named 'Warrawong', which is aboriginal for 'Water on a hillside.' Eerily, it was exactly the same size as the piece of land his father had cleared to establish an orchard. It was an old dairy, a valley with a dam at the bottom and six large, old stringy bark trees dotted about.

The indigenous understory had almost completely vanished, replaced by pasture grasses. The exception was an area of native Coral Fern which later became the basis for an artificial 'rainforest'. But viewed from the top of the hill, where the house was situated with a north facing aspect, the property presented beautifully.

'I didn't know what I wanted to do, but I knew I wanted to do *something*. It involved recreating *my bush*.' Such was the minimalist extent of his plans at the time. 'I certainly knew I couldn't live in suburbia. I knew if I did that I'd go mad. There's evidence for that because you can see how everyone who lives in suburbia now is bloody mad. You've only got to look at the news every night to see that.'

Warrawong appealed to John as a place where he could live happily, even though, when he bought it, the property was far from the kind of forested environment he had grown up with. In his mind's eye it was already transformed into a place of indigenous plants and animals.

No commercial ideas existed in relation to it. Warrawong was home, no more. Mathematics, which he loved, was meant to be John's lifetime career and he stresses that there followed a long period of stability in the teaching job when he thoroughly enjoyed what he did, in spite of the stresses created by the unusual extra-curricular activities which we will come to.

It is important to understand the state of awareness about natural systems at the time. We now take for granted certain attitudes and facts which were either not conceived of or were the province of a tiny handful of invisible amateurs and naturalists. Knowledge of the natural world remained anecdotal and poorly rendered. Perhaps the kindest thing to say is that misconceptions abounded.

'Conservation' was a word used by very few people. South Australia's national parks system scarcely represented the diversity of habitats in existence. The only large parks were in isolated mallee habitats which few members of the general public would have even heard of, with Flinders

Chase on Kangaroo Island being an exception. Little had been set aside for posterity in the Adelaide Hills and land clearance proceeded, out of sight, though on a reduced scale. In truth, after the frenzy of vegetation clearance immediately following the Second World War, little high quality agricultural land remained to be developed.

Within the mallee lands, only the existence of sand dunes in certain areas precluded farming and this led to the formation of conservation parks, while steep and rocky places were left uncleared in the hilly regions.

Animals once common over large areas were already locally extinct. In a cynical interpretation of the motivation of politicians in relation to the establishment of Flinders Chase, John suggested that the formation of that well-known sanctuary on Kangaroo Island was a trade-off to allow the guilt-free obliteration of animal species on the mainland, opening the way for total destruction of habitat and the dominance of a rural paradigm.

A good example of the prevailing mentality can be seen in the first task which John undertook at Warrawong. This involved revegetating the land.

'I asked at the Belair nursery (a government nursery) about what trees I should plant, and I was urged to use Pinus radiata. (a tree from California) *There was a special going at the time.*'

It would have been laughable except that it was where environmental awareness actually sat in 1969.

Such was the advice being given to those who wanted to do revegetation in the Adelaide Hills. John knew little about plants; his focus had always been on the animals.

'I didn't understand what makes the bush, the bush. I knew a Pinus radiata forest wasn't a nice place to walk through, though it was better than the main street of Adelaide.'

He credits two people with influencing his understanding. One was Brenton Tucker, who lived nearby and operated a fledgling nursery, growing native plants. 'Native', at that time, meant *any* Australian plant. The concept of *local species* and was yet to be derived.

It was the era when Australian flora was just becoming significant in the public consciousness. Western Australian trees were the 'flavour of the month'. They were 'showy' and Adelaide's streets were newly planted with everything from coral gums to bushy yates to willow myrtle and silver gimlet. Hundreds of streets and roads all around the state were adorned with varieties of WA trees which were later removed when enough time had passed to demonstrate their unsuitability in our climate or their structural incongruity in the restricted spaces where they were forced to grow.

Walking into Brenton Tucker's nursery, John was delighted at what he saw, even though the species weren't necessarily locally indigenous. He bought thousands of plants. Brenton grew to order and John made an agreement to buy whatever plants remained at the end of the season.

Keith Oliphant (brother of the former governor of SA, Mark Oliphant) also lived nearby. John became good friends with him and his wife Coral. Keith became what John calls a mentor.

Keith was, like John, multi-talented, a scientist and an artistically gifted man with a passion for the natural world and someone who exhorted John to exceed his own expectations. It seems they made quite a pair, enjoying a drink together, although Keith sounds like a very different kind of personality.

Two things give some insight. John related how Keith invented a process for colour photocopying. He took his idea to America to see if he could get a company interested in further developing it. A large, well-known company stole his unprotected idea and Keith returned to Australia a broken man.

In another incident, some controversy followed when John attempted to loan one of Keith's paintings to the Stirling Council for public display in their chambers. The painting contained a very graphic message about environmental destruction. Perhaps more than a little ahead of its time.

Keith Oliphant's property had a marked influence on John's progress to understanding the connection between plants and animals. There seemed, to John's eye, to be 'millions' of native birds at Keith's place, more than John had ever seen in the bush, and this was simply because of the year-round supply of nectar from flowering Australian plants.

'Plants and their pollination was one of the extraordinary things that happened with evolution and basically we ended up with a division between the northern hemisphere and the southern hemisphere. In the northern hemisphere most of the plants are insect pollinated and in the southern hemisphere many of the plants are bird pollinated. The flowers themselves allow for the pollination to occur with a bird. So we have bell-shaped flowers and we have the stamens situated in such a way that they put the pollen on the bill of a bird and not on the head of a bee. So an insect pollinating a plant that was designed to be pollinated by a bird can often not pollinate the flower. The bees can take the pollen but not do the job. In the long tubular flowers which were specifically designed to be pollinated by spinebills, the bees can't get down inside so they put a hole in the bottom to get the nectar out and the spinebills don't get any nectar anymore. The aim at Warrawong was to show how this worked and the way to do that was to get a year-round nectar flow. Once the birds moved around following the nectar flow but we've segregated Australia so much they can no longer do it. If you want birds you have to provide a year-round nectar flow.'

To this end the plants came from all over Australia because it was impossible to replicate the natural order with South Australian plants in a small area within a fixed climate zone. The fragmentation effect lends weight to the modern arguments for closely spaced reserves and 'corridors' which allow animals to travel between sources of food.

At this time the Adelaide City Council put up artificial birds in the parklands with coin-operated bird-call recordings! The first manifestation of the John Wamsley profile and forthright style came from this, for he made comment about this pathetic state of affairs in a public forum, though he doesn't remember where.

'There were no birds in the city of Adelaide beyond the very common species like magpies. The reason was simple. There was nothing for them to eat.'

Council's policy at the time was one of clear-cutting everything around the trees. There was no hint of an understory, native or otherwise. High grass or bushy growth was considered a fire hazard, a trap for litter and a hiding place for 'undesirable' people. Many of the parks had predominantly exotic trees. Rose gardens and exotic shrubberies were the norm. Such native plants as were available tended to be planted in inappropriate situations (e.g. as single specimens in lawns subject to summer irrigation) and were rarely very successful.

We still harbour a northern hemisphere mind-set over the seasons. Winter, being a time of extreme cold, is the limiting factor for plants in the northern temperate climes, whereas summer's heat and dryness is the limiting factor in the Australian climate.

Adelaide's parklands today offer a very different kind of environment, with large logs left as habitat and close-packed, local indigenous plantings of a kind which would have been unthinkable when John began developing Warrawong. I have even seen a tawny frogmouth nesting in a tree alongside an inner city apartment.

A new connection formed in John's mind between plants and animals. Over the next couple of years he did mass plantings at Warrawong with the specific aim of creating that permanent nectar supply. And the birds came.

'I realised I had learned something fascinating. Nature doesn't just do what it should do. There are things *we* have to understand about nature.'

The road where John lived, and still lives today, comes off Stock Road between Longwood and Mylor. 'The Stock Road orchid story', which John loves to relate, runs concurrently with his growing understanding of the relationship between living things and the critical decisions which are made, sometimes with the best intentions, but founded on mistaken premises.

Stock Road gained its name because it was originally a 'travelling stock route' with a wide verge to allow for stock to graze as they moved. In the remnant dry schlerophyl forest of these verges, John identified 45 species of native orchid. There are photographs of each one, taken in situ, on John's website. These tiny flowers are among the most complex and intriguing of all the state's flora.

*Today there are five species remaining on Stock Road.*

These exquisite plants and their fate were fundamental to John's growing understanding of the relationship between all living things within a given local system.

New catchment and environmental laws were introduced, with the best of intentions, and these laws prohibited stock from being grazed on the verges.

Paradoxically, the new laws led to the disappearance of the other orchids. Interactions in nature are never as simple as they seem. In John's mind there emerged a connection between the removal of grazing pressure, the growth of exotic weeds or too many small native woody plants and the loss of the orchids. It was clear that no one really knew what they were doing, least of all the government departments charged with looking after the landscape.

Keith Oliphant, along with a man named Peter Dormer from the Mount Lofty Ranges Association, called on John one day and urged him to stand as a local council member to redress the uninformed decisions that were being made. After assiduously doorknocking the district and talking up the idea that people were paying too much for the services they were getting, he succeeded in being elected.

Of this decision to run for council, John says, 'It was the most stupid decision I made in my life, but it was a good learning experience because I found out that the whole system was stupid.'

True to type, controversy and conflict dogged his term as a councillor. He sums up the state of affairs thus, 'There were two groups, the conservationists and the developers. The conservationists principally comprised the Mount Lofty Ranges Association. They were planting Liquidambar trees in the streets. A possum which eats the leaves of these exotic, deciduous trees will die. It's just so atrocious that you do such a thing.

'*The developers were basically Liberal politicians.*'

Politicians used prior knowledge of muted projects to buy up land and sell it back to the government at an inflated price. It was acceptable in those years for elected officials to use their position in this way. If John is to be taken at his word, and he was, after all, an insider with council affairs, cronyism and blatant opportunism, within the law, were the order of the day.

One Liberal member was basically running the council 'He gave the Stirling District Clerk his orders every morning.' This was also considered normal behaviour at the time.

John had voted Liberal all his life, but the outright and systemic corruption he uncovered challenged his political leanings. To this day, he has a profound lack of confidence in the public sector, although he has strictly conservative political leanings, with a conservative's disdain for left wing aspirations, notwithstanding that he is enlightened and progressive in so many ways.

In his determination to expose what was going on, John took to publishing.

'I decided to put out a monthly paper and I called it "Stirling Payers". The student union at Flinders University published it for me. We printed three thousand copies. I had people helping me and we stuck one in every door in the Stirling council area. Well, didn't the shit hit the fan!'

The 'Stirling Payers' newsletters are a fascinating historical artefact in their own right, quite apart from the complex and controversial matters they address. Each newsletter comprises four A3 sized pages, closely typed and professionally presented. One of the impressive features is a series of cartoons drawn by Keith Oliphant including one which is in the form of an intricately drawn landscape covering an entire page.

*Keith Oliphant's magnum opus*

John claims this cartoon is the reason Stirling Township has a sewerage system today.

The most interesting thing about the writings is how they validate the often strange stories John tells about this time in his life.

A couple of headlines and short quotes give an indication of the matters covered and the strident tone of the writing:

**Stirling floats on effluent.** 'Recently a group of civic minded people planted some trees in the main street of Stirling. The most interesting feature noticed while the trees were being planted was the rate at which the holes dug for the trees filled with a vile smelling liquid commonly referred to as effluent . . .'

**Local developer in shadow cabinet.** 'Mr. Stan Evans M.P. recently was named as being Shadow minister for Transport, Tourism, Conservation and Environment. This must show beyond doubt, the contempt that the established political parties hold for their constituents, especially in the so-called blue ribbon seats. The fact that tourism (sometimes called national prostitution) can be combined with conservation and environment must be beyond comprehension for most people . . .'

A growing environmental awareness led John more and more into practical measures to protect and enhance the landscape around him. As an elected member he was in a position to make changes, though overcoming the inertia of the 'Stirling Club', as he called it, was an exhausting business.

Cleverly, John used the Council's fear of exposure, coupled with his reputation for so doing, to gain approval for his ideas.

'I had to side with one group or the other, so I sided with the Mount Lofty Ranges Association, even though they were planting trees I knew to be unsuitable. One of the projects they were involved with was the planting of sixty Liqidambar trees along a roadside. I knew the details of the costs because, being in council, these details were available to me. The trees were donated by a local nursery and planted by volunteers, including myself, yet somehow two thousand dollars had been spent on this project.'

When John queried this exorbitant amount he was told that it related to the overseer's wages. This was clearly a nonsense, as there was no overseer on that job.

'I said to the chairman of council, "I reckon this would make a good article in the local paper, you know, because it's a bit hot. But look, I'll tell you what I'll do. I'll make a deal with you. If you give me a thousand dollars to plant trees on the roadside in Mylor Ward then this business will be okay. It's a bit unfair, two thousand dollars to plant sixty trees." So he gave me a thousand dollars. I went to Brenton Tucker (the native plant grower) and I said, "Here's a thousand dollars, let's do it." So we planted *four thousand* trees for a thousand bucks.'

Attitudes were only just beginning to change. Revegetation was a new word. Stirling Council's stated policy was to 'Clear and level all roadsides and plant with exotic trees.'

The reaction to John's work with his volunteer group, from elements of the public, was strange indeed to our early twenty-first century sensibilities.

'Well, bloody hell, that was considered the biggest waste of money you can ever imagine. Four thousand trees. One of the roads I planted was Williams Road and my neighbour lived on the corner. So here's the front page of the Courier (the hills paper). There were all these tree stakes and there was my neighbour kneeling down among them all and the caption read, "A Picture of Dismay". The article went on to say, *"After a lifetime of clearing the scrub from his roadside it has been replanted"*.

*Courier front page photo 1975*

'So, I had to go. It was unacceptable for a councillor to plant four thousand trees for a thousand dollars. It was acceptable for others to plant sixty trees for two thousand dollars. That's okay. What I had done was considered an absolute waste of Council money and I was thrown out at the next election for wasting all this money.'

*Planting native trees was a waste of money.*

There is probably no better example of the prevailing state of environmental awareness in the early nineteen seventies. Native Vegetation Clearance laws weren't enacted for another two decades and the deplorable over-clearing of the SA landscape, taking place out of sight and out of mind, was a long way from the public consciousness. Eucalypts, at least, the SA species, didn't make nice formal avenues. They were 'messy' and variable in their habit. One of the reasons for this variability was that we had neglected to cultivate them and thereby select the best varieties for formal use over the years. Exotics, often with centuries of selection behind them, were used instead. Today we treat our native trees and shrubs, at least selectively, with the respect once only reserved for plants from another country.

John missed out on re-election by one vote and The Courier reported, 'Three recounts of the ballot failed to alter the result.' 42 percent of residents, a very high percent for local government elections, voted in his ward.

'In my time as an elected member,' says John, 'I managed to change the by-law which required that the roadsides be cleared of existing native vegetation and planted with exotic trees. That's about all I achieved. The rest was probably a waste of time.'

I doubt that his time on council was really wasted. He relates a charming story of how he tried to get through to the elected members by resorting to a modern-day parable. One of the Doctor Seuss books is called 'The Lorax'. Written in 1971, it remains an early example of a creative work dealing with the newly-emerging paradigm of environmental awareness. It is the story of how one man's greed destroys a forest and along with it an entire ecosystem, all in the name of producing *the one thing that everybody needs* viz. another consumer artefact.

What John did with this book gives us one of the most striking insights into his character, especially with regard to the unselfconscious way he was prepared to push an important idea. John describes 'The Lorax' as his bible.

While still a member of Stirling Council he took along to a meeting an armful of the books and handed a copy to every member present. *He then proceeded to read it to them as part of the meeting.* It may have hinted at a certain eccentricity, but it was undeniably a *beau geste.*

This 'lesson' for the elected members was designed to influence them in a decision they were about to adjudicate on regarding a request to remove native vegetation.

'And when I'd finished, Councillor Forbes said, "That's a lovely story, now let's get on and give approval to remove these trees." So after I'd read that to them they passed a motion to allow the bloke to clear the trees he wanted to take out. You're wasting your time to talk to these people. It goes over their heads.'

Some things are worth doing for their own sake, regardless of whether they're futile.

Punctuating John's life there are discreet 'stories'. Some of them are so comically infused as to sound made-up, were it not for the corroboration of other people and the remarkable written records which have survived. One of these stories is the 'Photinia Story'.

Photinia, sometimes called by the common name 'Chinese Hawthorn', is the generic name of an introduced plant. It is widely planted throughout Adelaide and the hills areas, where it is used as both a hedge plant and as a feature. Under the right conditions it can grow to be a large tree.

Speaking about the ongoing Williams Road planting, John said, 'When we came to plant trees close to the Photinias, the landholder said he didn't want us to plant there because he liked the Photinias which were spaced at one every twenty metres, saying "That's how a roadside should be." So we were told we weren't allowed to plant there. And that gave me the shits. I was pretty upset with them all by this time anyway and thought, "You bastards!" And I sprayed them (the Photinias) on Christmas Day with diesel fuel and blackberry herbicide. In broad daylight with the landholder watching me off his veranda! Later he said he thought it was a council person spraying for thrip (an insect pest).

'When he walked out on his veranda, I thought, "What do I do?" But I knew what to do because I'd learnt. I'd learnt that you just have to look as if you know what you're doing. If you're caught you don't act suspiciously, you just keep going. He stood there watching me for about ten minutes and then went back inside. I assumed he'd gone in to ring the police or something so I kept going. And the Photinias died. It took a while, but they died. And he said he'd seen the person doing it but he couldn't remember what they looked like. He was high society, you see. He used to ride his horse around the block. He didn't talk to council employees. I used to get on very well with the council employees, but he didn't. I suspect the council employees knew a lot more about what was going on than they ever told anyone. When the pine trees were coming down (another story) they asked me one day if I could do it on a weekend because they got overtime!

'Councillor Forbes said, in council, "We'll sort this out once and for all, we'll replant them." So in due course this ute pulls up with these beautiful little Photinias in pots and they started planting them. And me being a community spirited person, I helped to plant them. And with each one, *I would break the roots off and throw them over the fence* and put the stick back in the ground. I did the whole bloody row of them, with the council officers there, planting. The landholder sat on his veranda, watching. See, one of the things I learnt is you can do anything and get away with it.

YOU PLANT THEM, HE PULLS THEM UP.
YOU CAN SWAP JOBS LATER.

*Keith Oliphant's take on the Photinia fiasco*

31

'They knew then that somebody had it in for the Photinias so they actually had someone stationed there to watch them. And they watched the Photinias gradually die.

'After that we were told we could plant there and we did.'

Remember that while this war in a tea-cup was going on, John occupied a position of considerable importance at Flinders University and also had a wife and three children watching from the wings. The single-mindedness of his seemingly petty actions was decades ahead of its time, as large swathes of exotic plants are now commonly removed from verges and creeklines to be replaced by indigenous species.

At the same time as the Williams Road native planting took place, there evolved an extraordinary saga involving trees of another kind. This is surely the strangest part of the whole John Wamsley story and like the story above, reveals more about John than almost anything else he did.

## CHAPTER FIVE

# THE MASKED MARAUDER

JOHN ADMITS, 'I WENT A little bit crazy at the time. I radicalised myself. I can see what happens to young people. It's basically because they have no choice.'

In order to plant the new trees along Williams Road it was necessary to clear the radiata pines which had seeded there. Pinus radiata covers huge areas of plantation forest in SA. The species was introduced into SA from California following trials as early as 1876 in the mid-north of the state. There are few natural controls to limit growth of the species in SA and in areas of high (600 mm and above) rainfall, the pines will self-sow, becoming the dominant species.

The demise of the Stock road orchids cemented the idea in John's mind that there was a connection between native plants, animals and biodiversity. Under the pines nothing much would grow, and certainly no orchids, so it was clear that pines were of no benefit in the greater environment, unless pines were all that you wanted. Again, we see the European tastes at work, for pines are the naturally occurring dominant species in large areas of the northern hemisphere.

At the same time, John noticed how messmate stringybark (Eucalyptus obliqua) trees were dying in one part of his property and he concluded that the culprit was the pines growing among them. Pines inhibit the growth of most (though not all) native vegetation, slowly creating a monoculture.

Further, a connection between plants and animals was already well-formed in John's mind by this time. The success of the plantings at Warrawong in attracting native birds cemented the relationship. Pines provided feed for only a very small number of bird species and that feed was seasonal.

We must jump ahead a little in the sequence here, for mammals, as John remembered them from his childhood, were the logical next step in building a living system, although the connection between mammals and the totality of a system would not at that stage have been formulated in his mind or in anyone else's mind. The desire to reintroduce mammals is tied in with the feral tree removal and at least partly explains John's obsession with pursuing the removals despite all the acrimony it brought upon him and his family.

Observations on his property had led to the monumentally significant conclusion that *mammals needed a protective fence if they were to survive the depredations of introduced carnivores*. There was no point introducing mammals if they were only going to be killed by foxes and cats.

Historically and ironically, the idea of a barrier to *protect* animals was only developed in regard to the dingo fence which was built to protect *introduced* animals and rabbit-proof fences were developed to protect *introduced* crops and pastures.

The radical notion of protecting native animals, which were traditionally the enemy of agriculture, must have seemed insane to the farmers who had spent their life effectively and brutally eradicating them.

Thus, concurrent with his developing awareness of the impact of introduced plants, John decided to build a feral-proof fence around his property and this came to be synonymous with Warrawong. It was not strictly the very first fence of its kind, although John's name has come to be associated with such constructions and no one had built a thoroughly researched and effective fence before.

Rex Ellis, the modern-day adventurer, tour guide, writer and naturalist built a feral-proof fence around a small area at McLaren Flat in SA in the 1970's, but John's effort was more sophisticated and it is his large-scale fencing efforts and the improvements he incorporated which are recognised today.

In Western Australia, a project to protect a native Swamp Tortoise utilised such a fence, but this didn't happen until 1992, long after Warrawong's fence was built. The important point is that the Warrawong fence *popularised* feral-proof fencing and put it squarely into the public domain. Significantly, the fence building also became integral to a much greater vision, allied with a practical demonstration of what could be done.

Efforts like this were a novelty in the early nineteen eighties. It is impossible to overstate just how primitive our concepts were in relation to natural history. Agricultural production was wholly divorced from considerations of the natural systems. We are only now beginning to understand how the two are connected.

I only mention the fence at this point because it created another incentive to do pine tree removal. For the kind of fence John envisaged to work, it had to be sufficiently clear of the surrounding vegetation that fallen trees or individual branches wouldn't touch it. This would have defeated the purpose of the structure as even one feral animal getting through meant disaster. Also, once the fence was built it would have been impossible to remove the pines without damaging the fence because some of the trees were massive. Removal of the exotic trees was absolutely essential to the slowly growing picture of a man-made paradise which John had niggling away at the back of his mind.

Accordingly, he obtained, while still a member of Stirling Council, a written permit authorising him to remove the pines, though only along Williams Road. Thus began a story which remains unrivalled in SA for its comic reality. Remember, in the early eighties, trees were trees.

There is a long article in the 'Payers' newsletter of December 1976, titled 'Groaping for the Truth', in which John chronicles the entire series of events. It makes for a complex story, such were the reversals in Stirling Council's decisions on the matter. They appear to have been happy for native tree planting work to go ahead, but perhaps unaware that pines would have to be removed in order for this to happen. Or it may have been the *size* of the pines involved and the attendant real or perceived public backlash against this removal.

The initial permission given to John for the tree project did not *specifically* say he could remove pine trees viz. 'Early in 1975 I was granted permission, by Stirling Council, to *rehabilitate* certain roadsides in Mylor Ward. I asked if Council wanted a plan for the projects and the then chairman, Mr. J. Rankin, said, "Carry on and report to Council from time to time." Unfortunately, nothing was minuted.'

After some initial negative reaction there seems to have been unequivocal approval. 'Councillor Bradsen told me that everything was okay and the engineer could now give permission for the removal of foreign trees. He also said he had been to look at Williams road and that the big pines *would never allow successful rehabilitation if I didn't do something*... On the 15th January (1976) I received written permission from Stirling Council to remove the damaged trees.'

This was not sufficient to allay the fears of some. 'A vigilante group was set up to watch me. . . The volunteer tree planters gave up under the harassment.'

On the 22nd of January the Chairman of the Council called to see John. 'He said he was concerned that the removal of the large pines would cause bad publicity.'

John's taped conversation reveals detail which is not covered in the newsletter:

'There was an outcry from the locals to the effect that some bastard was removing trees. Why were they doing this? The council told me I couldn't do it. Now I knew it wasn't as simple as that because I knew the rules of council. If you make a resolution, then in the life of that council, which is until the next council election, you can't change that resolution other than by having a question on notice and it has to be written down how everybody voted. There has to be a division, and they hadn't had a division, so I knew that rescinding my approval to remove those trees wasn't binding. I still had approval. I also knew that as soon as I told them so they'd give notice to council and call a division. So how do I get around this? How do I do it? Well, it's not me, is it? *I'm not doing it.* So I didn't let anyone see me doing it. Each night, a tree would come down. I used a bow saw for the small ones. I also found out there was such a thing as an electric chainsaw. So, anyway, things got warmed up a bit. It was quite incredible the way that it built up.

*The Chairman of Stirling Council inspecting a ring-barked pine tree in 1976*

'Then one night I cut down two trees across the road. There was one each side of the neighbour's driveway.'

If John wanted to make enemies he couldn't have picked a better way to do it. The neighbour in question was the same person who had been so dismayed by the planting of native trees on his verge.

'The Adelaide News got involved and published a very prominent article about it. The town clerk called me in and asked me who was cutting down the trees. I said I didn't know and he jokingly suggested that it was "Probably some organisation called G.R.O.A.P or something, for *Get Rid of All Pines,* or some such thing." So *he* invented it (the name). I thought what a fucking good name for it and so it became GROAP. On the 10th February I made statements to most of the news media on the damage pines were doing in the hills.'

Typically, I remember this imaginary terrorist group from so long ago because of its name. It was the very first reference I can recall to John Wamsley's activities, although his name wasn't at first associated with the radical action. My reaction mirrored that of most people, for trees were never considered pests, no matter their origin and the damage they did to the bush.

An organisation *which didn't exist* took on a life of its own and John milked it for all it was worth.

Somehow, dots were connected and John stood out as a suspect. When the media came along and asked if he was cutting down trees, he would tell them that he wasn't going to answer that question but he would tell them *why* it was being done. That there existed a problem with feral plants and this explained the necessity to remove them. On every occasion when it was possible he tried to educate the public. It wasn't the dramatic acts themselves that mattered but the *reasoning* behind those actions.

The whole concept of a feral plant was alien to all but a very few people involved in the infant task of bush care. Public outcry over removal of pine trees clearly points up the low level of awareness about biodiversity, a comparatively modern idea.

'They (the media people) would end up virtually clapping me and saying that it was a good thing and everybody should be doing it, because I had proved it to them. So they gave me a very favourable hearing.'

It was another matter with both the Council and the government of the day. What ultimately happened is hard to believe. From the newsletter:

'On the 10th February Stirling Council decided to revoke all permissions given to the Mylor tree planting group. It ignored paragraph 152 of the Local Government Act. *It offered a $200 reward for information leading to my conviction. It asked the police to charge me.*'

Somewhere among the factions of the troubled Stirling Council, paranoid conspiracy was at work. The Council's actions and utterances were schizophrenic. There is no other interpretation unless we think that John had his facts confused, but the newsletter is full of dates and other specifics to back him up.

Not wanting to wait for the police to act, if indeed they ever intended to act, the Council decided to take matters into its own hands. If the police wouldn't do anything the council would put John Wamsley on trial. An ABC radio announcement called it a 'Citizens' Trial'.

Chairman of the Stirling Council David Beaumont-Smith was to be the Judge, councillor Jentsch (whose verge had been targeted by the GROAP poisoner) was the prosecutor and a handpicked audience was the jury. In assuming John to be a no-show, they seriously underestimated him.

'It was full of people. I didn't bother to talk to any of them. I just walked down and sat in the front row. There were police everywhere. And so the trial opened.'

John confessed to being terrified of walking into that hall, feeling the way a man might feel in the bad old days when people could be lynched by such a court.

Oddly enough, the trial started with a resolution favouring what John was doing. Viz. 'That pines are a pest in the Adelaide Hills'. It was, apparently, okay for others to remove them, but it was not okay for John to do so.

'Councillor Jentsch got up and stated the case, saying "You are guilty of criminal vandalism, you have to prove your innocence." Those were his words.

'So I said, "Hang on councillor, you're not in Nazi Germany now, you're here." That brought a bit of a roar from the crowd behind me. And so it started. It didn't go on for long. I said "The chairman can tell you that I had been given approval to remove the trees." And he didn't say anything.

'Somebody at the back said "Is this true? Has he got approval to remove those trees?" David Beaumont-Smith admitted that I had been given approval to remove some of them but not all of them.'

John went on to ask if they had designated which trees he had approval for and which ones he didn't. The chairman had no clear answer. The matter of a *rescinding* of that approval came up and John asked if the proper notice had been given and proper process followed. He knew very well that such process *hadn't* been followed.

'The chairman went red in the face. As soon as that happened the audience knew something was up and must have thought, "What's going on here?" They all guffawed and started to leave. That was the end of the trial.'

The newsletter puts it this way: 'After a while they decided to hear me and the trial was adjourned when the more intelligent in the audience realised they were being had.'

I asked John if he spoke to anyone after this 'trial', but he said, 'No, I just went home. I don't think I had any friends.' His intake of medium solero sherry reached a flagon a day at this stressful time of his life.

It sounds like a circus, and so it was, but other parts of the story were more like a Monty Python sketch. A Canberra University friend of John's wrote to an Adelaide newspaper. In the letter he claimed to be a representative of GROAP (the imaginary terrorist tree-destroyers) and said that the organisation was intent on removing all feral pine trees in South Australia. The paper published the letter, naturally assuming it was authentic.

Not to let an opportunity pass, John took advantage of the fear and loathing. Best of all from this slapstick show, there is, on John's website, a short clip of the 'hooded man' incident, engineered by John, in which an axe-wielding member of the fictitious GROAP organisation is filmed attacking pine trees. It was assumed to be John in the hood but was in fact a university friend.

The media people were invited to this staged photo-opportunity as a way to get the message across about feral trees. The hood with eye sockets looks ridiculous today, but it was serious fare at the time. After ring-barking a pine tree for the cameras, the anonymous vigilante scampers off to continue his dastardly work.

The phantom axe-man was followed by the phantom poisoner, another friend who posed in a hood with eye-sockets and sprayed diesel fuel on every pine in sight. This time it was along the road where councillor Jentsch (who figures in the next fiasco) lived. John announced to the invited newsmen that GROAP had now mechanised their operations. 'We can do in ten thousand pine trees a day now.'

Madness and mass fear escalated. Pines were cut down along the freeway. John swears he never cut pines from anywhere but his own property verges. 'With all I had to do why would I be out cutting someone else's weeds down?' But John was *the* public enemy of his day and hysteria grew.

The reach of John's 'terrorism' is attested by what happened next. It was reported by none other than the governor of SA, Sir Mark Oliphant who was, as mentioned earlier, the brother of John's friend Keith Oliphant.

'Keith rang me up and said that his brother had just rung him to ask "What's Wamsley up to?" Because Don Dunstan (the premier) had just called a special meeting of the executive council which he (Mark) had attended, because he's the governor, and Don Dunstan had declared that *John Wamsley was an urban guerrilla and he'd ordered the police commissioner to lock him up.*'

So the plain clothes detectives duly came to lock him up, and as John so humorously tells it, 'I'd cut this little tree off, right in front of Warrawong. It fell, but it was hung up in another tree. I took my mind off the road for a while and I was shaking it to get it down. And down it came, straight on this fucking police car with three detectives in it whose job was to arrest me!'

When he produced a permit they threw it away, saying, 'You don't have a permit now, do you?'

One of those men was a detective Lacey, of whom John says, 'I found Mr. Lacey extremely aggressive . . . he arrested me. I declined to make a statement. During the interview Mr. Lacey had some interesting things to say, like, "You're a bastard. Everyone says you are a bastard. I haven't got fucking time to waste over this." And on it went.'

The charge was 'damage to a tree in an avenue worth more than two dollars' and this carried a maximum gaol term of five years. After a stint in the Adelaide city lock-up he was released on a $200 bond and the stipulation he 'not cut down or destroy any tree including genus Pinus'. But significantly the world now knew it was John Wamsley cutting down the trees.

'The only lawyer I could get was someone who acted for drug offenders because that's the class I was put in. We argued that the tree in question was only worth $1.76 and that it wasn't growing in a formal, planted avenue but was, in fact, self-sown. The proceedings kept getting postponed due to lack of evidence.'

The story ended well for John. Peter Duncan, the Attorney General at that time, returned from overseas and upon hearing of John's arrest was outraged. He spoke to John on the phone and went on to order that the charges be dropped.

Following the final hearing, when charges were dismissed, John was driven to the police station and here the police admitted that they had no right to arrest him. Someone from high up in the force (John doesn't recall who it was) spoke to him. 'If I didn't sue them for wrongful arrest, they would issue an order to all police in the state to the effect that if anyone was seen cutting down trees on a roadside and said that they had permission, the police were to take no further action.'

From the newsletter: 'In April the police realised they had been conned by Stirling Council and withdrew all charges.'

In John's brilliantly colourful words, it came down to a simple agreement. 'If you don't sue us for wrongful arrest *you can go and knock down as many fucking trees as you want*!

'I doubt that the police ever really gave a damn about anyone cutting down trees.

'The incredible thing is that in 2003 I was given the Prime Minister's Award for doing exactly the same things that Don Dunstan had me arrested for thirty years before.'

The exoneration may have come a little too late, but that will become evident as we proceed.

As a postscript, the newsletter relates that, 'In May Councillor Jentsch rang me and invited me to coffee. He said he had just realised that I did have permission to remove the pines. He said he had been embarrassed by it all. He said it was the fault of the engineer the clerk and the chairman. He said he wanted to get even with them. *He asked my help.*'

Strange how events come full circle.

A talk given by John at the time to a group of 'Young Liberals', and reported in detail by The Courier, is full of well-articulated arguments to support removal of pines growing near native bush. Today the logic is clear and arouses no controversy, but the pine tree story was the beginning of true notoriety.

John adds, 'At no time was I worried about what happened to me (apart from the threat of being lynched!) I couldn't give a stuff. If I couldn't do what I wanted to do at Warrawong then nothing else mattered.'

At a time when John had few allies and most of the world against him, a curious thing happened. No less a personage than the famous English comic, Spike Milligan, wrote a letter to one of the Adelaide daily papers. Spike took John's side, suggesting it was the councillors who ought to be ringbarked! Spike is another who marched to his own tune, so it is not so surprising he should have been sympathetic, but the fact that the matter came to his attention at all is an indication of how far John's notoriety spread.

The final lines of this saga represent a startling irony. Stirling Council were worn down by the war in their midst.

'And then in the end *the council came and removed the remaining trees* because what I was doing was too dangerous. The only thing they could do was to remove them.'

'There were about six hundred pine trees along Stock Road. It would have taken me years to remove them.'

Like so much of what seems important at a given time, the whole drama came to a point of capitulation and today exotic pines, along with a list of other woody plants, are recognised as seriously destructive invaders of Australian bushland. They are regularly cut or poisoned by both private landholders and government agencies. Feral trees remain one of the most insidious threats to our remaining remnant bushland. I met John through the Scott Creek Friends whose primary job is the removal of woody weeds. Our president currently works for Trees for Life. I have watched him drilling holes at the base of a large pine tree in the bush and pouring poison into it. Such are the changes in social attitudes wrought by time. This is the important legacy of that strange and absurd sideshow.

It was also the first example of John Wamsley as the source of ideas which today have become mainstream. For all its slapstick aspects, the pine trees story represents John's undeviating adherence to an idea whose genesis was the saving of wildlife and biodiversity.

Clearly, only someone as self-contained and careless of his own reputation as John could have weathered that storm of derision, but there is always a cost. 'After the pine trees were long gone,' he said, 'I didn't have a friend in the world.'

For most people it would have been more than enough trouble to make them settle to safer pursuits, but the pine tree removal was only the first phase. When one feral plant is removed it is almost inevitable that other unwanted plants will germinate in the vacuum. Such a plant was 'broom', a leguminous woody weed which became rampant when the pine trees no longer suppressed it with their shade and competition for water.

Huge piles of cut broom were left along the roadside after John cut them down. This led to his being ordered to clean up the mess. John's way of removing the heaps of branches was to set fire to them. This precipitated the next comical episode when the Emergency Fire Service arrived to put out the flames.

I chronicle these odd events as John presented them to me. As he lit one pile, the EFS would be putting out another, and so it went. The police arrived and asked what on earth was happening. John calmly told them, 'I've been asked to remove this rubbish and that's what I'm doing.'

The police officer asked, 'And what are *they* doing?' (meaning the EFS) 'They're putting out the fire.'

The officer began to join the dots. 'What's your name?' he asked.

When John told him he put his notebook back in his pocket, walked to his car and drove away. Apparently enough trouble was enough for one police force. John also related how on one of his tree-cutting days he felled two pine trees in such a way that one of them blocked a police car from behind and another blocked the same vehicle in front. I can surmise that the poor police officers on their patrols must have drawn lots to see who would attend on Stock Road.

There has to be some advantage in any public exposure, for John tells how he was coming home one night along a road below the hills freeway and how he was driving a little above the limit. A police officer pulled him over, ready to book him for speeding, but when he saw the name on the licence he had the same kind of reaction as the officer on Stock Road and directed John to keep moving.

The GROAP scenario doesn't represent the total of media exposure in those years. Then as now, people used roadsides to dump rubbish illegally. Rubbish was regularly dumped on Stock road during John's council term. He asked the media people if they would come and do a report for the paper. 'They would only put me on the front page if I could be photographed *carrying a gun down Stock road*. I didn't own a gun, so I had to rush around and borrow one from a neighbour. The neighbour said the gun (a 22 calibre rifle) didn't have a bolt. I said I didn't need the bolt.'

The photograph was duly taken. 'Next day there was a cop at my door asking about an unregistered gun. He asked to see the gun and then asked where the bolt was. I told him I didn't have a bolt and so it emerged that it wasn't my gun. The cop suggested I tell my mate to get it registered!'

As John puts it. 'If you want things to happen then someone has to walk the plank. You're not going to get the people who run the newspapers to publicise your cause *unless you make a fool of yourself.*'

The level of publicity is best demonstrated by the fact that John became the topic for one of the famous Michael Atchison cartoons in the Adelaide Advertiser. It showed a row of ring-barked trees receding around a curve in the road, with the caption, 'If you want me I'm around the bend.' I think John is proud of this and one has to admire the genius of the cartoonist.

"If anyone wants me I'm around the bend . . ."

*The Atchison cartoon in the Adelaide Advertiser 1976*

A pattern of almost obsessive single-mindedness is evident in the early episodes of environmental activism that characterised those years and that resolve affected not only members of the public but it had the effect of pushing John to the edge of his own limits.

The vigilante-style tactics of the feral trees 'war', the high profile generated by the newsletters and the other exposure put those close to John under great pressure. So much negative public attention couldn't help but impact on his family life. His children were harassed at school because of their father's reputation.

'I had no way to manage that and it put me in a terrible position.'

The protracted period of extreme action led, for the second time in John's life, to the point of collapse.

This time it would cost him his marriage.

CHAPTER SIX

# A NEW PARADIGM

MATERIALS WERE ALREADY ORDERED FOR a feral-proof fence when the personal crisis struck. John's mother-in-law said she could *prove he was mad because he had built a swamp* and his wife, Betty, cancelled the order for fencing material without telling him, claiming John was 'a bit stupid and would waste his money so she had to look after him.'

John promptly re-ordered the material but Betty cancelled the order again and because their money was in a joint account he couldn't do anything about it. 'She told everyone I was a nut-case.'

As is often the case, the collapse of his marriage took him by surprise. It had *seemed* a workable union up until that time but in hindsight he saw how his obsessive work ethic and the very public affair of the pines et al had placed unbearable strain on the marriage.

Unwittingly, John became like his father, for whom work was the beginning and end of all things. Referring to his father, John said, 'We were on different sides of the ball-park. He was a workaholic and that's why I didn't like him, but I grew up the bloody same.'

Such was the nature of mathematics that if he was sitting in a chair his children would have cause to ask him if he was relaxing or working. There is almost no physical action associated with mathematics. To work or to research is to merely sit and think.

After the painful breakup John admits to drinking a flagon of sherry a day. It represented the second nervous breakdown in his life and for a lifeline he turned to his new neighbour, Proo Geddes, a science teaching advisor with the Education Department. They had been introduced, thanks to Keith Oliphant, when John gave her advice about her newly purchased property.

Proo wasn't at home when John went there, distraught, but he let himself in just the same. Like John, Proo was born and raised in the country and also like him, she loved native animals. It was, to say the least, a fortuitous meeting. Proo spent her childhood on a wheat and sheep property called Ippinitchie near Wirrabara in SA's mid-north, just east of the Southern Flinders Ranges.

Like John, Proo is down-to-earth and straight-talking, although she conveys the sense her feet are firmly on the ground where John sometimes allows himself to be levitated by the big-picture.

Proo is a natural with animals, an 'animal whisperer' and chronic adopter of orphans.

Dramatic circumstances brought John and Proo together at Warrawong. The first Ash Wednesday fire in 1980 (as distinct from the second, fatal fire in 1983) tore through their district. Fire took hold under Proo's house while she was at work, completely unaware.

Without electricity for the water pump John watched helplessly until told by a police officer to get out because they were evacuating the area.

As he relates it, 'I phoned Proo at work and said, "Is your house insured?" She said it was. I said, "That's good, because it's on fire." Those were almost my exact words.'

Ironically, the fire started in a Stirling Council rubbish tip owned by the family of the same Liberal politician who was John's nemesis during his term as a councillor.

A remarkable document chronicles the events of that day (Ash Wednesday). For all of its matter-of-fact style, the blow-by-blow account is quite chilling. It is a hand-written letter, rendered in lead pencil and cursive script, to John's mother, sent just after the fire. To my sensibilities, it recounts something no less than heroic.

*Dear Mum,*

*Well, it rained last night, only five points but that was enough. Ash Wednesday they called this. I wonder how they knew. When I was in Council complaints always came in that the local dump was burnt, but he is our local member of parliament so nobody did much about it. Anyway, it was a hot day with a nasty wind and the dump was smouldering so I decided to stay at home. Just after I had finished lunch the siren blew. I looked out and saw it was heading for Proo's house so I went round to it. I didn't have time to get all her stuff out but she didn't lose too much. The wind had built up and the police ordered everyone out of Conrad Road. I went back home. I thought I had better ring Proo and tell her. She was engaged. I rigged up the tractor sprayer and filled it with water. I thought, I am glad my old man isn't here, he wouldn't like all that long grass around the house. I got through to Proo and told her that her house might get burnt down. I knew it already had but thought it better to break the news gently. What do you do when you wait for a fire?*

*I can now see the fire. It is in the pine trees at the top of Stock Road. How do you stop a fire like that? We put the kangaroos in the laundry. Well, it's not much point hoping it won't come it is bloody well here . . . the main fire came over the hill. I was in a paddock of short grass of about five acres. It didn't catch alight it blew up. The paddock was burnt. I hadn't had time to put my tractor in gear. How do you stop a fire like this?*

*I realized my trousers were on fire . . . Two hours later I looked to the north. Aldgate Valley was alight and the fire was heading for me . . . a cool southerly wind began to blow. I'm glad my mother isn't here she would have strange reasons for that happening. A copper hands me a can of coke and drives off down the road . . . The fire behind the dam is coming closer. It's not too bad it is climbing the gully against the wind, but there is no road between it and me. Wouldn't it be crook if after surviving the main blast I cop it from some piddling fire sneaking up where I can't get at it? The fire truck pulls into my drive . . . They charged off with siren blaring and ten minutes later they had stopped it. It was 11 o'clock. It didn't seem like 9 hours. The wind had stopped . . . The main fire is miles away. There is a glow on the horizon. It's very quiet. As the sun comes up the light and shadows on the smoke keep alarming me. We ring a few people to tell them we're okay. The day passes without any problems. In late afternoon a light drizzle starts and the smoke stops rising off the burnt grass. I put the tractor away. The power comes on. I have a bath and go to bed. This morning we went for a drive. I still don't know why I am not burnt out. I should have been. If I hadn't been here I would have been. Only for that fire truck being where it was I would have been. Only for those freak wind changes I would have been. I guess I had better give the CFS a donation. Anyway everything is okay.*

*Love John.*

Proo moved in with John. Prior to living with her, John used to shave 'once a week whether I needed it or not', but Proo didn't like the bristles and so the shaving stopped. The images of John from his very high profile days always show a man with a long, flowing beard.

Because they both had 'old-fashioned parents', they married. In 1982 their son, Shane, was born.

Proo embraced what John wanted to do at Warrawong and was thereafter an equal (or, in her words, not quite equal) partner in all his pursuits. In years to come she heroically carried on with the mission John started, even after he lost the will to do so.

Speaking of all that came about in ensuing years, John admits, 'I don't think I could have done it without her.' To the outside observer this is more than evident. Seeing them together it is obvious they form a natural team.

Emotionally, life normalised again, if 'normalised' is the appropriate word, but finances were problematic and remained so for some time to come. In order to complete the financial settlement of the divorce, John and Proo borrowed to buy Betty out and thereby retain Warrawong.

The financial pressure thus generated added a material urgency to their tenuous dreams.

Fence building recommenced. The job took a year to complete although the idea, according to John, was ten years in the making.

Proo gives a colourful account of the process.

'The building of the fence was a brilliant concept and ahead of its time. It was also an engineering feat. *It was also built by hand.*'

Work started in Dec 81 and finished in Aug 82. Proo remembers it very well.

'It was a mild, relatively dry winter and this allowed John to build right through the winter months, something he hadn't thought possible at the start.

'But first, after Betty cancelled the orders for the fence and John and I were together, John went down to Coopers to order the materials, but the price of steel had risen so much we couldn't afford it. So we saved some more but again more price rises and we still couldn't afford it. So in the end we purchased units at a time, the steel posts, then the wooden posts, the wire netting etc. But I do remember that all extras once building commenced came out of the housekeeping!

'John cleared a metre on either side of the fence line, mostly with an axe, mattock, and chain saw. At one stage he got the blade of the chainsaw stuck high in a tree and couldn't move it so he wrenched it and the chain saw came in half.

'Once the clearing was done the posts went in. The corner and strainer post holes were 6' deep. These were dug with posthole shovel and crowbar, but when the hole got to the last few feet, John would have to lie on the ground and scoop up the loose dirt with that essential fence building tool, an empty beetroot tin!

'Then the posts would be cemented in. Cement was mixed on a piece of flat iron to the age old recipe of making a well, putting in the water etc. Hard work. And for most of the holes the water was carried in with buckets on the carryall of the tractor.

'Once the posts were in place the straight wires were strung. John made a wire spinner and I would stay with the spinner with Shane in the bassinet and John would clamp locking pliers to the end of the strand and then walk off with the stand of wire over his shoulder, pulling as he went. You would have to ask John but from memory 2 runs were over a kilometre each. There were 8 strands to complete each section. And the terrible times were when the wire tangled off the spinner and with no means of contacting John I would have to stop the spinner and hope he realized then try and untangle things. High tensile wire is a fair bugger at getting into a tangle and hard as to untangle.

'The tractor didn't have any brakes so on one section (called Heart Break Hill) he would bring the netting in on the carryall of the tractor, reverse the tractor and back it onto a stump to hold it while he took the wire netting through in the wheelbarrow. One load tipped over and all the netting rolled into the dam. It was a very steep section.

'After completion the maintenance and care of the fence was very important. It had to be walked daily and any sticks etc cleaned off. The electric wire at the top of the fence allowed for an alarm and many was the night one of us would be walking the fence at 2am looking for a branch or tree or something else shorting out the fence. And would you believe so often it would be a poor old huntsman spider in an insulator causing the tell tail click, click of the short.'

While construction proceeded, John and Proo began looking for native animals to stock the property.

John approached the Adelaide Zoo because that was the first place he assumed someone seeking animals might look. They flatly refused his request, the idea of giving animals to a private sanctuary deemed outrageous at the time.

Proo joined the Marsupial Society to see if they could help. The advice from the society was to look under 'Birds' in the classified section of the Saturday Advertiser! There were plenty of birds for sale but no native animals, so she decided to read through every advertisement in the classifieds and sure enough, hidden in the wrong section there were some small marsupials for sale. Wrongly listed under 'basinetts', she found bettongs, a tiny species of kangaroo, very rare in the wild, as well as pademelons (another small species of marsupial) and albino kangaroos.

Someone in the unlikely location of Peterborough, in South Australia's mid-north, had a private collection which they were selling off. Few people in Australia at that time, at least among the general public, had even heard of the animals in the collection.

It was to be first in, first served at the Peterborough animal sale. After spending much of the day hastily building an enclosure to take the new arrivals, John and Proo made the trip to Peterborough in time for an evening transfer of animals. As it turned out, no other buyers were there. The Advertiser's mistake in misplacing the advert was to their advantage. True to detail, there were indeed two species of animal for sale and they obtained a pair of each.

One of those species was an animal John remembered from his childhood. 'I was about to realise they were pademelons. I hadn't seen one for thirty years. I remembered them well. They had a red neck and a yellow stripe on their hips. I had tried to look them up. The best I could do were red-necked pademelons. But they didn't have a hip stripe.'

This animal's presence runs like a thread through the whole of John's story.

The new animals soon demonstrated they were more than a match for the pen John constructed. They simply jumped over the wire, making excursions to the dam, but they returned to the pen each time because that was where they slept.

The perimeter fence still allowed determined foxes to get in. Foxes cannot be kept out of what has been their range. One way or another, they will get in. One benefit came from this behaviour.

'There were a few rabbits within the fence when it was completed. There were also a few foxes. The rabbits didn't last long. The foxes ate them. I was to learn my first lesson on foxes.

'There are two sorts of foxes as far as developing fox free areas are concerned. There are those who believe they belong to the place and those who believe they do not. The second group are easy to keep out. The first group cannot be kept out. They must be destroyed. If a fox believes an area is part of its range then it will do anything to enter that area. The day after the fence was "closed" at Warrawong Sanctuary, there were holes under the fence a person could crawl through.'

Two cats lived on the property. These were trapped and removed, but not destroyed. Remarkably, given John's later fearsome reputation as the nemesis of the feline species, he admits to releasing them in the Bridgewater area of the hills, hoping they 'found a good home'!

One of the pademelons was found dead, clearly the work of a fox. The other, a female, was missing, presumed dead. But what subsequently happened would be the catalyst for the idea of Warrawong not merely as a personal escape, but as a place for the public to visit.

Baiting took care of the remaining foxes in the sanctuary as well as a great many others outside it. Dead foxes were in evidence all over the place. John feigned ignorance.

'A few months later we bought four long-nosed potoroos, yet another diminutive species of kangaroo which few people would have been familiar with.'

Next came some red-necked and tammar wallabies, followed by some red (or *rufous* bettongs) from an enthusiast at Port Broughton.

With the addition of a few hand-reared orphan kangaroos, Warrawong Sanctuary was looking good. In 1983 Laurie Delroy of the South Australian National Parks and Wildlife Service (NPWS) gave Warrawong six woylies (brush-tailed bettongs). Laurie Delroy would be a supporter of John's vision for as long as he was in charge of the NPWS.

Two southern hairy-nosed wombats rescued from Yalata on the edge of the Nullarbor added to the numbers. These animals, destined for the cooking pot, both sustained injuries, one quite significantly, but this animal later became the star of the Warrawong show and is reported to have lived for 34 years.

John brought another wombat, named Nadine, to his university classroom to demonstrate a mathematical point. Nadine was there to demonstrate the concept of *'equivalence relations, equivalence classes and factor sets'* (sic). One student objected and John found himself threatened with dismissal. Nadine remained blissfully unaware of the trouble caused by her hairy-nosed presence.

*Nadine the wombat*

'If I couldn't show that I had taken it (the wombat) to class for pedagogical reasons, I would be dismissed.'

As a champion of logic John had no problem presenting a good case.

'My reasons were accepted but I was given a reprimand for *keeping it in the classroom too long.*' Just how long should a southern hairy-nosed wombat remain in a classroom? Surely one of the enduring philosophical problems confronting all mathematics lecturers!

Other animals graced his lectures. A possum and cape barren geese chicks, all brought to school tucked into his shirt. The possum was a great source of mirth as it would climb up to the top of his arm each time he raised his arm to write on the board. With few exceptions, his students were delighted to have a lecturer who combined humour with academia.

With so many animals now in place, maintaining the security of the fenced area became critically important. Proo remembered a potentially disastrous breach.

'One night I came home late, it was wet and dark. The gate opened, I drove through, pressed the remote and watched the gate start to shut as I drove up to the house. The rain shorted the mechanism and the gate re-opened. Next morning to our alarm there was an open gate. We looked in the mud on the road (Williams Road was a dirt road then) and sure enough there were all these bettong and wallaby footprints, hop, hop, hop up the road and then as we looked we saw all the footprints on the other side of the road hop, hop hop back and through the gate! We did a count next evening and all were present and correct.'

Incrementally, the sanctuary grew beyond an idea, but it remained a strictly personal refuge rather than a public attraction. A combination of financial pressures and the powers of natural regeneration colluded to propel it into the next phase.

## CHAPTER SEVEN

# THE SHAFT OF LIGHT

JOHN'S CAREER AT FLINDERS UNIVERSITY is a remarkable story. In the 16 years of his employment, along with the teaching load and several stints in administration, he produced 25 original research papers, but it all came tumbling down when a conflict of principles leading to a Commission of Inquiry spelled the end of his role as a Professor.

Ironically, no less than an obsessive ethicality lay at the heart of the matters brought before the commission. Put simply, John refused to lower his standards to suit the university's teaching policy. In all good conscience he couldn't do what he had been asked to do and was thereby accused of dereliction of duty. This represented the second time in John's life he had to face a 'kangaroo court', even if on this occasion it appeared to be officially sanctioned.

Teaching mathematics, and doing it properly, constituted a passion, not just a job, but for the first time in his life financial constraints meant he couldn't walk away.

The commission exonerated John but left him humiliated and broken. Unable to lecture, he received a part salary, paid indefinitely. Ironically, his opinions about a 'dumbing down' of university teaching have been echoed decades later, when the mathematics curriculum has been accused of not adequately providing students with a solid understanding of their subject.

Also for the first time in his life, John found himself struggling to make ends meet.

Born out of necessity, John's concept of 'Sola Wood' (used as a company name) derived from the considerable success of tree plantings at Warrawong, using Brenton Tucker's bagged seedlings and planting in early summer, a time not usually considered conducive to good survival rates. Phenomenal seedling growth followed.

'I had purchased some native tree seedlings from an Adelaide nursery. They were in tiny tubes. Although they survived, they simply did not achieve the growth rates necessary to establish a forest, say, in ten years. Brenton's seedlings were much better. He used six inch by two inch plastic bags instead of tubes. The seedlings looked much more vigorous. However, they still did not achieve what I needed. A seedling, a few inches high, planted in Autumn would grow about a metre a year. Just not good enough.

'Then one day Brenton mentioned to me that because of an extraordinary early Spring, he had some Eucalypt seedlings ready for planting in December. Normally his seeds planted in October would not be ready until the following Autumn. He had some Eucalyptus dalrympleana, grandis and saligna ready. I had a spot picked out where I wanted to plant a tall forest. It was covered with blackberries, so I thoroughly ploughed it all up with the tractor and planted the seedlings. Since it was our dry period I flooded the area with water immediately after planting and then left them to their own resources.

'The results, from this Summer planting, were absolutely astounding. By Autumn, when I would normally have seedlings just twenty centimetres high, I had saplings of over two metres. They just kept growing. The next year I went to special efforts to plant thousands and thousands of Eucalypt seedlings in Summer. After ten years I had amazing results.'

*Astonishing growth of Eucalypts*

The record of plantings and construction is impressive by any standard:

1969    1000 trees planted on the boundary
1970    1000 trees planted on the boundary
1971    Dam built
1973    1000 trees planted
1974    4000 trees planted on adjacent roadsides
1975    3000 trees planted above Fernery Creek
1976    3000 trees planted along Williams Road

| 1977 | 5000 trees planted including near dam |
| 1978 | Swamp built and 2000 trees planted |
| 1979 | 4000 shrubs planted on contour hill |
| 1980 | 4000 shrubs planted on contour hill |
| 1981 | 3000 shrubs planted on contour hill |
| 1982 | Vermin proof fence constructed and 1500 trees planted, including Platypus ponds. |

Much of the current character for the area around Warrawong derives from this time of intensive revegetation and it is difficult for an untrained observer to tell natural from planted bush.

Note that *all* of the tree and fence-post holes were dug by hand, with John's tool of choice, the mattock.

The idea for 'Sola Wood' was to grow Tasmanian Blue Gum seedlings to sell as woodlots. Landholders paid for the trees and paid for them to be planted. John planted thousands of seedlings, once again using nothing more than a mattock. Interestingly, Tasmanian Blue Gum plantations as we know them today had scarcely been thought of in South Australia.

An article in the Hills Messenger newspaper in 1985 had this to say. 'Eucalypts should be grown for fuel and to prevent the destruction of natural bushland (i.e. the logging of old growth forest), according to Mylor resident John Wamsley.

'Dr Wamsley outlined a plan for farming gum trees at a meeting of the Mt Lofty Ranges Residents' Association. And it is not all talk.

'Dr Wamsley recently bought a 40 hectare property at Tooperang, near Mt Compass. Twenty acres will be devoted to farming gum trees.'

When you consider the hundreds of thousands of hectares of Blue Gum plantations in evidence today, the scale seems almost laughable, but it is indicative, once again, of John's eerily accurate predictive ability.

'We will be planting 4000 eucalypts at Christmas and if it goes as well as I expect it will, we should be getting about 1000 tonnes per year within five years . . . The remaining 20 hectares will be planted with Australian wildflowers.' Never one to talk down a project, John added, 'It will ultimately be the biggest wildflower garden in the southern hemisphere.'

Coles made an arrangement with John to sell 10kg boxes of cut firewood. Not having enough blue gum, he decided to use mallee harvested from where it was being rolled at that time on a property near Maggea in the Murray Mallee. The farmer, while not interested in harvesting the wood himself, was happy for John to take what would otherwise have been burned.

From a Stock Journal article, 'John Wamsley will pay $50 a tonne for mallee logs cut, dried and packed according to requirements, and will travel up to 500 kilometres to get it.'

Compare this wholesale price to the price of cut mallee today and it is obvious again just how prescient was John's idea. It reveals, also, how resources once considered only fit to burn in the paddock have become valuable as population grows and availability of those resources dwindles.

Proo told me they had to disconnect their phone because of a flood of offers from interested landowners. But the price, just below $3 per 10 kg, which was necessary to cover costs and make a profit, was nevertheless too high for that time and people didn't buy the wood. Proo joked that she was one of the few who actually bought it.

Today such small quantities of bagged wood are sold at supermarkets and service stations all over the city and the price of wood has risen to where 'Sola Wood' could have worked very well as a business.

Of the Sola Wood enterprise, John says, 'That was my first failure at making money. Usually when I decide to make money it works very well.'

The stress of looking for a way to earn a living detracted from the pure enjoyment of living at Warrawong and the happiness of a new relationship and family.

Something serendipitous and touching waited its time, to change the paradigm again.

A well developed environment already existed, with 40,000 trees and shrubs, including what John called 'South Australia's only native rainforest' using ferns that once grew in the Adelaide hills. Five different habitats were simulated: grassland, shrub-scrub, dry and wet forests and wetlands. Reed beds and a series of twenty ponds and lakes, fed by a reticulation system, ran the length of the property.

On a quiet day, the next two decades of John's life declared themselves ready to be born, thus:

'One day, walking around the property, I thought I caught a glimpse of a pademelon. They only allow themselves to be seen very briefly and I remembered what a retreating pademelon looked like from my childhood experience.

'Next morning I took some bread with me and threw it where I thought I'd seen the animal. This pademelon came out and ate the bread! I threw another piece of bread and another pademelon came out. And then I threw another piece until I was surrounded by pademelons. *The female that got out had survived*. It was pregnant and produced young. They'd built a colony and I didn't even know they were there.

'When I was standing there in the forest surrounded by this ring of animals *it was like I had died and gone to heaven*.'

Immediately, he was thrust back into the bush of Niagara Park, his childhood home, where the small kangaroos used to graze at the forest's edge and he walked, barefoot, lost in reverie.

'I thought, bloody hell, this is fantastic! And it's better than I ever thought I could do.'

Just how long he lingered there we don't know, but after the initial shock of delight, pragmatic thoughts started to intrude. He was, after all, unemployed and perilously close to the financial abyss.

'I thought, *people would pay to see this*. This is what went through my head. I could open the place to the public and that would give me an out from my financial difficulties.'

The fence had worked. The last fox hadn't got the last pademelon. What it dramatically demonstrated was that all the animals needed was a place to be safe and they could do what nature gave them every facility to do. It wasn't even difficult once you gave the animals themselves a chance to determine their own fate.

On the first of January 1985 John put up a sign which read, 'Guided walks at dusk every day.'

*Warrawong Sanctuary*

Those small, unassuming animals had unwittingly started a powerful engine. The sign was the first step in a process which created a veritable empire.

Running the business was initially a low-key affair, without even council approval. John succinctly put it this way. 'They (the customers) gave me five dollars. I put it in my pocket and took them for a walk. Then showed them the gate. It went very well and blew everybody's mind.'

But business was slow. In the first year, they conducted 32 night walks.

Then, in February of 1986 someone from the Advertiser newspaper rang up. They had heard a rumour to the effect that 'you could see all these little animals.' It was fortuitous that their usual reporters were on strike and so they were looking for stories. Warrawong hit the front page.

The only negative was that word of Warrawong's success got through to the Australian Universities Superannuation Scheme which was still paying John at half salary.

'Obviously, I wasn't sick.'

The money stopped and that represented the end of any connection with the old world of lecturing.

When pressed about it, John says he didn't miss the involvement with mathematics. Once it stopped being a dream job he had little interest in it, but then as now he does daily mathematics puzzles (at a very high level) to keep his hand in.

Mathematics, he thinks, is a young person's game. The kind of mental gymnastics required to 'do' it are not for older people, though there are exceptions. Even concepts which are like pre-school topics to John remain about as accessible to ordinary mortals as a rocket trip to Mars.

Mathematics lecturing faded away. The pademelons had won.

CHAPTER EIGHT

# CONSOLIDATION

Close to the Almanda Swamp, where there is thick vegetation cover, Bandicoots are in evidence from their conical diggings and the occasional fleeting sight of an animal crossing the road. That they have survived to flourish there is miraculous. John likes to say that the population in Scott Creek is the last stronghold of the southern brown bandicoot in Australia.

Increasingly, I can understand how it must feel for him to know that animals like this needn't be so precariously balanced in the natural world, if only we had listened.

Right from his toddler years, circumstances prepared him to understand how to help the denizens of the bush, how to love them without romanticising or anthropomorphising them, nurture them without distorting their connection with evolution.

Warrawong was not conceived as a zoo. In a zoo, animals are reared from birth within artificial enclosures and their behaviour is modified by this upbringing. Evolutionary processes cannot proceed as they would do in the wild and this is important, because there are no permanently stable systems within the natural world. Change is ever-present. It could be argued that human beings are now the arbiters of change and this is fine if we are prepared to accept the kind of impoverished world we are creating. A world of ever-diminishing diversity. *A vanishing kind.*

John had this to say about zoos: 'So we have the ridiculous situation where our zoos are breeding wildlife that have nowhere to go. Here in Adelaide we are breeding Przewalski horses to send back to Mongolia. The reason that Przewalski horses disappeared in Mongolia is because the Mongolians ate them. At Taronga zoo they are breeding Golden Lion Tamarins to send back to Brazil. The reason Golden Lion Tamarins are disappearing in Brazil is because they make cute pets. If the public's view is changed, and that is happening through education programs in this case, then there is no need to carry out captive breeding.

'We have the incredible situation of our zoos stuffed full of rare and endangered animals on birth control because there is nowhere left for them to live in the wild. Then we have incredible statements like, "our zoos are arks holding these animals until the day comes when they can be released back into the wild." Surely if the wild is unsuitable today, it can only be worse tomorrow.

'Warrawong Sanctuary also introduced the average Australian to their wildlife. When Warrawong opened to the public, the curator of Adelaide Zoo publicly stated, "People do not want to see tiny kangaroos, they only want to see big kangaroos." A few years later he lamented, "What we need here at the Zoo are more tiny kangaroos; that is what people want to see."

'Australians could now see woylies, bettongs, pademelon, bandicoot and quoll.'

Whether John consciously realised it or not, Warrawong attempted to recreate the bushland at Niagara Park, the natural system as he knew it from nearly half a century before. Over that time the world he grew up in endured quiet devastation and few were aware of it. Even fewer cared.

The behaviour of animals as he remembered it was wild behaviour without human imprint. Until that first cat and fox proof fence appeared in SA there was no place in Australia deliberately set up to protect native animals in situ.

Large areas of land augmented the conservation ledger once the shocking extent of vegetation clearance in SA and elsewhere pricked the conscience of governments (especially with the advent of satellite imagery), but after protection from clearance, nothing more was done with the land. Management plans and the routed wooden park signs couldn't help the wildlife.

While preventing vegetation clearance is a huge and admirable step in itself, it cannot benefit the animal species if introduced predators are allowed to do as they please. Rabbits also play a huge part in the drama, removing vegetation which other animals depend on for their survival. The feral cat's range covers the entire continent of Australia, north to south and east to west. The fox's range is from east to west and as far north as the tropic of Capricorn, beyond which the humidity is not to its liking. Rabbits occupy a similar range below the tropics. In Spain, from which country our rabbits originate, there are no less than twenty nine predators to keep these animals in check. This is the difference.

Sheep quickly spread throughout the semi-arid zone and cattle made incursions even into the extreme environments of the centre. These grazers had a profound impact on the vegetation and hence the animals which used it.

Vast areas are, in one sense, biologically dead because the interaction between plants and animals is broken. Little, if anything, was understood in earlier years about the relationship between plants and wildlife, the way in which plant species distribution and abundance is dependent on the presence of the animals who recycle nutrients, graze, pollinate, spread seed, open up areas of the soil and keep the forest or woodland floor from becoming choked with organic litter.

Even for John, with the benefit of intuitive understanding, this complex inter-dependence represented a fledgling science. Whether or not he understood the many roles his beloved animals played, his prime concern was to first save them from complete destruction. The bushland plants could recover as long as the seed-stock was there, but the animals, once their DNA vanished, could never come back.

In time, the earth can rejuvenate itself, but we are talking hundreds of thousands, if not millions, of years, and this is of no use on any human time scale. For all normal purposes, the loss of species is forever.

To say that Warrawong's beginnings were humble or tentative is to scarcely do justice to the original motivation. John states categorically that, 'I had no plans to open to the public. I didn't do it for money. *I didn't do it for any reason other than to have a place where I could get up in the morning and be happy.*' For some people, the surrounding physical environment is critical to their mental health. It really was that simple and accidental, but fortuitous.

A few animals at a time, over a period of years and parallel with the growth of its plants, Warrawong developed into the sanctuary spawned in John's imagination.

In a very real sense, it became a sanctuary for John as well as for the animals. It is obvious that the stress-related symptoms generated by the necessity to remain at Flinders University simply fell away once he embraced the 'new' persona. The persona which had been there all along, perhaps, in the end, at war with his Mathematics Professor image.

Together, John and Proo knew what few people outside the professional wildlife fraternity knew, namely that Australia's native animals, while extraordinarily diverse and unique, had disappeared over most of the continent. If our animals were large and visible by day we may have been more conscious of their demise. Most of our wildlife appears only when we go to sleep. This is profoundly important in understanding our alienation from them and our lack of awareness of their fate. Both John and Proo grew up in contact with and, just as significantly, emotionally bonded with, native animals.

Ultimately, the sanctuary would contain potoroos, bettongs, bandicoots, pademelons, wallabies, platypus, quolls, kangaroos, possums and swamp rats, but the animals were acquired one species at a time, as circumstances allowed.

Interestingly, an official from the tourism commission came along in those early days and told them the idea for Warrawong wouldn't work. That they needed to have at least some of the animals in cages at the 'shop-front' to attract people. Nocturnal animals weren't going to interest anyone. Later, the same tourism people admonished them for not putting their sanctuary on the advertised tourist circuit. Of course, this was after it had become a runaway success.

Proo explains the rationale for nocturnal walks: 'With the decision to open to the public came the question of HOW to do this.

'All but the big Kangaroo species are nocturnal. Zoos answered this question by having nocturnal houses, but we felt the magic of what we had done, seeing such rare and unknown species in the wild, feeding, fighting, carrying nesting material in their tails was so much more powerful than collecting up one or two of each and confining them in a cage or pen for people to view during the day.

'So with just that in mind we worked out routes and paths, purchased suitable torches and invited in groups of people.

'Taking a group of 20 or so people on a nocturnal walk involved having stories to tell and we had many stories to go with seeing the animals. The walk was also designed to start on sunset, for the groups to walk "into the night" and to last 90 minutes.

'There was the story of how we had planted the property, the reason for the fence and why it was important, the importance of dead wood for habitat and hollows in the trees, the fast growing eucalypts, the 10/80 (poison bait) story and how the many species extinct across eastern Australia had survived in Western Australia because of a family of plants full of 10/80 and the tolerances these native creatures have – an advantage over foxes and cats There were the stars, walking in moonlight with no torch light, and along the way the rustles in the undergrowth telling us where to point the torch to highlight a wallaby or a bettong or a possum high in the canopy. As darkness settled we would be able to hear and see bats hunting over the Black Water Lake. Sometimes other rarely seen species like owls crossed our path, hunting at night, gliding through the trees after an insect or small rodent. The waterways had many easy to see species such as ducks, grebes, swamp hens, coots and tortoises as well as the Platypus, and there was much information to tell about them.

'In the Little Forest we would ask everyone on the walk to hug a tree and put their ear to the trunk to hear the sounds of the tree.

'So the aim within the 90 minute timeframe was to take a walk full of diversity with stories, information, animals unrestrained by pens and cages. The magic of being out in the night.

'As the walks became known a staffer from the Tourism Bureau came to visit. Of course he came at10am and couldn't comprehend what we were on about. He told us to put our animals in cages; tourists don't go out in the dark.

'This attitude also became a problem with signage. We were advised by letter the only way we could have signage was if we were open 9-5 as well as the Nocturnal walks.'

*Nocturnal walks at Warrawong represented the first such walks offered in Australia* and the first of many 'firsts' for John and Proo in their conservation and education endeavours.

For every animal procured there is a story. In order to obtain southern brown bandicoots from Scott Creek Conservation Park, John offered to get rid of the northern brown bandicoots he already had because they were not indigenous to SA. The NPWS was concerned that these animals, which they had sighted at some point, posed a vague threat. 'They could escape and take over the country!' as John said. What he didn't tell them was that his specimens of the northern species had already died, because the climate of SA didn't suit them. With this ruse he got the Bandicoots from Scott Creek.

Swamp rats, so called because they lived in long grass usually associated with swamps, were taken from private property in the nearby Kuitpo area.

'I built this habitat for them with pipes under the ground. The interesting thing was, after a week I lifted up the edge of the enclosure and let them all out. They all went down and lived in the car park! So much for my construction. We ended up with a massive colony. They did very well at Warrawong because without the cats they were fantastic.'

Some, like the northern brown bandicoots, came from as far afield as Byron Bay in northern New South Wales. It seems extraordinary that a native animal which was once so common in Australia could only be found by travelling thousands of kilometres.

The Byron Bay purchase almost didn't happen. John and Proo left Adelaide with $500 allocated for the purchase. This was all the money left over after insurance paid off the mortgage on Proo's bushfire-ravaged house. En route to their destination, and still in South Australia's mid-north, Proo inadvertently left the purse containing this precious cash on the roof of their car after a brief stop. John relates how furious he was about it, cursing and swearing and how despairing of getting it back, but as they drove forlornly back along their route looking for it, a fifty dollar note blew up and across their windshield and stuck there. And then another. They stopped and as they watched the cars go backwards and forwards, so did the notes. The purse had been run over and destroyed but miraculously they got all their money back and continued with the trip.

Possums, being naturally occurring, were not confined or blocked by the fence and made their own way to the sanctuary. Kangaroos derived from rescue animals. Their numbers had to be controlled (due to their size) and so the kangaroos were all desexed. They had individual names which John used when interacting with them on the public walks.

A pair of Eastern quolls came from the animal house at Flinders University. Others of this species were smuggled in (John's words) from Tasmania but were on record as having been bred from the original Flinders pair. The university then gave them more quolls under the guise of improving the biodiversity of the colony. Sometimes a little bending of the truth is necessary in a good cause!

Warrawong's animals roamed free and survived on natural browse. The fence existed to keep unwanted predators out, not to keep animals confined.

Some of John's casual utterances say a lot about him as a person, though it is not necessarily possible to quantify what we are learning, eg, 'I had less trouble telling the kangaroos apart than I had with people. *I wish people were as different as kangaroos.*' He went on to say, 'When I met Proo, she was the first woman I could tell from the others, so I thought *I'd better hang on to this one!*'

At both dawn and dusk, groups of people assembled at strategic spots where they viewed whatever species appeared and received information about them.

'Wally' the wombat was the only animal who had his own enclosure. John used Wally's well-established natural routine to great advantage.

He would say, 'Come out now, Wally.' And the animal would dutifully appear. 'Have a scratch now, Wally,' and Wally enjoyed his scratch. 'Roll over and do your back now, Wally,' and so it went. Wally never let him down.

Antipathy towards the Warrawong concept came from certain elements within the government departments connected with wildlife management in these early years. 'I used to go on my walks and say how hopeless government departments were. They had a monopoly on animals and it was stupid.'

Whether for reasons of perceived threat to their jobs or simply a desire to keep wildlife management 'in house', there was almost a zero tolerance for private involvement in wildlife management beyond the small private zoos which existed to display animals in cages.

Warrawong's animals had to be obtained wherever they could be found, even if it meant 'smuggling' them out of Tasmania. The government culture was against private conservation initiatives, but public culture was the very opposite; people were delighted and charmed.

John has repeatedly stated that there was support from the wonderful people 'on the ground', like the park rangers, and from the very top, where he had a good relationship with the CEO of the NPWS, Laurie Delroy. It was Laurie Delroy who authorised the collection of southern brown bandicoots for Warrawong from the remnant population at Scott Creek Conservation Park and later authorised the trapping of platypus on Kangaroo Island.

Certain middle managers in the NPWS, Zoo and Museum gave John cause for concern and he has reiterated this on many occasions. I have tried to be objective. The one firm proof of organised opposition lay in the existence of a brochure circulated by the NPWS. The brochure only came to light when a member of the public wrote a letter to the newspaper making certain claims about Warrawong. When John threatened to sue for defamation the letter writer defended himself by producing the brochure from which he had obtained his spurious information. Unfortunately, John failed to keep this document.

But another story serves to illustrate how forces were arraigned against Warrawong. There were two species of bettong in the sanctuary, the eastern and the western. These animals, one kind from Tasmania and the other from Western Australia, are naturally separated by a vast distance and represent distinct species. Those concerned with wildlife management wanted to maintain them as separate entities. It was not permitted under law that the two species should interbreed.

John wrote about this in one of his publications. 'Someone realised that we had both *Bettongia penicillata* and *gaimardi* (the two species of bettong). Someone else realised that we were not a zoo and that all of our animals lived together. Someone else remembered that one day over one hundred years ago there was a report that *gaimardi* and *penicillata* interbred at London Zoo. And then someone else realised it was illegal to hybridise native animals. Unfortunately for us, *these four people all turned up at the same dinner party*. We were in serious trouble.'

John insisted that his bettongs were not interbreeding. 'People from the NPWS turned up with traps and syringes. They trapped every single bettong, or so they said. They took blood samples and left. A couple of weeks later came the result.'

John says of this, 'The biggest win I had in my life was that there wasn't any interbreeding whatsoever. Zero. And that put me on a pedestal as far as Laurie Delroy was concerned, because he saw that I knew something the experts didn't.'

The incident serves to illustrate that even without formal training in zoology, John possessed knowledge *which none of the so-called experts in this country apparently had and it was gained intuitively through observation of animals in the wild.*

Stressing the point more than once, John wanted me to understand the principle at work among animals where breeding is concerned.

'If you take an ant from one of those colonies of meat ants (Iridomyrmex spp) which make their nests on pathways and you put that ant in the next adjoining colony, it would be accepted by the neighbouring ants and could even live in the colony. If you took an ant from that colony in turn and took it to the next, the same would happen, and so it would go, right down the line.

'But if you took that first ant and placed it in a colony a long distance away, it would be killed by those ants because it would be seen as too different to themselves. To that colony it would be alien.

'The same happens with animals in the wild. They won't accept and interbreed with individuals from a far off colony. Being born in captivity, in cages, and growing up with one another interferes with this natural selectivity. Hence zoo-bred animals will interbreed where Warrawong's animals wouldn't.'

All of the animals introduced to the sanctuary thrived, though this success in building up numbers brought its own special problems. The animals weren't caged, but the area in which they could live was limited, even with several additional blocks of land purchased to expand Warrawong. The young of species like swamp rats and bandicoots passed through the fence, meaning that, in spite of predation, the area around Warrawong abounded with them because their numbers were sufficient to outpace the predators.

Larger species like wallabies and rufus bettongs were a problem because they were too successful. Culling was no doubt necessary, but impossible once the sanctuary operated as a busy commercial venture.

Proo says of this, 'We know in hindsight it was a problem we failed to address. We failed to have a trapping area and we failed to have places off the tourism circuit, the public circuit, where we could deal with things like that if we had to.'

Culling and vermin control are two of the less palatable aspects of wildlife management, things which the public can't always digest. 'There are those animals that regulate their numbers and those that don't. Those that don't have to be disposed of somehow.' Being able to put the surplus animals somewhere else is the ideal situation, but it has to be a place both suitable and safe. There lies the dilemma.

Of those situations, such as that on Kangaroo Island, where koalas represent an introduced environmental disaster, John asserts that, 'There is no doubt that the kindest thing you can do is cull.' Unfortunately, there is little public sympathy for culling, but the alternatives are often brutal, with species breeding to the point of starvation.

Not one feral-free place existed in Australia where it was practicable or legal to translocate Warrawong's surplus animals. When you consider the size of this gigantic land mass we live on, it was a staggering and disgraceful reality.

This need for room ultimately drove the next phase of the sanctuary story, with the way forward destined to be littered by obstacles.

The simmering enmity shown by some government managers towards the Warrawong enterprise had a legal manifestation when John and Proo applied for the right to put up an advertising sign on the freeway. Such signs advertising private tourism destinations are common now, but it was a source of conflict in 1998, when Warrawong lodged a case alleging that certain commercial activities by Cleland Wildlife Park contravened the principles of Competitive Neutrality.

Cleland Wildlife Park (CWP) is a government-run venture near Mount Lofty at the top of the ranges. It had a large sign at the freeway exit to advertise its presence. Warrawong asked for the same thing, but was refused permission. Competitive Neutrality laws had been introduced in federal parliament whereby it was illegal for the public sector to wield an unfair advantage over the private sector in a similar business.

In the first action taken under the new laws, Warrawong took the SA government to court over the issue and won their case. The SA Competition Commissioner found clear similarities between the operations of both entities, as both were about the same distance from the city and both displayed native animals.

The Competition Commissioner found, 'CWP held a much larger market share than Warrawong and possessed the market strength to act as a "formidable" competitor to existing and potential private sector operators.'

One of the outcomes was that the Cleland sign reduced in size and Warrawong got a sign of the same dimensions. The theme of government versus private conservation comes up repeatedly in John's writings. Perhaps he wouldn't have minded so much about the level of subsidy to public zoos and sanctuaries if those zoos and sanctuaries were doing their job, as he saw it, in helping to halt the wave of extinctions.

Some of his statements give unequivocal voice to his feelings about the role of government. The failure of successive governments to address the problems of mass extinction become inseparable, in his mind, from political ideology. This is an extract from a preface to a paper written by John titled 'We can do it if we wanted.'

'There have been two great confidence tricks carried out on the world in the twentieth century. One was called communism. The other was called conservation. Both failed. The reasons for their failure were remarkably similar.

'The basic philosophy of communism is that the most important asset a people have, is the means of production. Therefore, it argues, that ownership of the means of production should be vested in the State and the State will care for it. Hence both will flourish etc. It failed because the State could not give a stuff. The State is incapable of caring. The State is a political animal, not a caring animal.

'The basic philosophy of conservation was that the most important asset a people had was the environment. Therefore, it argues, that ownership of the environment should be vested in the State and the State will care for it etc.

'If the Australian Governments had spent twice as much on conservation over the last twenty years, we would have lost twice as much. In fact, it is easy to correlate the loss of wildlife, in modern times, with conservation expenditure. Queensland's biggest drop in numbers of bridled nail-tailed wallabies happened after the National Parks took over their management. Queensland's loss of the bilby happened after the National Parks took over their management. The same goes for the Northern Territory's care of the mala and Victoria's care of the barred bandicoot.

'If we gave the government the job of producing our food we would all expect to die of hunger. Yet we hand over our wildlife, the very soul of our country, to a non-caring State.

'I would gladly give my soul to the devil, to roast in hell for an eternity, if I could save one species of wildlife in exchange. Yet I could do nothing. I sank into a sea of despair. Maybe tomorrow will be better.'

These last comments are meant to lead into the developing story (in the same writings) of how John addressed the problem with his own private initiatives.

In the same vein, John paints an amusing picture of politicians. 'Conservation, the dictionary says, is the result of conservative action. Fifty years ago, good conservation was at the heart of Country Party policy. Today they seem to have lost the plot. Why must the most right wing conservative become a raging socialist the minute he is made Minister for the Environment?'

In spite of some twisting of semantics, the idea is clear. Our culture, at that time, and perhaps still today, with qualification, dictated that something as esoteric as conservation could only be the province of government. This thinking is closely allied to the idea, strongly developed later in our story, that wildlife and ecosystems suffer because they do not and cannot be allocated a monetary value.

It is not surprising, given the kind of sentiments expressed above, that John and Proo became a bit wary of potential government inspectors, but there was a humorous side to it. Warrawong advertised its bird population, especially the diversity and sheer weight of numbers near the nectar bearing plants as 'The world's largest aviary.' Of course, it wasn't an aviary in the conventional sense because there were no walls or ceilings of wire. This is the aforementioned 'two-pounder' principle at work.

'This bloke turned up one day and sat in the tea rooms, watching the birds outside He was obviously a government spy. And Proo said (to John), "You're in trouble now". And there he sat all bloody day. He had scones and a cup of tea. In the end I went and sat down and asked how he was going and he said, "This is fantastic". And it was. It was fantastic. The birds had migrated from Coral Oliphant's house 15 years before. *He turned out to be a retired bank manager.* So we were close. They look very similar to government spies!'

Notwithstanding the tussles with government departments, these were the golden years. Finding money hadn't yet become an issue. Both public and media support remained constant and enthusiastic. As a speaker John was always in demand and Warrawong provided one of the standard roll-outs for television current affairs or documentaries.

Economic success and notoriety were, however, secondary to the real job in hand, for taken over a span of fifteen years, the breeding numbers for Warrawong are truly impressive.

'The brush-tailed bettong, Australia's smallest and then rarest living kangaroo, increased from 6 individuals to over 300. The long-nosed potoroo, Australia's most primitive 'real' kangaroo, increased from 4 individuals to over 100. The Sydney sub-species of the red-necked pademelon, the last colony of this sub-species left in the world and John's childhood familiar, increased from just 2 individuals to over 30. The southern brown bandicoot, the last remaining species of South Australia's 8 species just 150 years ago, increased from 4 individuals to over 200.'

John concluded with the salutary observation that, 'The only difference between Warrawong Sanctuary and any other bit of Australia is simply that Warrawong Sanctuary is fox and cat free.'

Warrawong regularly made the shortlist for Tourism Awards and drew praise for its achievements from people all over Australia and the world. The man vilified as a destroyer of pine trees became synonymous with a new awareness within Australia about natural heritage, and the story had only begun.

# CHAPTER NINE

# SOMETHING UNIQUE

IN THE CLEAR WATER OF the Almanda Creek (part of John's current stamping ground) I have seen small, unspectacular native fish called Galaxias and have been delighted at the sight. Our streams within South Australia are mostly so utterly changed and degraded that it is rare now to find aquatic wildlife. Even the tadpoles, common when I was growing up in the nineteen fifties, are hard to find, but there were once other, larger animals in at least two of our rivers. Mammals unlike anything else on earth.

I have seen how John works with water in a creek, logging the stream bed to slow the flow and create habitat, transplanting sedges and other riparian plants from wet areas of the park and even reshaping a pool or spring outflow to create forms pleasing to the eye and to provide habitat for the abovementioned Galaxias.

Nothing is as it was in 1836 when Europeans came to this state. We will never know what it originally looked like, but we can help nature along and try to create something which will enable plant and animal species to become self-sustaining.

Sections of the Almanda creek are quite exquisite, where permanent water flows past tall native fern, sedges and rushes, gypsy-wort and native lobelia. Before John first started working on the creek it was smothered to head height in blackberry. Others joined him when they saw what was possible, leading slowly to the recovering display visible today.

This intuitive drive to work with the landscape in the most cooperative and disciplined way and to allow that which is put back the best chance of survival led to an almost unique achievement.

I speak, of course, about the successful breeding of Platypus. No other story is so closely connected with Warrawong. Platypus occupy as unique a place in our psyche as they do in our natural history.

The Platypus achieves almost mythical status. I attempted, unsuccessfully, to see one, spending some time on the banks of the Rocky River on Kangaroo Island. It was an intense and special experience to be there on a calm day, with a very gentle rain sprinkling the water while I waited for something more substantial to disturb the surface. On Kangaroo Island it is still possible to see streams in their original condition, running with pure, tannin-stained water from catchments wholly within a conservation zone. The vegetation is as it should be, wild and dense. It is not surprising that Platypus were successfully introduced. What is more, Kangaroo Island has only a limited problem with feral animals and this is only at the more developed Eastern end. There is still a chance to eradicate them.

Attributes of the Platypus are universally known. The strangeness guarantees its notoriety. When first described in 1799 it was thought to be a hoax, a compounded animal made from several species sewn together. But in defiance of everything rational, it truly exists. A semi-aquatic, filter-feeding egg-laying mammal, the only representative of its genus, with the bill of a duck, the tail of a beaver, the webbed feet of an otter, a pair of venomous spurs on the hind legs of the male, the ability to locate its aquatic prey by electrolocation (like a shark) and with a waterproof fur once sought after for human use.

While they have been protected from hunting since 1905, their future remains uncertain due to human-led degradation of the streams they inhabit. The IUCN gives its status as 'near threatened'.

Breeding of this strange and beautiful animal had been achieved only once before, at Healesville Sanctuary in 1944, where one specimen was produced within an artificial stream enclosed by a tank. David Fleay, the man who brought this about, spent the rest of his life trying without success to duplicate his own feat. A visit by John and Proo to Healesville convinced them they should introduce platypus to Warrawong.

The last reported wild sighting of this animal from the SA mainland was in 1976 at Renmark on the River Murray.

John boasts, 'I knew more about animals than anyone else in this country.' A big statement perhaps, but supported by his hands-on experience and a string of unique achievements. Thus he knew he had a good chance of duplicating the Healesville experience. The respect from Laurie Delroy, the head of the NPWS, meant John had his wish to take platypus from Kangaroo Island granted.

Because these animals are introduced, rather than indigenous, on Kangaroo Island, there was none of the legal trouble associated with their removal, but an application process needed to be followed, and John had an interesting take on it. It appeared to him easier for groups or organisations, rather than individuals, to get what they want.

'I decided that I should form a group of people with the intention of bringing back platypus to the mainland of SA.' To this end, prominent people were asked to become part of the group, but this was to teach him a new lesson. 'There's no way in the world that a committee can make a decision about anything. It just doesn't work that way. If there's something serious to be done then someone has to do it.'

Accordingly, John wrote a submission to the NPWS and in the meantime began to study platypus in situ. 'I spent a fortnight sitting on the banks of the Rocky River on Kangaroo Island, watching platypus, because I decided, long ago, you don't learn things about animals by looking in a book, you learn by sitting and watching them.' The observations gave him confidence.

He brought back handfuls of mud to see what small organisms lived in it, studied the riparian plant-life which grew where the animals lived and began attempts to increase the alkalinity of the water in his dam to match that of the Rocky River, but even in this he ultimately had to rely on his own ingenuity because the 'experts' could only tell him what worked in a controlled situation. The solution was to fill part of the water channel with limestone rock.

The application to the NPWS 'went through surprisingly well', so Warrawong had permission to take two platypus from Kangaroo Island.

'The News' (formerly Adelaide's afternoon paper) reported, 'He is going ahead with the scheme after it was refused status as a Bicentennial project. He says this means there are only pseudo-conservation projects, such as the tropical conservatory.'

While the conservatory he refers to is a stunning addition to Adelaide's contemporary architecture, and its aim was to educate people about biodiversity in other parts of the world, it is not hard to take John's point. The platypus project, which dealt with one of our own special, vulnerable species and, moreover, a species extinct on mainland South Australia, was denied money from the large pool of funds available. Presumably because the project was in the hands of a private individual. Yet money was forthcoming for something which promoted ecosystems outside South Australia and which contained plants from other parts of the world.

Channel Seven, one of Adelaide's local television stations, generously offered the services of the station's helicopter and a crew to film the whole thing. John still expresses gratitude to this company for helping with the project when no one else would. Helicopter flights are expensive and logistics in such an undertaking were otherwise daunting. Technical advice on the actual capture process came from Dr. Tom Grant, who was Australia's leading expert on platypus, but he was unable to take part in the process on the ground due to other commitments.

'With the film crew came this other bloke who knew all about Platypus. He'd been on Platypus catching expeditions and was an expert on catching them.' John felt relieved to have this man on the team, because he had no experience of his own with handling Platypus. In NSW he had never seen one.

The method involved placing a gill-net across the place where Platypus swim. It is necessary for someone to be present at capture because Platypus are air breathers and can drown if they are unable to surface.

At midnight, in bitter cold, John decided he'd had enough and retired to bed, only to be woken at around 1.30 am with the news that 'they nearly got one.' The whole thing was filmed and it showed that the 'expert' had let his animal get away, jumping in the water and tentatively poking at the Platypus. The film crew and the expert then decided to call it a night.

Suddenly finding himself again the man on duty and now a little desperate, John determined to give the expedition a chance to succeed. But he hadn't planned to do the catching and had never caught or handled a Platypus, so now he was flying blind. There were two capture sites but it wasn't possible to monitor both of them in the dark without getting injured in the dense vegetation or disturbing the platypus they were there to catch.

This is what happened: 'By God it was a cold night! At about 2 o'clock there was a "plop" in the pool (of the river). I couldn't see it in the dark, but I realised a Platypus had gone into the net. I jumped into the water and wrapped the whole net around the Platypus. I was soaking wet and I didn't have a change of clothes. All I had was a flagon of port. It was a young female Platypus and that was all we got but the next morning the ranger turned up with another young female he'd picked up at a crossing. So we ended up with two females.'

All the careful study and water engineering paid off. The platypus thrived in their series of pools, finding the food they naturally ate, the small invertebrates which they filter from the water like a duck.

A year later and after another trip to Kangaroo Island he caught two males. The News article also said, 'Getting the platypus to breed and live happily at Warrawong is a big problem, he says, and he is "terrified".

'But he has one kilometre of the Onkaparinga (catchment) on his property, and a deep "black-water" (that is, tannin-stained) pool, which is their natural habitat. "They're juvenile so they won't breed for three years," he said, "and if we lose them, we'll have to understand why, so we don't repeat the mistake. I haven't a zoo mentality, I'm quite patient."'

That patience paid dividends. 'According to the experts, the males didn't breed until three years old, but mine bred at two years because they had no other dominant males to worry about and they had some older ladies to show them what to do.

'When I said there were young in the swamp, nobody believed me. The males weren't old enough to breed. So I organised Dr. Tom Grant to come over and do a catch. And we caught a young one.'

*The first successful breeding in forty years*

John said his $20,000 breeding program, which allowed the egg-laying mammals, or Monotremes, to live in their natural surroundings, 'Succeeded where million dollar efforts by major Australian zoos failed

'We've been a hundred percent successful as platypuses usually only have up to two babies and we've also learnt that males can breed when two years old.

'The births came after a series of failures in breeding programs in zoos around the country. Melbourne zoo abandoned its $2.2 million Platypus breeding program 18 months earlier after no success, while Sydney's Taronga Park zoo and Queensland's National Parks and Wildlife Service had failed in similar programs.'

Taronga Zoo sent a congratulatory letter:

> '*Dr Dedee Woodside of the Conservation Research Centre at Taronga Zoo joins me in extending to you our warmest congratulations on the birth of platypus in your sanctuary. You have clearly provided them with an entirely suitable environment and an appropriate mix of individual animals, and have this happy achievement as a result.*
>
> '*We look forward to hearing of some of the details of your facilities and the circumstances which have led to these*

*young animals appearing. We are currently studying our captive conditions at Taronga Zoo, and would like to apply elements of the conditions at Warrawong (where appropriate and where we are physically able to) to our own captive environment. I will contact you shortly and would like to arrange to visit your facility, at your convenience.*

*'Once again, our congratulations on the birth of the platypus, and on your obviously successful re-introduction of platypus to the mainland of South Australia.'*

It was signed by F. Dominic Fanning, a Research Fellow from the Platypus Breeding and Conservation Research Program.

There could scarcely be a greater accolade. Compared to the people in Government programs, John was an amateur, yet he succeeded where they had not.

I asked John if platypus had originally been indigenous to SA and in connection with this he spoke of a strange incident.

'There used to be two Platypus skins in the Adelaide museum. One had a tag saying it was from the River Murray in SA and the other from the Onkaparinga River in the Adelaide Hills. Mysteriously, once I bred the platypus, they (the skins) disappeared and the museum claimed the animals weren't native to SA, saying, *Wamsley's just having you on.*'

This incident is part of a series of pieces of evidence which I have tried to be objective about, but which point to the veracity of John's repeated claim about a deliberate campaign to discredit him.

The next phase in the breeding program necessitated obtaining a bigger water supply. John sought money from Toba Aquarium in Japan. They gave him $240,000 for the chance to acquire a platypus, should the law be changed to allow export of native animals.

The money was to be used to set up a 'Platypussery', complete with an underwater viewing area. 'I explained to them that they may not get a platypus. That I would do my best. And I did my best.'

John is understandably incensed by the intransigence displayed at the time. 'Each year, two to four platypus leave Warrawong and are eaten by foxes. If you could get them a home you could get millions of dollars to help save Australia's wildlife, but the greenies don't think that's the way to do it.' The Japanese never got their Platypus. 'The greenies insisted the foxes have them instead.'

John's remarkable achievement is still sometimes omitted from articles about platypus breeding and reintroduction in Australia. There is a confusing double-speak at work. If his Warrawong platypus breeding area doesn't represent a 'captive' environment, then he has successfully reintroduced the animal to the wild, yet he is not necessarily credited with this feat.

Stories circulate about platypus sightings in the Adelaide Hills, even now. John is still called upon from time to time to comment in the papers about such sightings. It is comforting to believe that escaped animals may have survived in one or two places, but the reality is that without protection from introduced predators, the chances of survival outside the Warrawong dams are very remote.

Out of thirteen nominees, the Harry Dowling Award for Excellence in Tourism was given to Warrawong in 1988. The Perpetual award, retained by Warrawong for a year, was in the form of a large piece of polished red gum surmounted by two bronze platypus.

An estimate of the platypus population at Warrawong in 1999 put the number at about twenty animals.

The cycle of breeding in the Warrawong dam continued, long after the sanctuary ceased to exist, unseen, forgotten and unremarked by government. A rebuke to us all.

## CHAPTER TEN

# EXPANSION

THE EUPHORIA OF WARRAWONG'S GOLDEN years were never to be matched in the grand plans and deceptively exponential growth to come. Complication piled on complication.

If John and Proo had stayed with Warrawong alone and kept a couple of staff, they might still be going today, but that wouldn't have done much for wildlife in the greater sphere.

Warrawong became almost overwhelmed by its own success in breeding animals and this points up the one major drawback of the venture; the property was too small.

Several adjoining blocks, purchased and added to the original area, greatly expanded the sanctuary, but it is simply not possible to replicate a natural, self-sustaining ecosystem, complete with animals, on such a piece of land.

It should have been a comparatively easy thing to scale up and repeat the process somewhere else. Simply buy a large area of land, fence out the nasties and put some animals there to multiply, but the opposition likewise scaled up, as we shall see.

About a hundred kilometres North East of Adelaide lies an unusual area. Goyder's Line, the imaginary demarcation of the ten inch rainfall isohyet, dips dramatically in the rain shadow of the hills to assume its most southerly extension. Within this area is found the corresponding southern-most range of the vegetation known as arid woodland, interspersed with great swathes of mallee, a low-growing series of Eucalyptus species.

A piece of this priceless country came up for sale at a ridiculously low $50,000. John and Proo named the property Yookamurra, which is an Aboriginal word for 'yesterday', a reference both to its vanished natural heritage and the hopes for restoration to yesterday's glory. The property contained that rarest of assets, namely, old-growth trees.

Without hard evidence, John used his knowledge of the bush to estimate the age of some of the trees, making claims of several centuries or, in the case of trees where the lignotuber had spread into a ring of growth, perhaps going back to the time of Christ. He likened it to an ancient bonsai forest (the mallee species rarely exceed several metres in height) and lamented that whilst people would flock to see old growth rainforest they would tend to overlook the wonders of old growth woodland in the dry areas.

To quote from John's written account, 'This sanctuary was located in the Murray Mallee. It consisted of over 1000 hectares. It contained some of the last old mallee left in the world. Of the twenty most endangered species of mammal, ten once lived in the Murray Mallee.

'Two hundred years ago one fifth of Australia was mallee. Today it is all but gone. It has either been pulled over or burnt. It takes 400 years for a mallee trunk to develop a hollow big enough for a numbat (a small termite-eating marsupial) to live in. Mallee national parks burn every thirty years. There are no old mallee trunks in mallee national parks.'

Impressed by the ancient trees, John purchased the land. One of the sympathetic people from the NPWS advised him that there was no better area of mallee to be found for sale. It had the added advantage of being comparatively close to Adelaide, an important feature in any commercial venture.

During his public talks, John touched on the problem of how to raise money for his visionary plans. At one of these talks, an accountant named David Macklin was in the audience. After the talk, he approached John and told him that he knew how to raise the needed money. It involved setting up a private company. Once this is done, it is possible to solicit shares from people by offering a prospectus. Thus was 'Earth Sanctuaries Pty Ltd' created, setting the scene for the growth of a unique experiment. David Macklin became one of the longest serving members of the company's board.

A man named Bob Brown (*not* the former Greens leader) from the Bird Society purchased $50,000 worth of shares, offsetting the expense of buying the new property.

Yookamurra meant a lot in terms of John's vision for wildlife. If your mission in life is to save a continent's wildlife, your thinking has to be continental in scale. 'If I was going to turn around Australia's record on wildlife, then I had to make about 1% of Australia fox and cat free. So that was my aim, and the first step in that was Yookamurra.'

At the immediate practical level, Warrawong's population of animals grew so successfully that more land had to be found to accommodate them. Part of the battle for success at Yookamurra involved politics, and part of it purely material considerations. The political war started when Yookamurra hadn't even commenced operating as a sanctuary.

I quote here again from John's own writings: 'In an effort to bypass the problems which occurred with Warrawong Sanctuary a special agreement was entered into with Susan Lenehan, the South Australian Minister for the environment. This agreement set out very clearly the aims and directions of Yookamurra Sanctuary. The whole 1,113 hectares would be fenced with a fox, cat, rabbit and goat proof fence. The fence would be designed so that big kangaroos and emus would be able to cross it.'

This last part of the design was a stipulation from the NPWS and embodies one of the troubling objections thrown against early feral-proof fences. Any design which allowed the passage of larger animals would impact the effectiveness of the fence for smaller species, but John had no choice in this matter. In light of current practices, there seems to be no good reason for the provision and I must add this to the growing list of arbitrary obstructions which, to John, constituted a deliberate campaign to frustrate his vision.

The less-than-ideal fence created an ongoing headache in the management of the property, for foxes occasionally got through and set feral control back on high alert. Once carnivorous native animals are already released within a sanctuary, they must be rounded up and protected from any baiting which is carried out.

Continuing John's 'vision statement': 'The feral animals would be eradicated. Woylies, boodies, sticknest rats, numbats, bilbies, western barred bandicoots, red-tailed phascogales, chuditch, banded hare wallabies and bridled nailtail wallabies would be reintroduced. The agreement was signed by John Wamsley on behalf of Yookamurra sanctuary and Susan Lenehan on behalf of the South Australian Government. Surely there would be no problems now.

'Before the agreement was even signed, an officer of the South Australian National Parks and Wildlife Service spoke with the directors of Yookamurra Sanctuary, John Wamsley and Proo Geddes. He said that as far as the National Parks were concerned the *agreement was meaningless*. He said there was no way in the world they would allow the reintroduction of any wildlife back into Yookamurra Sanctuary.' (apart from foxes, cats, rabbits, goats and sheep)

I struggle to understand this kind of attitude, when both parties were supposed to be on the same side, but what subsequently happened involved behaviour even more irregular for a government department.

John and Proo were immensely frustrated by this duplicity and decided that the only way forward was to buy animals *in situ*, that is, purchase land with the animals already on it. To this end they investigated and purchased a 1000 hectare property at Buckaringa Gorge in the Flinders Ranges, part of a pastoral run. $200,000, which had been set aside for the first reintroduction of animals at Yookamurra, provided the capital.

Here on a hillside there lived one of the last colonies of the endangered yellow footed rock wallaby, a remarkable creature which can live on difficult rocky slopes, seemingly defying gravity in its ability to move in all directions. By John's account, the NPWS management were horrified at the prospect of this land falling into his hands because it took control of an endangered species out of their provenance, but the sale went ahead.

This is what happened: 'On a visit to Buckaringa Sanctuary, Proo and I were amazed to see *staff from Adelaide Zoo catching yellow footed rock wallabies on our land without either our approval or knowledge. This would be exactly the same as our staff entering the zoo and stealing their animals.*'

This actually happened.

'I approached them, took their photographs and asked them what they were doing. I gave them the choice of appearing on the front page of every newspaper in the world or negotiating a reasonable introduction program for our rare and endangered wildlife.'

As outrageous as it seems, it was necessary to use blackmail to get a fair deal. Once more John encountered corruption where there should have been responsible governance and he had to play their game.

I do not believe this behaviour mirrors anything which happens today, but there can be no doubting John and Proo's account from those years.

Having embarrassed the authorities over the Buckaringa incident, the work of reintroductions at Yookamurra proceeded.

A couple of anecdotes from project manager Bruce Jackson serve to illustrate the ongoing difficulty associated with obtaining animals for the sanctuaries.

'There was a meeting with Laurie Delroy and a couple of other managers from National Parks plus John, Proo and myself. We were talking about animals at Yookamurra and all sorts of different things and one of the middle managers said, "We can't do a lot (to help) at Warrawong because you've got species at Warrawong that shouldn't be there," and John fired back with, "*Name one!*" And the manager froze. He couldn't do anything.

'There was a guy over at Nhill who had the Little Desert Nature Lodge. He bred mallee fowl. Someone in the department said that we couldn't take mallee fowl chicks, captive bred ones, from there and put them in Yookamurra because they were on *that* side of the river and didn't come from *this* side of the river. That's what you were battling against the whole time. Mallee fowl can fly hundreds of metres.'

Feral eradication at Yookamurra represents a unique story in itself. The land was a haven for rabbits and a meal ticket for the foxes which preyed on them. Total removal of rabbits from 1000 hectares was to be, in John's words, 'A world first.'

The help of Margaret and Don Gillies, who sold their home and set up in a caravan on Yookamurra, became critical to the project. They worked tirelessly to count the rabbits on the property, because it was necessary to quantify the numbers before attempting removal. 'Buck heaps', where the animals marked their territory, sufficed as a measure of population density in a thoroughly systematic process of eradication.

'Eight hectares were fenced off with rabbit proof fencing. The rabbits inside this area were carefully monitored. There were four rabbits using sixteen buck heaps. However, the female rabbits were using the buck heaps as much as the male rabbits. So they became "rabbit" heaps from then on.

'The whole 1,100 hectares of Yookamura Sanctuary were then marked into 200 metre by 200 metre grids. Each grid was carefully checked and all rabbit heaps counted. This work was carried out by Margaret and Don Gillies. Without their help Yookamurra Sanctuary would not have worked. Six thousand rabbit heaps, 1500 rabbits. The slaughter began. (using 1080 poison oats)'

Logistically, the surveying and physical gridding of the sanctuary was a daunting task, not attempted on such a scale before.

Strangely, the killing of rabbits sparked controversy from some quarters.

'Tim Jeanes was a freelance journalist working in the Barossa Valley. The local paper, the Barossa and Light Herald, grabbed the story. "Thousands of animals slaughtered at mallee sanctuary," the headline glared. On page nine they said they were rabbits, but who reads page nine of the Barossa and Light Herald?'

Objection solidified, thus:

'A demonstration organised to protest the building of the sanctuary fence involved some bikies and local greenies. The bikies started off being on the side of the greenies, but when I gave my talk I made sure to convince them they should be on *my* side.'

John told me he did this by answering their questions at length and answering the other questions in a cursory manner. Clever.

'It wasn't long before they told the others to piss off. I had enough sense to know what side I wanted to be on if there was going to be a fight.' A wise orator knows how to manipulate his crowd.

The article in the local paper also had the effect of alerting one Christine Pearson. According to John, 'We were not very nice people killing all these rabbits and by the way, *it is illegal to kill a feral cat in South Australia.*' Much more of this later.

After four weeks of baiting with 1080 poison, Margaret and Don did a recount. 120 rabbit heaps were still in use meaning that 30 rabbits remained.

John relates, 'A friend suggested that what we needed were some hunting dogs. He was in a hunt club. He would soon get rid of the remaining rabbits. About 30 people turned up with about 300 dogs.

There were dogs fighting everywhere. One dog would not come out from under the car. It had lifted its leg on the electric fence. It was a very hot day. After a couple of hours the friend announced there were no rabbits and they all left.

'I thought an advert in the Adelaide Advertiser might do the trick. "Wanted. Professional rabbiter with dog needed to clear residue rabbits from 3,000 acres. Full board. Top wages."

Hundreds replied. None were professional rabbiters. None had dogs. And then one call from a woman claiming her husband could do the job. He would contact me when he returned.

'Adam O'Neill came with his dog and his gun. Within six weeks there were no more rabbits at Yookamurra. He left saying he thought he had also got all the foxes bar one, which he said was a dog fox (a male fox).

'Nothing was taking the baits. No fox footprints could be found. The first of the native animals were released. They were all very quickly killed by a fox. We learned a lot about this fox over the next 8 months. It would not walk on dusty ground, therefore no footprints. It would not eat anything once it was dead, even if it had killed the animal itself. It would simply kill and eat a little while doing so before moving on to the next animal.'

One has to admire the intelligence and adaptability of some animals, even if they are feral. It took human ingenuity and the sedative Diazapan dusted onto live baits to finally conquer this fox.

John's own dog, known, for good reason, as 'Sid the Wonder Dog', had the job of finding the strychnine baits once they had done their job. It was necessary to remove all the baits to avoid poisoning the wildlife (of the carnivorous kind) which might be introduced.

Sid was no less a legend than his master.

'He was a very protective dog. If anything sort of attacked Sid, he'd take care of it. I did a lot of off-road work and any bushes which hit the car, Sid didn't think that was acceptable and he'd bite them. So every now and then he'd disappear out the window because he was hanging on to a branch that didn't break off. So I'd have to stop and get him in again. He was a funny dog. He thought it was his job to make sure that nothing attacked the car.

'He liked chasing foxes but he didn't chase kangaroos because I told him not to. He was very easy to train and he convinced me that if you train dogs properly you can get the ferals. But you'd need to have the right person in charge.'

For the job of finding and collecting the baits, Sid wore a muzzle, preventing him from eating the poison. But there were mishaps, when a bait somehow got past the muzzle. Sid survived two episodes of strychnine poisoning, on the second occasion it was only because John ran red lights at high speed to get him to a vet. Only later did he have time to ponder the ethics of what he did for Sid.

We will give the last word on rabbit control to Dave Chinner, a retired officer of the Vertebrate Pest Board, who said, 'Only John Wamsley could have done it.'

## CHAPTER ELEVEN

# THE MAN WHO SHOCKED THE WORLD

RABBITS WERE GONE FROM YOOKAMURRA, leaving just a few feral cats to be eliminated.

Cats are known to prey on at least 400 species of vertebrate animals in Australia, including 28 species red-listed by the International Union for the Conservation of Nature (IUCN) and have contributed to the extinction of 16 species of mammals.

Wherever you stand on the issue of numbers and the scale of the problem, the results are a disaster for Australia's wildlife. Feral predation is not the only source of destruction, but it may be the most intractable and thorough factor at work.

Rabbit removal without feral cat removal would only lead to more native animals being taken, because rabbits are a major food source for cats. The process is called 'prey-switching'. It was imperative the cats be eradicated.

One of the neighbouring property owners near Yookamurra was upset with the feral eradication initiatives because he considered there existed a nice natural balance in place between foxes, cats and rabbits! The logic is undeniable, but there is a whole world of other life which can achieve a balance if given the chance and what is more, the feral 'balance' could only lead to the destruction of the overall relationship between plants and animals, hence the ultimate loss of the natural system as it was originally constructed by the earth.

Not even John and Proo, with all their experience of habitat restoration, understood the true legal picture when it came to cats.

'The realisation that it was completely illegal to kill a feral cat in SA hit us all like a bomb,' John says. 'How could we save our wildlife if we couldn't destroy feral cats? Now that Animal Liberation were watching us, it would be difficult to carry on without ultimately being caught.

'It wasn't our job to educate Australians on how to be Australian. It was our job to create safe areas for our wildlife to live. To do this we had to destroy the cats. *We would have to change the law.*' Naturally.

That law was a rather strange affair, for it said that you couldn't destroy a cat as long as it was *owned* by someone. Thus, if you killed a feral cat, anyone only had to say it was *their* cat and you could be in a lot of trouble. Because there was no registration process for cats, ownership was just a matter of *saying* that you owned it. Effectively and without intending to, it stopped the removal of feral cats. This was of no concern to anyone except John, because feral cats weren't a public issue at the time.

It so happened that around this time Adam O'Neill, who had eradicated the last of the rabbits and all but one of the foxes from Yookamurra, gave to John and Proo the gift of a massive feral cat skin. It came from an animal Adam shot in South Australia's Flinders Ranges.

It also happened that the annual Tourism Awards night was imminent, with Warrawong Sanctuary once more short-listed for an award.

Proo has never really been acknowledged as the originator of the controversy which was soon to break upon the world. We can blame her artist's eye.

'Proo looked at the cat skin and put a couple of little safety pins in it. She put it on my head, saying, "*You're wearing this tonight.*"

'I had to publicise the fact that I wasn't allowed to save wildlife because I wasn't allowed to kill cats that nobody owned and were out there. They shouldn't have been out there anyway. I had to get some publicity on that. Here am I, I think I'd only shot one cat in my life, but I had to act like I went around a bit like in the pine trees all over again. You've got to build it into a story.'

As with the pine trees and the gun toting episode, John says, again,

*'You're not going to get the people who run the newspapers to publicise your cause unless you make a fool of yourself.'*

The video clip on John's website, taken from the documentary, 'The Platypus Man', says it all. Into that very formally dressed gathering of people who came from all over Australia for the awards ceremony, there intruded a six foot two inch, broad shouldered man with his partner by his side. On his head, and flowing down his back in a carpet of lynx-like markings, was the pelt of a very large cat.

*The 19191 South Australian Tourist Awards. From the ABC TV documentary 'Platypus Man', produced by Piper Films Australia.*

Its disembodied face stared from sightless eyes and the directional ears were still. Not a wild species, but a huge specimen of Felis cattus, the domestic cat gone feral. John's own heavily bearded face perfectly complimented the feline headgear. Indeed, the two entities, the cat and the man, appeared almost of a kind.

The gathered throng truly didn't know where to look. Their priceless expressions are captured for posterity in the video. Such an image had never been seen before in all the western world. It would forever define the man, John Wamsley, in the eyes of all who subsequently heard his name.

In spite of the stunt, Warrawong took out the top award.

Today, three decades on, if I mention John's name and people do not immediately react, I only have to say, 'You know, the man in the cat-hat,' and most people then get who I mean.

The reaction was immediate and intense. John jokingly says that he knew where the news got to in the world by where the death threats were coming from. But the death threats really came.

'A photograph appeared on the front page of the Adelaide Advertiser. It made every major newspaper in Australia. It enraged Australia. It enraged the world. *The education lesson had commenced.* On the day it appeared on the front page of the Advertiser, the various environment ministers were meeting in Adelaide. Cats were suddenly on the agenda. The timing could not have been better.

'I received hundreds of death threats. Animal Liberation ran a massive campaign to stop people visiting our sanctuaries. Television discovered the cat-hat. It went round the world. The story grew more bizarre at each telling. It was soon joined with cat recipes etc. Everyone wanted a cat-hat. Warrawong Sanctuary sold hundreds of them. Ironically, visitor numbers fell markedly during this time. There was more sympathy for cats than for wildlife.

'*Yet with each telling a little could be said about the damage done by cats.* Slowly, very slowly, the message began to get through. This was more than just a publicity stunt. This was serious conservation. Within a few years every state in Australia would pass legislation on cats. A group of animal liberationists turned up at Yookamurra, headed by Christine Pearson.'

'The demand for "cat hats" was enormous. We were offering $35 per tanned full cat skin. We were selling cat hats for $50 each and couldn't get enough to meet the demand. We sold thousands. Our cat traps were selling nearly as well.

'I even talked of the concept of writing a cat recipe book. The public loved it. They couldn't get enough. All their lives they had submitted to the continual torment of indecent neighbours letting their cats run amok. Now was the time for revenge.

'There is no doubt, in my mind, that the biggest problem our wildlife faces is from domestic cat owners. Not because domestic cats destroy wildlife but because their *owners* destroy wildlife projects. Gradually, it all turned around. Cat owners even began to look a little embarrassed when they admitted they owned a cat. Some began to talk of "responsible cat ownership."

'The new law in South Australia was very clear. Any cat on a national Park or Sanctuary could be destroyed by an authorised person.'

Under the SA dog and cat management act, 'Any unidentified cat (i.e. feral cat) can be seized, detained, destroyed or otherwise disposed of, if found straying in areas where cat management officers have authority to exercise their powers.'

It is so important that we understand the *intent* of John's actions. Just as the 'GROAP' story, in all its absurdist manifestations, was designed to educate the public about the damaging effects of an introduced plant, so with the cat story. Only it was something much more destructive than pine trees. Cats and their owners were possibly the number one cause of the shocking reductions and extinctions within Australia's wildlife. This continent has the well-known and unenviable record of the worst extinction rate on the planet.

Ironically, John may have killed only one cat in his life, this being the unfortunate neighbour's cat he shot as a child. John expresses it comically, thus, 'There wouldn't be many people in the world who have killed less cats than me!'

Yet to this day, there are many who see the stunt as an end in itself. As the action of a cat-hater rather than the action of someone who loved wildlife. John puts it succinctly, thus, 'Wherever I went I was asked to tell the latest cat joke. There is no doubt that we got more mileage out of cats than we ever got out of wildlife. That is a measure of the problem. *Why do Australians think so little of their wildlife?*'

John has never resiled from his action on that night of the awards. His emails carry the famous image. If that is how people choose to remember him, at least it means the message is still getting through, even if subliminally.

## CHAPTER TWELVE

# THE GOLDEN TOUCH

THE FENCE AT YOOKAMURRA, DESIGNED to let through larger animals, may not have been what John wanted, but at least it could be built and enabled considerable success with introductions. An expensive and sophisticated affair, it featured a section of mesh at the bottom level which descended to create a 'skirt' over the ground. The upper part had strands of electrified wire through which determined larger animals like kangaroos and emus could pass.

Of this style of fence, John says, 'It was pretty good. It kept most things out.' But it was not what it ought to have been and if a fox got through it caused a real headache.

Buckaringa, the land in the Flinders Ranges, never got its fence.

It went like this. 'Development approval from the council stipulates that a development has to be started within one year and completed within three years. After the council approval you have to get approval from the mines department. Then there are other departments for further approvals e.g. the National Parks Authority.

'By the time you get all the approvals, the original council approval has lapsed, so you have to start all over again.'

Meanwhile, animal numbers steadily increased at Yookamurra. They arrived in the same varied and sometimes tortuous way they came to Warrawong. First to be introduced were woylies (another name for brush-tailed bettongs) from the excess stock at Warrawong. Southern hairy-nosed wombats, mostly hand-reared by Proo, also enjoyed the ideal environment. Wombats seem to have a greater affinity with humans than most other native animals. This may be a result of their superior brain-to-body ratio. In his talks during the public walks on Warrawong, John used to tell people how the wombat was the most intelligent of the marsupials. Referring to one of the wombat 'stars' in the sanctuary, he would say, 'When you saw him sitting over there he was *thinking*.'

Four releases of government animals failed. These were more woylies from the SA Museum, stick-nest rats and mallee fowl from the NPWS, then stone curlews from Adelaide Zoo. In each case it was because the animals had to be released according to the faulty methods set down by the donating departments.

'After much argument the National Parks and Wildlife Service agreed to release stick nest rats, but only if their release methods were used. All failed. Whether this was planned or not can only be conjectured. Some bled to death because their tails were cut off (as a means of marking them). Some were taken by birds of prey due to their oversized and colourful radio collars.'

Further to this, John told me that, against his wishes, the edges of the special enclosures into which they were released were raised up on the night of their release to allow them freedom of egress without giving them time to become acclimatised to their new surrounds.

There was more. 'Adelaide Zoo agreed to release stone curlews (a large native bird), but only if their release methods were used. They failed. Their feeding was stopped while they were still in a restricted area and they died of hunger. Was this planned? We will never know. It just seems strange that every independent release we have ever done has worked. Every release ever carried out by the NPWS or Adelaide Zoo failed. Adelaide Zoo promised to release some bustards (another large bird) at Yookamurra but it never happened.'

I take John at his word in regard to the failure of government releases. It points up the great disparity between academically educated wildlife specialists and those who learn through observation, as John did. The numerous methodologies which John, Proo and their managers developed for animal translocations were remarkable for their time.

Stone curlews, also called 'bush thick-knees' are an impressive, large and somewhat strange-looking bird once common over most of the country, and still so in the tropical north, but now rare in the south. Their night-time cry can be an eerie intrusion in isolated places.

The bustard or bush turkey is another large ground-dwelling bird increasingly rare in south eastern Australia.

Mallee fowl were promised (from the newly established Monarto Zoo east of Adelaide) but they never eventuated. These are ground-dwelling birds whose nest-building is truly astonishing, being major constructions of sand and organic matter which are used to incubate the eggs. These mounds are perhaps three metres across and half a metre high. The male attends to the nest and regularly checks the temperature of the incubating chamber, using a heat-sensing ability in its beak which we do not yet understand and adding or removing material as necessary to maintain the optimum temperature. Their status in SA is 'vulnerable'. The nest mounds remain for decades long after being abandoned and these mounds are often all that remind us of their former presence.

A big breakthrough came when Western Australia offered to supply, for a price, numbats for Yookamurra. Fifteen numbats, a small and beautiful termite-eating species with distinctive stripes across their back, were successfully released and their numbers soon built up to about fifty.

Authorities opposed this release because they didn't believe numbats ever existed in the area. Their belief derived from a lack of fossil evidence, but John and Proo were sure numbats belonged there. The range of this animal is within exactly the same kind of country found at Yookamurra, only most of this habitat occurs a little further north. This is the Goyder's Line effect again.

Proo says, 'Yookamurra is within the original map distribution but they (the government) asked us to prove it with fossil evidence.' A lifetime of searching might not turn up such evidence.

As John so dryly put it, 'The government might have been afraid that the introduced numbats would interbreed and hybridise with the extinct ones!'

Following the acquisition of numbats, burrowing bettongs, or boodies, were another successful transplant from WA. This animal is the only macropod which makes burrows. Formerly one of the most widespread and common animals on the continent, they were rendered extinct on the mainland by the 1960's and only existed on some off-shore islands.

Woylies brought from Warrawong had their own story. 'The NPWS insisted on counting our woylies at Yookamurra. Although you can walk across Yookamurra sanctuary at night seeing woylies everywhere, they (the NPWS) said there were no woylies at Yookamurra. This was to be the start of a well thought-out plan by the NPWS to discredit Earth Sanctuaries. All the literature to be published on the saving of the woylie from extinction would fail to mention the work done by Warrawong, Yookamurra and later Scotia Sanctuaries.'

John's idiosyncratic take on these events is not surprising, given the more obvious and seemingly senseless obstruction that his company encountered over the years of operation and my own experience in researching his work has demonstrated that his contribution is sometimes completely overlooked.

Reintroduction of bilbies, now one of the best known of our endangered mammals, to Yookamurra had its own original and convoluted path.

'By 1991 we had been promised bilbies by the Northern Territory Conservation Commission. No one even knew what a bilby was. We had big plans for bilbies. Easter, 1991, saw the first sales of Chocolate Easter Bilbies at Warrawong Sanctuary. It was obvious from the start we were on to a winner (bilbies superficially resemble a rabbit). With careful planning and proper selling, the bilby was to be the first Australian mammal to fund its own saving. The plan was so simple. It did have, however, one big flaw. Another group of people registered the name. I don't think they wanted the Easter Bilby name, but I think they didn't want *us* to have it. They didn't use it, they just stopped us from using it.'

It was the 'Foundation for Rabbit-Free Australia' who snapped up the unregistered name. Chocolate companies Haighs, Pink Lady and Darrell Lea all donated tens of thousands towards the conservation of bilbies, and this is commendable, but it was John and Proo who popularised the concept. Sadly, chocolate bilbies are now scarcely in evidence at Easter.

Worse to come: 'The South Australian National Parks and Wildlife Service decided our bilbies would go to Adelaide Zoo instead of us. In 1994 two pairs of bilbies arrived at the zoo. Our dreams were shattered.

'You couldn't have these things. Nobody could. You weren't allowed to own endangered species, basically, but it was just that I already had licences for platypus and woylies, amongst others, so I had my foot in the door. There was no way in the world that the Northern Territory Government wanted me to have their bilbies. They didn't mind the SA government having bilbies, but not me. Not a private company. It's much better for them to become extinct.'

There is at least a good ending to the story, for John still obtained his bilbies from the NT government as a separate issue.

'Alan Holmes was just appointed the CEO of the Department of Environment and his first job was to convince me why I couldn't have Bilbies. At a meeting they spent about half an hour telling me why I shouldn't have them and at the end of that I spent about an hour telling them why I should and they said I could have them. But I created a fair bit of bad press for them. They were in a difficult position because the public thought I should have them. It was on the radio when I got offered them. They asked me to go on and debate it with the Northern Territory CEO. Again, he went on about why I couldn't have them and I said that basically the only hope that the bilbies had was if I got them because I could demonstrate that if he kept on the way he was they'd all be gone. In the end he "lost it" and said, "All right then, you can have your bloody bilbies!" He said it quite loud and the announcer said to him, "Are you serious?" And he said, "Yes, I'm bloody serious!" or something of that sort, so the bilbies came in due course.

'If I hadn't got those six Bilbies I would have been totally radicalised.' This wouldn't have been pretty!

Within 21 days of being released at Yookamurra the bilbies produced young. Despite the repeated success of John's breeding methods, *nothing might have come about if governments had their way.*

John has written much about this time, when the conservation work being undertaken by Earth Sanctuaries was hindered, overlooked or misrepresented. There is a fine line between obstruction and simply adhering to arbitrary rules for their own sake. The NPWS opposed the construction of a feral-proof fence at Buckaringa, but the Development Assessment Commission came out on the side of the sanctuary, saying that 'Sanctuary development promotes the objectives of the Development Plan.'

In John's written words from that time, 'This is extremely important because here is a case of a government department ruling that another government department is not acting in its own best interests. The NPWS, in this case, was proven to be acting for purely malicious reasons against Earth Sanctuaries.'

This may yet be a matter for interpretation, but John was in the thick of it, so to speak, and we may accord him some insights which aren't so apparent today.

And is lack of recognition the same as obstruction or deliberate misrepresentation?

'All the literature published on saving the woylie from extinction would fail to mention the work done by Warrawong and Yookamurra sanctuaries.'

Professional jealousy may be a more feasible interpretation, but John found the cold shoulder treatment akin to conspiracy.

Horizons were about to widen for Earth Sanctuaries and John's ambitious adventure unwittingly sowed the seeds of its own destruction.

CHAPTER THIRTEEN

# GOING EXPONENTIAL

IN 1993, IN FAR SOUTH western New South Wales, right on the border with South Australia in habitat known as 'Scotia Country', Earth Sanctuaries Pty Ltd purchased over 65,000 hectares of land. It straddles the area of the Woorinen Dunefield, a place of parallel calcareous dunes where the habitat varies from mallee to black oak (*Allocasuarina decaisneana*).

Being further north and having deeper sands, it differs in its vegetation communities from the mallee at Yookmurra. There are extensive areas of spinifex in the understory beneath the mallee. Spinifex is a prickly grass whose clumps grow in a ring, forming a most intriguing pattern from above. It will only grow on deep sand ridges or sand plains and provides good shelter for the small animals which are adapted to its seemingly impenetrable foliage.

Scotia, as it came to be called, was contiguous with Danggali Conservation Park in SA and part of a vast, uncleared mallee expanse north of the river Murray which was only opened up for pastoral use in the earlier part of the twentieth century.

An article by John in Earth Sanctuaries News said, 'If the bureaucrats delay Buckaringa we will probably start Scotia Sanctuary as our next project. It is good to have a choice of projects to work on.'

Frustration at Yookamurra led to Buckaringa and frustration at Buckaringa led to Scotia. An ultimately unfortunate pattern of enforced expansion formed while all that really concerned John was the imperative to use his knowledge in the service of saving wildlife.

Scotia's purchase meant the size of the sanctuaries augmented in the race to acquire one percent of Australia before luck ran out. The corporate structure likewise grew, with Earth Sanctuaries now a public company.

'You can do little jobs. And that was the choice when I had Warrawong. Warrawong was wonderful, there's no doubt about that, but compared to what had to be done it was virtually nothing. There is this problem of scale, and National Parks and Government weren't doing anything.'

A later publication summarised the ambitious plans for Scotia. 'When complete, it is planned that Scotia Sanctuary will return to NSW a total of fifteen species and increase their number tenfold.'

At the time of that article, about six years after the opening of Scotia, 7,900 hectares had been fully fenced and work commenced on a further 19,300 hectares, setting it up to become the world's biggest feral-free conservation project. Compare this to the 1,100 hectares of Yookamurra. The article concluded thus: 'Because of its size and location, Scotia Sanctuary will be a showcase to the world of an entire biosphere in balance.'

The figure John puts on a Scotia-sized project is ten million dollars to set it up and one million dollars a year to run it. A long way from the comfortable scale of Warrawong.

It looks optimistic and risky, in hindsight, to have proceeded with something as ambitious as Scotia at that comparatively early stage in the company's story, but it makes sense in light of what John says of this time. 'Money was pouring in. People loved us.' Scotia appeared too tempting to resist.

Yet even Scotia represented just a small beginning, because John's plan to save Australia's wildlife required a hundred reserves of that size. One billion dollars to set up and one hundred million a year to run. John says now he 'must have been delusional', but such was the euphoria and confidence surrounding his work, he believed in the possibility of it all.

Through running Warrawong, John and Proo developed business skills, but a multi-million dollar budget using shareholders' money put them in another league altogether. They were to learn that conservation values make strange bedfellows with corporate goals and this was the one factor to come through in all that John said about the Earth Sanctuaries saga.

Like its Yookamurra counterpart in SA, the Scotia fence was not the fence John wanted to build, for it had to let through all native animals but somehow stop the predators. John suspected collusion designed to stop him between the SA and NSW governments. Perhaps this is fanciful, and it wasn't collusion but simply similar suspicions and fears.

Scotia developed in sections, due to the vastness of the area to be fenced. The first step involved fencing and then clearing feral animals from 4,000 hectares. Four times more ambitious a task than that at Yookamurra and Adam O'Neil, from the Yookamurra project, was again the man to do the eradication.

A manager called Greg Martin had oversight of fifteen people for the work of installing the fence and other infrastructure.

The contingent included ten young unemployed people hired under a government scheme as trainees. According to Greg, none of them had ever lived in the bush before. The fact they stayed for the full term of the project, some for as long as three years, is remarkable in itself. Living conditions were crowded and difficult until new accommodation was built. The isolation, extreme heat and the repetitive nature of the work tested everyone.

John visited Scotia irregularly, but there was other contact as Greg often drove a truck to Adelaide to pick up supplies, and there was a monthly report. According to Greg, John's instruction in relation to the report was, 'If you write more than one page, you're sacked!'

As for phone conversations: 'John's not good on the phone. You're lucky to even get a goodbye!'

When I mentioned my own experience of John as someone very easy to get on with, another employee from those days remarked that 'John may have mellowed over the years.'

The final testament lies in the loyalty of members of his staff over many years, in spite of the difficulties encountered in the latter part of the Earth Sanctuaries story.

Greg confirms what John said about proceeding in spite of not having clear permission:

'We had to keep moving. There were a lot of eyes on us. We didn't have all the permissions.'

The fait accompli principle once more.

'The Western Lands people said the fence had to be at least about five or six feet high to stop the introduced native animals, which were perilous to the local land holders around us, getting out.'

This 'peril' seems to lie in the fact that if an endangered species is found on private land in NSW then that land would be acquired by the National Parks Service.

'And the Department of Environment (the two departments didn't talk to one another) said it had to allow animals to migrate so it can't be any more than three feet high. These were the types of things that went on all the time. We had to keep moving. If we had sat there and waited for permissions it would never be built to this day.'

The days of support from the top were over. John again: 'As soon as Laurie Delroy (the SA head of the NPWS) retired the others just gave me shit all the time. They thought it was their job to make life as difficult as possible for me. And that was the normal way that a government department would react towards me. I know why. *They were supposed to be saving wildlife but they were losing everything like they are now.* The interesting thing is that while Earth Sanctuaries was operating the SA National Parks budget was increased every year and as soon as we were closed down, down it went. So the stupid bastards were getting more because of me anyway, but they were too silly to understand it. At the ranger level you've got wonderful people. The CEO (when it was Laurie Delroy) was a wonderful person. In between, the middle management in all government departments are a waste of money. You'd be better off without them.'

The litany of government failures with threatened species continued, but perhaps it was to Scotia's advantage in at least one instance and it may have been that the government conservationists were slowly and reluctantly beginning to concede that John knew what he was doing. The story of the bridled nail tail wallaby is, unfortunately, a validation of what John publicly said at the time, and continues to assert today, about government initiatives.

This animal, whose zoological name, *Onychogalea fraenata*, has a musical ring which matches the elegance of the species, was described by John Gould, the naturalist and wildlife artist, as 'One of the most beautiful and graceful objects that can be conceived.'

Originally there were three species but by 1929 they had all but disappeared. With no confirmed sightings for 35 years they were presumed extinct, but a population of 2,400 animals were found living on a remote Queensland property. The government bought the surrounding land, but within half a year the population reduced to 700 animals. This came about because the dingoes, which, ironically, controlled the feral fox and cat population, were removed. The fox and cat numbers came back with a vengeance.

Scotia obtained a group of the wallabies for $12,000 each. A quote from the website of the Australian Wildlife Conservancy, which now manages Scotia Sanctuary, has this to say about the current situation: 'Over the last 20 years, the bridled nailtail wallaby population on National Parks has declined almost to extinction, while the population on AWC land (at Scotia) has increased to more than 2,500 animals.'

*This represents over 90% of the entire population of this species in Australia.*

Furthermore, this population of what is still an endangered species owes its existence solely to John Wamsley's initiatives, at a time when private conservation was not only frowned upon by government but sometimes actively opposed.

Scotia was the pinnacle for Earth Sanctuaries, a testament to the hard work and passion of the people on the ground and the single large reserve where John's vision could be tested.

In John's typical language: 'I was a "nut case" for thinking it could be done. The fact it's *been* done is interesting. Nobody's come back and said, Oh, sorry for calling you a nut case.'

## CHAPTER FOURTEEN

# DIVERSIFICATION

THERE WAS, AND REMAINS TODAY, an irreconcilable conflict between the needs of conservation and the needs of a corporate entity. How this manifested in the case of Earth Sanctuaries as a business will come later, but right from the start, as evidenced by the problems at Buckaringa, in particular, and Warrawong or Yookamurra to a lesser degree, uneasiness persisted as a private company invaded the exclusive province of government agencies. To this day there is still no successful, large-scale model of a profit-making company doing the work of wildlife conservation.

The year is 1995. This time the private versus government stoush becomes very public and great detail remains on the written record. John wrote this piece for his shareholders:

'Earlier this year, a letter was published in the Mount Barker Courier. It was written by Gary Ling of Mylor. It stated that John Wamsley should repay the thousands of dollars in assistance the South Australian National Parks and Wildlife Service had given him. In his defence Mr Ling produced an amazing document. It was, he said, given to him by the SA NPWS. It was a list of all the assistance that had been given to Earth Sanctuaries projects.

'For the first time this mysterious assistance, often alluded to in the past, was in writing. It was an incredible document.

'Cleland offered Warrawong Sanctuary a pair of red-necked wallabies.

When Warrawong went to pick them up they were told they had changed their mind. This was described as assistance given to Warrawong sanctuary.

'A ranger came one night to watch Warrawong catching platypus. This was assistance given to Warrawong.

'Yookamurra allowed the NP to carry out a comparative count of the bettongs at Yookamurra. This was assistance given to Yookamurra.

'The NPWS demanded that Earth Sanctuaries give them Buckaringa Sanctuary in exchange for other land. This was described as assistance.

'And so the list went on. It did not mention the fact that NP used Warrawong's inventions in relation to rat control or releasing bandicoots.

'It did not mention that the dingo fence uses Yookamurra's inventions in relation to the earthing of electric fences in arid zones.

'However to the credit of the management of our National Parks they did come and discuss the document. They did agree it was rubbish and they did agree to amend it.'

A copy of the revised document appeared in print for the benefit of shareholders. The NPWS was fair and reasonable in this new version. It is divided into headings covering each issue. Under 'Southern brown bandicoots', it says, 'In 1988 a permit was issued to John Wamsley to take four bandicoots from Scott Creek Conservation Park. These bandicoots and their progeny remain the property of the Crown. All costs were borne by Warrawong Sanctuary. These bandicoots have now colonised the area surrounding Warrawong Sanctuary. Twelve bandicoots have been returned to DENR for release in other parts of the Mt Lofty Ranges.'

Note that the progeny 'remain the property of the Crown'. Attempts to value the animals as part of Earth Sanctuaries' assets had to ignore this fact.

Regarding the ill-fated Buckaringa project, there was no immediate agreement about the true state of affairs. 'We are still negotiating this paragraph. We will let you know what we come up with.'

But John has the final word. 'The NPWS say that when they made an official submission to the SA Planning Authority opposing the development of an Earth sanctuary at Buckaringa, they actually weren't officially opposing it.'

The fact that such a convoluted disagreement took place is less significant than what it says about the attitude of certain people in the NPWS. It also explains John's mistrust of government and his certainty there existed something not quite a conspiracy but having much the same effect.

While these distracting skirmishes were happening, Earth Sanctuaries increased the value of its shares at each issue and sought to validate a method of putting a dollar value on wildlife and conservation outcomes.

More land added to the company's portfolio, this time on South Australia's Yorke Peninsula at Cape Elizabeth. It was given the name of Tiparra Sanctuary. This beautiful property appeared in the company's prospectus thus: 'Tiparra Sanctuary is nearly 2,000 hectares of coastal dunes, samphire swamps and former cropping land south of Moonta on SA's Yorke Peninsula.

'Astride Cape Elizabeth, this property juts out into the gulf with mudflats and reef, stretching towards the crumbling Tiparra reef "Lighthouse Station". The reef itself has an enormous diversity of marine species.

'Both the samphire swamp and the old cropping land continue to benefit from the withdrawal of farming pressure with quite spectacular regrowth of natural vegetation.

'ESL's plan is to undertake a joint development with the District Council of Yorke Peneinsula, which controls another 1,000 hectares of sand dunes adjoining the Tiparra Sanctuary land.

'It is hoped that about 20 kilometres of coastline can be included within the sanctuary

'Because this sanctuary is likely to include "joint" development and "joint public land" it may take several years before the main sanctuary development work can proceed.

'Animals which can be reintroduced include woylies, stick nest rats, plains mice, hopping mice, southern brown bandicoots, hairy nosed wombats, tammar wallabies and boodies.'

The optimism is clearly evident here and the sanctuary, had it become a reality in such an interesting and accessible part pf SA, had great potential. Like the attempted Buckaringa development, the site took advantage of existing 'passing trade' and facilities.

That region of Yorke Peninsula is easily accessible from Adelaide in no more than a two-hour drive and has become a fast-growing holiday and retirement destination. There are ample shopping and service facilities in the

'Copper Triangle' towns of Moonta, Kadina and Wallaroo. A Cornish festival and mining history tours complement the beautiful coastal attractions.

Like the experience in the Flinders Ranges, there is everything but wildlife to see and the Tiparra Sanctuary, combining the beauty of the coast with a range of successive habitats and educational tours, would surely have been a success.

Proo explained, 'Foxes and cats work the intertidal zone along shorelines and the plan to protect these areas by fencing was again innovative and exciting.

'As was the planned accommodation viz. houseboat-style cabins floating in the shallows, able to rise and fall with the tide. Glass bottoms would allow the observation of marine life passing underneath.'

Shareholders were allowed in for weekend tours during which they camped on the property if they wished, but little else was destined to happen. The main local government objection arose over the necessity to extend feral-proof fencing out into the extensive intertidal area, thereby interfering with visual amenity and with the assumed right-of-way for four wheel drive enthusiasts who liked to test their skills (and risk getting bogged) on the exposed strand.

I think the most remarkable acquisition of all may have been Neptune Island, out in the Southern Ocean off the bottom of South Australia's Eyre Peninsula. People are familiar with it from weather reports or shark-boat tours, though the number of visitors remains low. The automation of the island's lighthouse left the lease up for grabs and ESL managed the island for a time.

'The last lighthouse keepers had the right to stay on so they contacted us to see if the island could be run as a sanctuary.'

Visiting this remote speck constituted an undertaking in itself.

'Neptune Island. It was a big granite rock. It had a lighthouse which meant it had three houses on it and it had a lovely lagoon. The lights were changed to automatic and the lighthouse keepers were told the island was theirs to use. There was no salary for these people so the idea was to run it as a sanctuary. So we had people come and stay for a week on the island, fishing or whatever we could do for them and that way we could make it pay for itself.

'I went to have a look at it. Proo organised it. We went out in a bloody yacht. Talk about terror. The bloody thing. You wouldn't believe it. Going out, there was a gale warning. They shouldn't have taken us out. They would have got into trouble if they'd been caught doing it. My god it was rough. When we got there I was so sick I couldn't get onto the wharf. I couldn't even stabilise myself.

'Compared with coming back, going out was a mill-pond. You know how waves curl over and break? We were in there in a yacht. A lot of the time the mast was hitting the water. We didn't have life-belts or anything. Shane was sliding around the bloody boat and I was in a state of terror over what was going to happen to him. It was just madness, what we did. After that I never got seasick again. We were dropped off out there and picked up ten days later. It was fantastic. Great white sharks. Seals. Sea lions. Mutton-birds used to come in their millions.'

Proo remembers things this way: 'When we were invited to do a project on Neptune Island, the big question was how to get to a small island in ocean waters. I couldn't find a charter boat licensed to go outside coastal waters and eventually found a yacht willing to take us.

'We guessed the waters would be rough and so I invested in "Seabands", glucose and ginger tablets to try and allay seasickness. The night before we left there was a big storm over Port Lincoln that left boats wrecked and washed up on the shore. So we set sail in the aftermath of the storm. The yacht couldn't sail into a raging head wind and so they used their engine and we slogged it out at 3 knots an hour for 9 hours. Waves were crashing over us and the yacht slammed into every one of them. Shane succumbed first, then John. I have 3 distinct memories of the crew who sailed us out. One was the immense cheerfulness at being lashed with the waves, another was the unnecessary information that bananas were very good for seasickness. Why? Because they taste the same going down as they do coming up! Thirdly, as our nauseous feelings set in, the crew had a morning tea of metwurst sandwiches which they freely offered around!

'We all crawled onto the jetty when we got to Neptune Island. On the return journey we simply flew before the wind.

'After our stay we staffed the island for some months, but the promised transfer of the island from the Commonwealth Lighthouse Department failed to come about and so we withdrew our staff and waited until the place was in S.A. N.P.W.L control. We reapplied but were not chosen.'

Amusingly, John has the final comment. 'The government gave it to some guy who was running away from the law.'

It occurred to me when hearing all this that John would have made a great lighthouse-keeper. Perhaps his ideal job!

A letter from one of the staff on the island attests to the joys of life in what was and remains an unspoiled haven for marine wildlife:

'G'day Warrawong People. This is Tim, one of the field workers from Earth Sanctuaries over here at South Neptune Island . . . Things are fairly good over here. It is hard work though trying to eat all those crayfish and abalone and then there is all the other fish we gotta eat . . . we snorkel with the fur seals and sea-lions. There is also a big Groper that swims along with us. The sharks are a bit of a worry (this is where they filmed most of "Jaws 2") . . . I even had the big bull sea-lion touch my hand with his flipper . . .'

Land acquisition remained perhaps the least expensive part of the ESL operation. Ironically, the land they were buying rated very cheaply precisely because it had no conventional commercial potential. The property called Dakalanta, on Eyre Peninsula, purchased as a potential sanctuary, is a good example. Being heritage listed, the property's natural portions could not be grazed, farmed or cleared. This in turn meant it attracted a very low price, but it was part of the problem which ultimately sank the company, for 'environmental assets' scarcely rated in the valuation of land.

John worked for years to come up with a way of valuing the environmental assets in such a way they would stand scrutiny and become part of the company's true, redeemable worth. The animals were given a collective value of $4,000,000.

The animal that John remembered from his childhood in NSW serves as an example of how difficult it is to make conservation popular.

'Warrawong Sanctuary contains the last of the Sydney sub-species of red-necked pademelon. This subspecies is distinguished by having a cream hip-stripe. There are about forty individuals left in the world. We are desperate to find a suitable area for them so that we can increase their numbers. We attempted to develop a sanctuary at Byron Bay for them. However the "greenies" stopped it. We attempted to develop a sanctuary in the Hunter Valley for them. However the "greenies" stopped it. We are about to attempt another one, this time in Western Sydney. Would you like to guess what will happen?

'The problem, therefore, reduces to one of simply being able to put a high enough value on them so that we are allowed to save them.

'*We put it to 200 people chosen at random from the Sydney telephone book, what they thought the Sydney subspecies of red-necked pademelon was worth. The Sydneyites gave it the thumbs down. Only one person surveyed thought they were worth anything.*'

Today we have yet to agree to put a price on pollution, let alone anything positive like wildlife or trees.

Early on in our interviews I asked John if he thought he could have achieved more by adopting a less confrontational approach. Proo answered the question for him by saying that John, 'Only bites when he's been bitten.' Meaning he isn't confrontational for the sake of it.

The early experience of bullying coloured so much of what he did during the years of public engagement.

Boarding schools favour the strong and ruthless. 'It's bad enough to be bullied at ordinary school where you can get away from it after hours. At boarding school you can't get away.' So it was with being in the spotlight.

John confesses that he fought back and did whatever horrible things he could to avenge himself on those who tormented him at school

'I'd often take a snake to school and any bully would end up with it down his shirt and screaming in terror. Bullies haven't got much guts, you know, they're easy to terrify.'

This necessity to find a way to survive explains a lot in John's subsequent history of unilateral action. When you are picked on as a child and there is no one to help, it is necessary to depend on yourself and sort out the problems alone. If you have the strength. And if they hate you anyway what have you got to lose? Certainly not a popularity contest.

'Being bullied, growing up like that you grow up in a funny way. You don't tend to trust anyone.'

From his copious writings it is obvious he enjoys a tussle and holds mistrust in reserve for those who at any time work against him, although he will always sit down and talk, eye to eye.

One-on-one he is always personable and ready to use humour to help with the process of communicating. This is my experience of the current John Wamsley, but he may have become a gentler antagonist with the years.

In the unfolding story of the sanctuaries, while the energy lasted, he didn't care for convention or opposition. Nothing gets done if you are distracted by these things. Only the animals were important and that figure of one percent of the Australian landmass. How little it sounds for the sake of something irreplaceable.

Feral-proof fencing itself, the core feature of the sanctuaries, aroused opposition in some quarters, even though we have in Australia the dingo fence, the longest man-made structure in the world, longer than the Great Wall of China.

'They were pretty daunting fences, I suppose. People hadn't seen them before. Most people haven't got much of an idea of doing big things. They're very tiny in their own tiny world. You've only got to look at Facebook to see that. Most people couldn't give a stuff what happens beyond that.

'There were people who said, "There has to be a better way. Fences take away your liberty." There's never been something put forward in its place. There's never been anything that works in its place. Some things can slow the destruction, like National Parks do, but you can't stop it and you can't save endangered species without fencing, not unless you put an enormous effort into feral control.'

Australia is the most fenced country in the world, so the opposition is quite strange. Grazing activity has extended to every possible corner where water is available. It is only the absence of ground water which has caused some arid or semi-arid parts of the country to be left intact. The Earth Sanctuary plan was, by comparison, asking for very little and for only a tiny contribution from the gross national product, but it assumed the proportions of an impossible undertaking.

The optimism and excitement persisted while ESL remained an unlisted company and the stress of running the company, while considerable, was offset by the rewards of seeing things happen on the ground.

John and Proo have a profound love of animals, treating them like children. There is video footage of Proo waking up with a joey which has slept with her and footage of John holding quite a large kangaroo like a baby in his arms. The runaway success of the breeding programs must have been exceptionally exciting and rewarding. This was, after, all, what the whole journey was about.

*John with Buster the red kangaroo*

With each month that passed there seemed to be new horizons opening up. 'The Environment' was a sexy concept in the nineties. Everyone wanted to go green.

Among other contracts, ESL took over the management of a property on Kangaroo Island at Hanson Bay. This beautiful spot has cabins and other accommodation overlooking the beach and the estuary of the South West River. It has, like other parts of Kangaroo Island, an unusual number of animal species, including pygmy possums and bush thick-knee, the ground dwelling bird whose introduction was thwarted by government incompetence at Yookamurra.

After years of hard work and a certain amount of struggle against opposition or broken promises, Yookamurra Sanctuary won its first tourism award in 1996 when judged SA's best example of Environmental Tourism. Numbats were spreading throughout the park.

Work proceeded on clearing land for the fence-line at Buckaringa and at a shareholders' weekend the feeling was all positive in spite of the eight year delay in obtaining title.

The area of Yookamura grew with purchase of an adjoining property, known as Graetz's block, taking the total area to over 5,000 hectares.

Scotia's first-stage fence was officially 'closed' by the Deputy Prime Minister, Tim Fischer, creating *the world's largest feral-free fenced area.*

Improvements at Warrawong included a new restaurant and kitchen. The public profile of this founding sanctuary constantly expanded. 'Media interest is still exceptional at Warrawong, our latest overseas guests including an American film crew from Hollywood.'

An international ecotourism travel award put Warrawong *at number two in the world.* This represents an enormous achievement.

Yet at around this time, with all the positive news, it is surprising to read, 'We are developing a buffer zone around the whole area (of Yookamurra) to frustrate *those who have been sabotaging the project.* Now that we know who these people are, it makes life a bit simpler. This buffer zone will be 40 metres across (this is further than a cat can be thrown). It will be inaccessible to people.'

It is a bit like winning the popular vote but losing the election. Feedback from the public stayed overwhelmingly positive while specific opposition consistently intruded.

I have the impression there was never a day without multiple problems to solve. Proo refers to '$2 days', when she and John would gladly have handed over the lot for $2. 'It was mostly,' she says, '. . . on a Friday. On Fridays some terrible disaster would happen. Someone would be denied something. We'd get a letter from the department saying we couldn't do something and everyone in the office would sigh. Those were the $2 days.'

Finding good managers to look after the sanctuaries proved one of the great stumbling blocks. John couldn't possibly oversee all of the Earth Sanctuaries projects, even if he didn't have to attend board meetings (which he hated) and carry out his duties as General Manager of the company. Adding to the stress, sparring between John and the Adelaide Zoo management became very public when Professor Mike Tyler sued Earth Sanctuaries for defamation over an article in a newsletter.

Surprisingly, amidst the conflict, John retained his sense of humour and conspired to go along with the bogus 'platypus cloning debate' on ABC radio. He claimed the scheme had been so successful that there was a 'platypus glut' and asked South Australians to 'open their hearts, their homes and preferably their muddy backyard pools to the excess platypus.'

'The ABC switchboard lit up with people wanting platypus, offering advice and commenting.'

Eventually, people checked their calendars to find that the date was April 1st!

The viability of the ESL corporate model had yet to be tested on the open market, but what could not be doubted was how expensive were the company's goals. The combination of an uncertain public reception for the share valuation and the headlong push for more land or for another Warrawong to fund the larger sanctuaries, began to assume somewhat scary proportions. John says, 'I knew I had a tiger by the tail.'

The focus turned East, to where the large population centres seemed to promise a steady return. NSW may have been John's birthplace, but he wasn't comfortable concentrating efforts there. Both John and Proo felt that in some indefinable way, the cultural climate differed from that in SA.

John knew there was a cliff-edge to fall from, but there were cards still to play. The further he pushed, the stronger would be the legacy for wildlife, regardless of his own fortunes. Never one to be shy of bold statements, his Managing Director's Report of 1998 included these words:

'Scotia Sanctuary will save over one quarter of the world's endangered mammals. It will do this with virtually no assistance from the public sector . . . It is, without any doubt, *the greatest conservation project ever carried out anywhere in the world.*'

And ESL was about to join the big league in fact as well as in expansive statements. This media release from January, 2000 accompanied the company's listing prospectus.

'Earth Sanctuaries Ltd, a $70 million Australian company dedicated to the preserving of Australia's wildlife in its natural habitat, will be *the world's first listed conservation company.*'

In 2000, ESL invited the public, through its prospectus, to subscribe for 6,000,000 shares at an offer price of $2.50 each. The prospectus listed the ten properties either owned or under contract to earth sanctuaries, including those in the Eastern States.

As Managing Director, John also had this to say: 'The earth is billions of years old and for most of this time it was slowly evolving into a veritable paradise that we inherited. However, sometime over six thousand years ago we took control and reversed the forward evolutionary processes. In my opinion, it was not an apple that Eve gave Adam, but a firestick. Since that time we have not husbanded the Earth, we have destroyed it.

'There are many indicators demonstrating the lack of success in our management of our inherited paradise. Two are the desertification of the Earth and the loss of species. These two indicators alone demonstrate the problem and probably the solution.

'Here in Australia, wide-spread desertification of our country has paralleled our loss of species. Of the sixty species that have become extinct worldwide in the last 500 years, 20 are Australian.'

No attempt was made to sell the ideas falsely. The 'real' income was to be derived from eco-tourism, not from trading in endangered animals, even though a large part of the company's assets were held in these animals.

A great deal of energy was about to be expended in battling the anti ESL lobby in NSW, and that energy had to come from John. No one else put their reputation on the line and walked that very public plank.

The ESL train had by this time become unstoppable, and, set to automatic, it headed East.

## CHAPTER FIFTEEN

# THE JOURNEY TO THE EAST

THE EARTH SANCTUARIES STORY, LIKE so many stories of innovation, started in SA, the 'Cinderella State', as some like to call it, but it was to be in the East that the experiment would stand or fall.

With Scotia basically up and running, the biggest battles were still to come. Scotia was fundamental to John's plan, being the large area where populations of animals could thrive, changing their own conservation status by becoming 'common'. The kind of reserve which could be sustainably managed and later augmented with other acquisitions of land. But not even the board members of ESL fully grasped the principles. They appeared to want something more akin to a theme park and they wanted it close to the big population centres of the East. John never felt easy about the push to Eastern Australia, but he recognised that the large, core Sanctuaries of Scotia and Yookamurra could only be sustained with help from the smaller, more accessible sanctuaries which had a good chance of generating significant income.

Although there had been opposition to John's plans in SA, there are intrinsic differences between SA and the lands east of the divide. SA has very little high rainfall country and such areas as we have were often cleared very early in the history of settlement. Those places which somehow survived intact into the latter part of the twentieth century were mostly released for farming after the Second World War.

By the time that ESL was operating, SA could boast very little in the way of true forest or tall woodland and most of the low woodland, which is comparatively easy to clear, was long gone. Likewise, any remnants of the vast malleelands of what became the grain belt of the state were invisible to casual observation from the main roads or, as in the case of the mid-north of the state, entirely obliterated. Large expanses of scrub still existed (the largest mallee areas in Australia, in fact) but these were outside the agricultural zone in places difficult for most people to access.

Whatever the true case, there was a level of opposition to 'development', even of the ethical kind which ESL advocated and this translated into lobbying at the political level.

There had been, at least some of the time, a friendlier association with elements in the SA government. The then premier, Dean Brown, was instrumental in allowing Yookamurra to finally obtain bilbies and Alexander Downer (a then federal member for the SA seat of Mayo) actively helped by facilitating the acquisition of animals. David Wotton, the environment minister, was sympathetic. SA was also, as previously stated, the only state in Australia which allowed native wildlife (with the exception of endangered species) to be owned, bought and sold.

A smaller population in SA led to smaller government (numerically) and this in turn led to at least some ease of access. Further, John was a local hero in SA, where to people on the eastern outskirts of Sydney he was an interloper, notwithstanding that he was born there.

The initial response was heartening. John met with Premier Bob Carr and commented that it was, 'The best meeting I ever had with a member of parliament!

'It's absolutely wonderful that we have a premier of a state with not only an understanding of what needs to be done to save our wildlife but also the determination that it *be* done. He thought it (Canyon Sanctuary) was a fantastic idea and he said yes to it. He gave me a person within the government to liaise with, who would look after me.'

This early optimism was only repeating a pattern which had occurred a number of times before.

The issue of corruption in government came up repeatedly in conversation with John. His early experience made it unsurprising that he would expect to find this corruption and many years later his suspicions have been born out in the scandals surrounding property deals and members of parliament. Regarding approaches by politically-connected people, when he was seeking approval for his developments, he says, 'There is no doubt in my mind that if I had paid up I would have got what I wanted.' This cannot be verified.

Several different threads were running together in the ESL story. The tide of optimism, the land acquisitions, the imminent public listing of ESL shares and the conflict with authority which culminated in a lawsuit must all have been churning in John's mind as he prepared for his own 'Journey to the East'. But overriding it all there remained an unstoppable, or, perhaps more accurately, stubborn momentum.

The workload must have been very great, with efforts divided between SA, Victoria and NSW. No one else had John Wamsley's expertise and insight. This put him under tremendous pressure and the problem of finding good managers would not go away.

The lawsuit issue alone would have taxed a less motivated man. Earth Sanctuaries countered with its own lawsuit against Mike Tyler for comments attributed to him in 1996, but after considering how much the action was costing, a settlement followed.

John's methods and temperament were not always in step with his board and here may be the beginnings of a sense of alienation from the corporate entity which he created. But with his role already mapped out he had to see the dream through to its conclusion.

To this day, John talks about the muted 'Canyon Sanctuary' in a disused colliery, west of Sydney, as a place absolutely ideal for his purposes. Not only did it have superb habitat for wildlife, but it was serviced by a railway line from Sydney with its own spur line. Thousands of people might have readily accessed the sanctuary.

Part of the marketing strategy entailed completing the sanctuary in time for the Sydney Olympics in 2000. It combined spectacular scenery with the proposed wildlife experience, making it unique among ESL's properties. The coal mining heritage comprised, among other things, 'more than a million dollars' worth of reusable and recyclable infrastructure like roads, a rail spur line right into the sanctuary, power, unpolluted water and massive water storage and reticulation.

The land could be acquired cheaply, for taking the lease off the hands of the mining company saved that company the cost of removing infrastructure.

In every respect it was a great buy. Of course, there's always a catch. Opposition mobilised, and this time there was no doubting its source. Opposition from the NSW National Parks was not opposition to a sanctuary as such, but opposition to a sanctuary in that particular place. ESL was urged to take up another parcel of land closer to Lithgow. This land John labelled 'The Pagodas' as it is filled with 'breathtaking pillars of rock'.

The logic is, as John said at the time, hard to follow. He put their 'case' in this way:

'You (Earth Sanctuaries) can develop the "Pagodas" but you cannot develop Canyon into an Earth Sanctuary.

'Therefore, (they argue) you must scrap millions of dollars' worth of infrastructure at Canyon and rebuild it all in the "Pagodas"

'You cannot fence to prevent wildlife crossing main roads and railway lines at Canyon, but at the "Pagodas", where wildlife now has safe passage (without road or rail lines) you can do as much fencing as you like.

'You must "rehabilitate" 50 acres of cleared and degraded land at Canyon, but at the "Pagodas", of course, (no problems) you can clear fell 100 hectares or more of virgin bushland. In fact (they say) suit yourself. Do you need to clear more?

'You cannot, of course, build a sanctuary adjoining the Blue Mountains National Park, but of course you can (can we help you?) build a sanctuary adjoining the Wollemi National Park.

'The argument is simply that Canyon must become a NSW National Park and the "Pagodas", next to Wollemi (or anywhere else really) should become an Earth Sanctuary.

'This is not logic. It is nonsense! It is the language of "Green Bureaucrats". It has nothing to do with conservation.'

As usual, it is possible to interpret what happened in different ways. John believes that the National Parks deliberately made it difficult for him in order to dissuade him from setting up in their state, yet it seems they were prepared to allow a development as long as it went where they wanted it to go.

The fight assumed, for John, political overtones. He finished off by saying, 'We do, however, live in a democracy. There is an election on March 27th. Find out the facts. Do not be fooled by nonsense.'

It came down to the Liberals, who seemed to support the development, versus the incumbent Labour government. Successive Earth News publications urged people to contact politicians to find out where they stood on the issue, although ESL steadfastly denied any political bias.

'ESL is, and intends to remain, apolitical. It has no political allegiances. It is not interested in saving governments, Oppositions, or the faces (or necks) of politicians of any persuasion.'

Then Premier Bob Carr wrote a letter to John, outlining why his government changed its mind over the Canyon issue. What is clear from this letter is how big an issue it had become and just how daunting was the task of campaigning which John subsequently took on.

*Dear Dr. Wamsley,*

*As you know, I am an enthusiastic supporter of the Earth Sanctuaries model as a means of protecting our native wildlife. I believe that Earth Sanctuaries provide a model that is complementary to our existing National Park system.*

*Since our meeting in March 1997, I understand that the Scotia Sanctuary south of Broken Hill has been proceeding well.*

*Clearly my support for the Earth Sanctuaries model does not, and should not be taken to mean that I am supportive of all Earth Sanctuaries proposals in all circumstances. You will recall that when we met in March last year, you gave me a very brief outline of what was then a very preliminary proposal for the Canyon Colliery site near Bell in the Blue Mountains.*

*When you then submitted your proposal through my office it was clear that part of the project involved fencing land within the existing Blue Mountains National Park. It was made clear that my government would not support any proposal that involved fencing part of the National Park.*

*However, my department was keen to facilitate negotiations with the relevant State Government agencies once a clear proposal was presented to the Blue Mountains Council and the State Government regarding how Earth Sanctuaries planned to establish an Earth Sanctuary at Bell. At no time did I give any assurance that the government would assure a long-term lease for the land at Bell.*

*Nicholas Rowley on my staff has had the task of assisting you in liaising with the government. Given the strong community resistance in the Blue Mountains to the fencing of the Colliery site I was keen to explore whether alternative sites could be found for an Earth Sanctuary to be developed closer to Lithgow and not bordering an existing National Park.*

*Following a visit with an officer in the Premier's Department to the sites identified, I am informed that you still wish to proceed with the Canyon Sanctuary proposal.*

*Together with the Lithgow Council I am still willing to provide all possible assistance with regard to sites you visited in Lithgow. However, given the likely conflicts that will occur if the canyon Colliery site is to be developed as an Earth sanctuary, I will not be supporting this project.*

*Once the lease held by Coalpac over the Canyon site expires in 2005, the lease will not be renewed, and the necessary rehabilitation will be completed as soon as possible. It is my Government's intention for the Canyon site to be added to the existing Blue Mountains National Park. In the near future, the area of vacant Crown Land where the mining lease does not extend to the surface will be gazetted as an extension of the National Park.*

*I trust this clarifies my position with regard to the Canyon Colliery site.*

*Yours Sincerely etc*

Note the discrepancy in this letter, for in one sentence it mentions 'fencing land within the existing Blue Mountains National Park' and later talks of the Canyon site being 'added to the existing Blue Mountains National Park.' Perhaps Mr Carr was a little confused.

The people of NSW did not support the ESL bid in their voting, although it can hardly be said that the sanctuary was the only issue in consideration, even in the Blue Mountains seats.

I remember a long television piece which followed John as he 'campaigned' and which showed his deep disappointment when the results went against him. The Canyon project was obviously special to him, given the energy he put into promoting it. It may have been symptomatic of some unspoken desperation, knowing that so much depended on getting a sanctuary set up near a major city, or it may have been a desire for acceptance in the State of his birth, but this is my interpretation and only a part of the story.

John wrote with great authority, passion and eloquence after this defeat:

'So this is the real position in NSW. This state has lost more species of mammal over the last 100 years than Africa has over 500 years. It has lost more species of mammal over the last 100 years than the whole of North and South America together have lost since Columbus discovered them in 1492. NSW expects to lose as many species of mammal in the foreseeable future as the world has lost over the whole of modern history.'

He was also completely accepting of the voters' decision. 'Labour won. And Labour won because it read the mood of the electorate better than the coalition. This is what democracy is all about. Someone once said that democracy was awful but the alternatives were worse. ESL accepts that decision.

'We do not apologise for attempting to change the direction of conservation in NSW. We saw the opportunity. It did not work. We would do the same again without fear or favour, no matter who was in government, no matter who was in opposition.

'I repeat, we are completely and totally apolitical. For us it was one hundred to one odds for an even chance to save our wildlife. We had to lay that bet. We lost. We are sorry about that.'

The push to the East was not over and the board of ESL were determined to focus the company's efforts on the eastern seaboard. John and Proo were never quite comfortable with that. Warrawong, though long profitable, could not provide enough capital, but in hindsight this was the point at which *expansion* might have instead become *consolidation*. John admits that as things got bigger the decisions became less rational. There existed a momentum which took on a life of its own.

A neat picture emerges (again, *in hindsight*) of a situation where valuable but undeveloped assets like Buckaringa, Tiparra and Little River (in Victoria) plus the less valuable land at Dakalanta could have been sold off to fully fund the infrastructure at Scotia. However, in light of John's greater plan it is possible to see how scale was important and I suspect that it was this idealism which fuelled the fire and drove the decisions. A litany of stalled or half-finished projects followed.

Seemingly undaunted, ESL announced, in October 1999, three new sanctuary projects:

'Murrawoollan Sanctuary (700 hectares) fronting the Hume highway between Bowral, Moss Vale and Marulan in the NSW Southern Highlands. A contract has been signed for the land, pending successful development application with local Mulwaree Shire Council.

'Blue Mountains Sanctuary (1500 hectares) near Lithgow. (the 'Pagodas' site) A fantastic site. Real brush-tailed rock wallaby country.

'Little River Sanctuary (1,060 hectares) is between Melbourne and Geelong, adjacent to the You Yangs Regional Park. Contracts have been signed pending a successful development application with local Geelong City Council.'

Throughout all this time, hope of establishing Buckaringa never waned, with shareholder weekends and frequent mentions in the newsletters.

Tiparra awaited approval for the unique kind of barrier necessary to prevent feral animals from negotiating the inter-tidal zone. As the only mooted sanctuary with coastal exposure, it represented both an asset and a challenge.

Dakalanta remained a distant priority, never receiving serious consideration, although it was no more isolated than an area like Scotia. All of the purchased (as opposed to optioned or leased) properties were owned outright, with no debt and this remained a positive factor for ESL right through to the end.

Hanson Bay on Kangaroo Island continued to be successfully managed by ESL and wildlife numbers increased along with visitors to the cabins.

*In 2001, ESL had ten areas of land spanning a total of over 90,000 hectares.* The resources and logistical requirements to effectively manage such a large holding were obviously considerable. The scope of these purchases illustrates the optimism of the early years.

Alongside the corporate concerns, day to day conservation went on and this illustrates the almost schizophrenic nature of the Earth Sanctuaries dream, with work in the field driven by passion and an awe of nature, while the hard-nosed reality of finding money and qualified people to keep it all going involved a totally different set of skills and aspirations.

The problem of how to fund the larger reserves necessary to the greater plan were ever-present and grew exponentially with the purchase of Yookamurra and Scotia.

Something workable *had* to be found in the East. Neither the company nor the animals were ready to be abandoned.

## CHAPTER SIXTEEN

# GOING PUBLIC

THE MORE I HEAR OF the opposition Earth Sanctuaries faced, the more I am inclined to sympathise with John's penchant for seeing conspiracies and the more I must question my own long-held beliefs about what passes for effective conservation.

The setting aside of large areas of land, while admirable, may not in itself result in conservation of biodiversity if those lands are left to degrade as a result of feral animal or plant incursions and the absence of reciprocal relationships between animals and plants. It is not that land should be left unprotected from clearance, but that land so reserved should be properly managed.

If the management strategy is to do nothing, then we must accept the outcome, which is to say, we must accept an impoverished biodiversity with an ever-diminishing biota.

Earth Sanctuaries' philosophy recognised the role played by animals in controlling organic litter beneath the tree and shrub canopy, thereby reducing both the frequency and severity of fires.

Criticism took many forms, including an intimation that the breeding of platypus, listed then as 'vulnerable' rather than rare nor endangered, as they are today, was more about publicity than conservation.

The fact John returned these animals as a breeding entity to mainland SA, where they were formerly extinct, is conveniently overlooked.

It is eminently clear John's vision was ahead of its time, for it is only now that his strategies are being widely adopted by other agencies.

What has not been tried again is the formation of a publicly listed conservation entity.

Two big things happened in late 2000: the long awaited public listing of ESL shares and the appointment of a CEO.

The share issue raised 12.1 million dollars. I suggested to John he seemed pleased enough about the share results in his newsletter reports, in spite of the performance being less than hoped for.

'Well, you could hardly say you weren't happy, could you? Not publicly. You could go home and curse it to your wife and say, "Bastards!" But no, I was quite happy with it because the important thing was to be able to raise money as we needed it and I thought I'd achieved that . . . the share price didn't really worry me as long as I could get more money for conservation if I wanted to.'

Ironically, as the company grew and assumed a corporate persona, some people ultimately had a change of heart. Proo explained, 'A lot of the people who bought shares did so because they thought they were being charitable and then when they saw it was a big company they decided they didn't want to be part of it.' But this was significant only later.

'Ethical Investment' was the catch-phrase for a time, but like so many other initiatives which were part of the evolving 'green' awareness in its day, including things like carbon off-sets reducing the environmental footprint of new buildings, it became marginalised and associated with the extreme end of the investment spectrum.

John gave the matter of assigning value to wildlife a great deal of thought. No one in the early part of the new millennium successfully integrated such a valuation system with a business model, in spite of the existence, after 1998, of the Australian Accounting Standard for Self-generating and Re-generating Assets (SGARAS). This acronym featured much in conversations about ESL's unique and fragile business model.

It had much to recommend it as an application to wildlife valuation but wildlife was not strictly within its scope and did not figure in the documentation. SGARAS concerned itself with valuing things like orchards and other income-producing assets.

Oddly enough, there was a substantial cost applicable to obtaining endangered wildlife from the government, as evidenced by the $12,000 per head for bridled nailtail wallabies at Scotia and the $5,000 per head for numbats at Yookamura, so the rules were interpreted in a novel way, even if the recipient of the wildlife never actually *owned* the animals. *Wildlife remained the property of the crown.* As previously reported, John was prepared to 'put up and shut up' where this was concerned, because it was ammunition for his own plans to develop an accepted valuation for wildlife.

Applying logic to the calculation of a value for wildlife, John started this way:

'To set up the mathematics of an Earth Sanctuary one has to make a number of assumptions:

That 100 Earth Sanctuaries each of 1,000 square kilometres be developed over the next twenty five years.

That the National parks system fails to save our wildlife.

That without Earth Sanctuaries, Australia would lose 100 species of mammal over the next 25 years.

That Earth Sanctuaries can save this 100 species.'

A number of assumptions are made. I would be inclined to trust John's judgement in the matter of losses, given his intimate knowledge of the needs of native animals and the probable outcome of government programs, based on what he knew of their record at that time.

'I should probably further develop the meaning of the word "lose" used above. I understand that in today's world we can store genetic material and hence lose nothing. I understand that we can keep a few hundred alive in zoos "in vitro" and hence pretend that we have lost nothing. I would like to broaden the meaning of the word "lose" a bit here to mean something like, "for all practical purposes lose" or "the animal cannot be found in the wild filling the niche it evolved to fill" or something.'

Most critical in the corporate model was the need to put a monetary value on wildlife.

'What seems to have happened, in the case of environmental values, is that probably *in a well-meaning fashion* we decided that these things should not have a value at all. We thought they should somehow be *above valuing*. We would somehow all believe they were so valuable that we were all happy to pay whatever was necessary to save them. In fact, what has happened is a "worst case scenario". We have put a value of zero on these assets and therefore there are no funds to save them other than welfare funding.'

In reality, it came down to a simple formula:

Under normally accepted accounting standards, assets can only be valued at their recoverable value.

Under wildlife regulations, rare and endangered wildlife cannot be sold.

Therefore, according to the Australian Securities Commission, all rare and endangered wildlife have to be valued at zero.

'The problem we had was really a circular argument. The assets of ESL are wildlife. We had to value our assets at zero. Therefore our shares had an asset backing of zero. Therefore we could only issue shares at zero. Therefore we couldn't make it work.'

Yet it did work, at least, for a time. The optimism within ESL, at its peak, was palpable.

The total value of all the company's wildlife, at the height of its profitability and under a formula created by John, was $3,845,000.

ESL's total assets at that time were $35,244,797, meaning wildlife represented more than 10% of the worth of the company. This became crucial in the company's story.

As enthusiastically as he wrote about corporate matters or the economic basis for conservation and in spite of the mathematician's insights he brought to bear on financial planning, John was never comfortable with running an increasingly big company. Then as now he hated meetings, always preferring to be out in the field getting his hands dirty or organising for others to do so.

Responsibilities outside the boardroom and the need to put ESL on an even more professional footing convinced John to step sideways and allow someone else to be the principle driver at a corporate level.

When I asked him if there was a catalyst for this move, he said, 'Just the overload. The workload was too much and I realised I couldn't continue like that or I would have burnt out. And I enjoyed doing the conservation side of things. I didn't enjoy doing the company things and the meetings. I suggested that *we put on a CEO to run the company* and I'd become the person who does the conservation.'

It cannot be overstated how critical this move was, for it marked the beginning of the end for the dream that had been Earth Sanctuaries. The difference was immediate for John, who still attended board meetings. It may have been designed to relieve him of the pressure he was under but it meant in reality he now had to bow to the ideas of another person.

'Up until when the CEO was appointed, I would go into the board meetings and say what I thought should be done and they would agree with it.'

There is no hint of pessimism in newsletters at the time, yet there was already a juggling act going on, with multiple balls in the air and mooted developments leapfrogging one another in a critical race to find a 'cash cow' to fund the real reason for the company's existence, that is, the large Scotia-scale reserves which were the only truly workable long-term ventures in the wildlife dream.

## CHAPTER SEVENTEEN

# SERVING NATURE AND MONEY

I WAS PRIVILEGED, ONE EARLY SUMMER morning at Scott Creek, to encounter close hand a rare and spectacular animal.

While I stood among low trees and dense understory, there appeared above my head a wondrous creature which had me babbling like an excited child to my fellow bush carer.

The animal in question was a square-tailed kite, gliding effortlessly and silently just above the treetops. I confess to having been deeply affected by the sight of this bird, not just for its striking beauty but for knowing that in SA, where it is classed as endangered, there are estimated to be no more than a dozen pairs.

This kind of experience is what John and Proo were offering Australia, only valuing the experience in a philosophical sense had to be translated into material valuation within the marketplace. It was all a long way from the reality of being a numbat or a brush-tailed bettong. The animals could not know how hard it would be to translate love into hope for their survival.

All effort concentrated on establishing a profitable sanctuary somewhere in the eastern states. A quandary existed in the development sequence. In order to bring Scotia to the point where it would generate the kind of income necessary to maintain itself, that is, about one million dollars per year, it was first necessary to make an investment in infrastructure like international standard accommodation and an airstrip to handle larger aircraft. And only full completion of the boundary fencing offered a chance for the sanctuary to function in the way John intended, mimicking natural cycles.

Raising the necessary money to do these things required a high-turnover site close to a major population centre.

Failure to secure approval for the Canyon site removed the very best option from contention, but it didn't stop ESL entering into other contracts. The scope of operations seems, at a glance, to have been hazardously large, with three separate properties all awaiting permits for sanctuary development.

'On 18th August 1999, Canyon Sanctuary Pty Ltd (the company set up to develop the original Canyon project), a wholly owned subsidiary of ESL, exchanged contracts for the purchase of approximately 700 hectares situated on the Hume Highway near Marulan. The purchase price is $775,000 . . . The contract is conditional upon the Purchaser obtaining development consent for a wildlife sanctuary, ecotourism lodge and visitors' centre on the property on or before the 16th of February 2000.'

The intended sanctuary took the name 'Murrawoollan', to honour the aboriginal word for the area. It means 'beautiful place'. Half of the property had been cleared for sheep grazing and the other half comprised grazed native bush. The proposed wildlife introductions included the formerly endemic red-necked pademelons, these being the animals John delighted in as a child.

'You Yangs Sanctuary Pty Ltd, a wholly owned subsidiary of ESL, exchanged contracts on 20th September 1999 for the purchase of 1,061 hectares approximately 55 kilometres south west of Melbourne and 35 kilometres north of Geelong. The property adjoins the northern end of the You Yangs Ranges. The purchase price is $3,750,000 . . . the contract is conditional on the purchaser obtaining a planning permit . . .

'The elevated site has excellent views of the Melbourne CBD skyline, the You Yangs and Brisbane Ranges and Port Phillip Bay. Only 50 minutes form Melbourne, 30 minutes from Geelong and 50 minutes from Tullamarine airport, You Yangs Sanctuary will be convenient for Victorian, interstate and international tourists to access.

'All but 30% of the land has been completely cleared for sheep grazing and cereal growing, the remainder is uncleared native tree and shrub regrowth. An extensive revegetation program is planned to bring the area back to pre-European standards.

'You Yangs Sanctuary could be perfect habitat for eastern quolls and brush-tailed rock wallabies. It has wonderful granite boulder outcrops and formations which they like to live amongst.

'A stunning feature of the property is a heritage listed, large, 127 year old granite block homestead. Restoration in conjunction with heritage authorities is planned.'

$3,750,000 represented a huge sum of money for a company the size of ESL and while this money might have enabled the completion of a great deal of the infrastructure at Scotia, there remained the immediate problem of securing a steady source of income. Little River, as the You Yangs site came to be known, held out promise of becoming to Victoria what Warrawong was to South Australia.

Ideas and requests for collaboration were never in short supply. In a novel and potentially very public project ESL entered into an agreement with the indigenous Wann people for development of a sanctuary on the 25 acre 'Brick Pit' site which was part of the industrial land to be remediated for the 2000 Olympics. This agreement fell through when some members of the community objected to the proposal. It would have been invaluable advertising for ESL and a spectacular attraction, incorporating the pond where the pit has been partially inundated. Today it boasts an elevated walkway and is home to the endangered red and green bell frog.

Finally, ESL paid $1,193,000 for a property in the Blue Mountains. This was the 'Pinnacles', the alternative (supported by the NSW government) to the preferred Canyon site. Here sat another purchase doomed never to be developed and which tied up a large amount of the company's money.

'ESL believes it is important to establish an Earth Sanctuary near Sydney and has entered into a contract to purchase 480 hectares in the Upper Blue mountains near Lithgow. The directors are hopeful of being able to purchase a further 1,000 hectares to enlarge this holding.

'An hour from Katoomba, about forty minutes from Lithgow, some two and three quarter hours from the centre of Sydney, this proposed earth Sanctuary has typical Blue Mountains escarpment views across wet valley floors to breathtaking sandstone cliff faces and rocky plateaus.

'The spectacular escarpments-on-the-horizon vision contrasts with the quiet, almost secret sound of the crystal clear creeks which bring permanent water and rainforest habitat.

'Already on the high-visitation Blue Mountains-Lithgow tourism circuit, this site, too, is ideal terrain and habitat for local, Australian and international visitors to see and be part of Australia as it was 200 years ago.'

Another, parallel story unfolded as these plans were being laid, for the company began to feel the pinch from the real world of share trading on the open market, which allowed no room for sentiment or aspiration. The share price at listing in May of 2000 was $2.50, falling to $1.42 by December of the same year and trading was slow.

1999-2000 saw a paid dividend of 50 cents per 100 shares. It is reasonable to assume early investors in ESL were driven by more altruistic motives than their later counterparts who purchased on the open market, for there was little hope of a significant return in those early years.

An OECD Workshop Paper managed to put ESL's dilemma into reasonably intelligible words. I have quoted in full because this statement summarises the problem so well.

'... a commercial operator such as ESL must balance its environmental objectives with the need to establish a financially viable and attractive investment option for potential investors. On the one hand, the company may wish to *retain profits to create additional sanctuaries and thereby expand its conservation activity*. In the case of ESL, the company has expressed a preference to *limit the dividend paid to shareholders* so that profits may be ploughed back into the company to allow it to pursue its conservation objectives. However, the chairman of ESL has acknowledged that it may need to *increase* its dividend to attract investor interest to be able to further its conservation goals.

'Similarly, a sanctuary's key revenue generating asset is likely to be the habitat and fauna contained in the sanctuary, yet *this asset is difficult to value and cannot, currently, be realised*. This can also affect the financial success of a company and by implication, through lack of funding, its conservation success.'

The model had this contradiction at its heart and John commented that the board members were always scared it would come back to bite them.

56 per cent of ESL's total revenue for 1999-2000 came from the growth in native animal numbers on its properties. Note that this asset is non-realisable. The outgoings for that period were nearly 10 million dollars, most of that for sanctuary purchase and development. The business model was fragile, but there was no reason to think the SGARA's principles would have to change and John had high hopes the new CEO would find ways of keeping the company afloat.

A lot depended on the CEO's performance and the decision to so alter the pyramid of authority within the company represented a huge step.

Stepping sideways sounded like a good plan for someone like John who was passionate about the field-work and by any standard exceptionally good at setting up the necessary systems on the ground. What actually happened only increased the stress.

'And so we put on a CEO and that CEO *almost immediately started making decisions that I totally opposed* so therefore I never could just concentrate on conservation. I was put under a bigger and bigger load.'

On another occasion, John said of this time, 'I tried to step down when I appointed a CEO. I told her, "Your job is to raise funds, to manage the money. I'm doing conservation." But she kept insisting that I take part in discussions on money matters, which I didn't want to do. They (the board) basically wouldn't let me step down from the money side of it. It didn't assist me in any way, putting on a CEO. I thought it would take a load off me, but it didn't. And any decisions she made were decisions that I couldn't handle. So she just made things worse for me. Gave me more to do, because I had to go to the board and tell them why this was wrong.

'For a while I did that but they sort of ganged up on me with the finance director.'

The CEO could scarcely have been said to enjoy a 'honeymoon' period at ESL. Only a matter of months after her appointment the tone of her article in the June 2001 newsletter no longer exhibited the kind of optimistic rhetoric shareholders had come to expect and which was invariably forthcoming from John.

She begins thus: 'Shareholders may have noticed a drop in the share price recently . . . we are not aware of any specific cause for the drop. It appears a number of sizable (given our thin trade) share parcels have been sold by institutions.

'Our options have so far raised $757,325 as of the 7th June 2001 thanks to our shareholders and to those taking up John Wamsley's offer. This has been the most successful part of our strategy to raise equity for Little River Earth Sanctuary and the Company operations.

'Don Stammer (our chairman) and I have made numerous visits to Australian institutions to attempt to raise funds for LRES. In the current market, this has not been successful. Socially Responsible Investment (SRI) is further ahead in the UK than here and I have a program of meetings to try to raise the necessary funds there.'

Proo comments on this time: 'She was clearly an intelligent and capable person but she had no idea about a few really key things that had made Earth sanctuaries. One of those was our education capacity. Not at sanctuary level but at keeping the shareholders in. We had wonderful shareholders who supported us and really got involved and we played that. We made sure that the newsletters that went out were full of positive information and positive stories. She couldn't pick people up and carry them along and she couldn't sell the financial message. When you look at CEO's or managing directors it's a very complex role and if you haven't got the big staff to handle it . . . I mean, if they'd "milked" John the right way, he could rally the troupes and bring everybody along, and if we had a better capacity to raise funds . . . it's funny, because you hear it all the time and all over again, if you look at Earth Sanctuaries we were always looking for money except straight after a prospectus if it had been successful. We then had some funds and we'd get on with things and then we would be running out again and people would have these ideas, like, "You go to an investment company."

'Campbell Boag ran an investment company that was looking at "green" investments. It was his idea that we had to upgrade the board and John had to step aside. Another idea was to go to the fundraising arm of one of these big accounting firms. So we went to this guy and he said we could raise all sorts of funds but he never raised a cracker. And then there was another idea to go to one of these investment companies that buy businesses and strip them. They come in and invest a lot of money but they generally change the business completely as well, to suit themselves.

'So everyone pulls these ideas in and off you go on that tangent and mostly nothing came of it. But you spend so much time and so much effort. That's why it was hard for John who wanted to build sanctuaries and save wildlife and do those things and he was always back in the humungous turmoil of ESL. And I say turmoil in the sense that we were always trying to work out how to survive, I suppose. I don't think I would have said it like that then, but that's really what it amounted to.'

There remained the intractable problem of who to hire in order to fulfil the very divergent roles demanded by business and conservation.

'Who do you hire? We had Richard Ryan on the board. He'd been in charge of billions of dollars. Don Stammer was an investment banker. But who do you put on to save wildlife in a financial setting? You had to actually have some empathy for the wildlife. You had to have some understanding of conservation and you have to be able to move in the financial world. Out CEO nearly got it. She flew to London and came back with money but she couldn't sell that message and being head of the Marine Park Authority was a government job. There was nobody with a business background that was interested in conservation.'

She had to oversee the early land sell-offs which presaged the much larger sales to come. Thus:

'You will notice that there is an advertisement for the sale of Dakalanta in this "Earth News". As we are focussing the company's efforts on Little River Earth Sanctuary and our east coast projects, the Board has decided to divest itself of some of its properties. As well, we received advice from the SA government that we could not fence the intertidal area at Tiparra. As a result, ESL is selling Tiparra, Dakalanta, spare blocks at Yookamurra and the undeveloped part of LRES.'

While this hard reality unfolded, the *spirit* of ESL stayed as strong as ever in the eyes of the dedicated shareholders and for purposes of national recognition. The CEO's article went on to say: 'ESL received National Tourism Accreditation, Greg Martin has been awarded a fellowship by the Land and Water Research and Development Corporation to spread the message about the role of our small native mammals in soil structure and quality. Yookamura and Scotia had successful shareholder weekends and one of our major shareholders, Toba Aquarium, joined us on a wet and stormy weekend for a Platypus census and we are offering mail-order sales of our merchandise.'

One shareholder who attended at Little River had this to say: 'When we see the fencing and the work involved, we can begin to appreciate the magnitude of the vision. Everyone we met associated with ESL in any way is imbued with this same dream and vision, and this enthusiasm is infectious. It took some effort to be there, but it was worth all of it, to meet other shareholders and other enthusiasts, and to know we are part of something so worthwhile to Australia and our futures.'

Proo wrote about the release of bilbies at Warrawong. 'The early morning of March 20th was a huge celebration attended by over two hundred people to witness the release of this endangered animal icon just in time for Easter. A total of nine bilbies were translocated from the successful breeding program at Yookamurra . . . By 6.05 am on the Tuesday morning, the Warrawong car park was nearly full. There was a sense of eeriness and excitement in the last half hour before dawn. Groups of people were making their way to the entrance, and the decking was a sea of people . . .'

Finally, this from a shareholder: 'I am grateful to have the opportunity to share ESL's vision and contribute to the future of our native wildlife. The value of these precious creatures is truly priceless. No amount of money can buy back an extinct animal. That is really worth investing in.'

Again, public sentiment and enthusiasm wasn't matched by investor funds.

Only months later, John and Proo stepped down from the board to become 'consultants' within the company, while the share price continued to fall and the board made decisions which would rip the heart out of both ESL and its founder.

CHAPTER EIGHTEEN

# THE BEGINNING OF THE END

ALONGSIDE SCOTT CREEK CONSERVATION PARK and sometimes separated only by a line on the map, is the Mount Bold Reservoir Catchment Reserve. The two areas combined represent the largest intact area of bushland remaining in the Adelaide Hills, where only 5% of the original vegetation still exists.

A biological survey undertaken in the early 2000's determined that this area contained an extremely high biodiversity and perhaps this helped to sway the government when, during the 2006-2008 drought, there appeared a proposal to raise the height of the dam wall to increase storage capacity. This idea, luckily abandoned in favour of a desalination plant, would have destroyed a large swathe of habitat.

John used to wander through the catchment to enjoy the bush until he was caught and told to stay out. In South Australia the catchments are mostly closed to the public, though no one seems to know why this should be so. Some of the best preserved bushland in the state exists in these long-isolated places.

During a conversation about the probable historical occurrence of small pockets of temperate rainforest in the Mt Lofty Ranges, John insisted that the best remnant of this vegetation once existed in a valley in the Mt Bold Catchment Reserve, but that it was cleared so the area could be planted to Pinus radiata.

Sadly, the vegetation of the catchment is poorly maintained, with entrenched outbreaks of feral plants infesting the creeklines. On the face of it, the relevant authorities assign little value to the precious biodiversity they 'own'.

There could scarcely be a better example to support John's argument that placing a value of zero on something is no way to save it. What is more, it must be a 'tradable' value, not just an imaginary one.

The idea is put forward in reverse for 'Carbon Credits' within industry. If clean air has no tradable value, it won't even figure in the business equation. If businesses have to pay for the right to pollute, they will think hard about how much pollution they produce and those industries which produce less pollution will have a cost advantage over those that produce more. If we can't, as yet, agree about putting a price on the very air we breathe, what hope for the small, secretive, nocturnal animals, out of sight and out of mind in the bush?

It is important to understand what happened next within ESL's accounting system, for it was pivotal in the company's story and crucial to the animals who went about their own business of survival, oblivious to the machinations of the law.

The Australian Accounting Standards Board (AASB) is an Australian Government agency that develops and maintains financial reporting standards applicable to entities in the private and public sectors of the Australian economy. In the early 2000's, the AASB implemented the broad strategic direction from the Australian Financial Reporting Council to adopt *International Accounting Standards* for financial reporting.

This brought Australia's accounting practices in line with global practice. For most companies adopting the new standards, this meant getting used to some new ways of reporting things, with little or no change in the day-to-day running of the company or the calculating of its assets. For some companies there may have been a saving due to lack of duplication in financial reporting.

In ESL's case, it represented a psychic shift, because assets previously taken into account were written off, resulting in a staggering $10.5 million loss (as outlined in the financial report of the company for 2001).

The value of things like feral-proof fencing no longer counted. The properties held by ESL had to be valued at what they would bring if sold as pastoral or farming land. Further, included in this devaluation was a new classification system based on that used by Environment Australia for wildlife which meant a write-down of $0.5 million.

Later, according to John and Proo, the change in accounting standards brought into play another set of international rules, namely the United Nations Convention On International Trade in Endangered Species of Fauna and Flora, or 'C.I.T.E.S'.

Also known as the 'Washington Convention', this came into force in 1975 and Australia is a signatory to it, along with most of the world's nations. It is designed, with all good intent, to prevent unscrupulous trade in vulnerable species, although it allows bonafide organisations like zoos to swap wildlife for breeding programs.

The regulations go like this: 'CITES works by subjecting international trade in specimens of selected species to certain controls. All import, export, re-export and introduction from the sea of species covered by the Convention has to be authorised through a licencing system. Each Party to the Convention must designate one or more Management Authorities in charge of administering that licencing system and one or more Scientific Authorities to advise them on the effects of trade on the status of the species.

'Appendix 1 includes species threatened with extinction. *Trade in specimens of these species is permitted only in exceptional circumstances.*'

It is unclear why the convention was applied at all in the case of ESL, given there had been no international trade transacted and the only proposition on the table was from the people of Toba Aquarium, who sought to obtain platypus, which were not a threatened species.

The result of applying this convention, for ESL, represents an example of where the spirit of a regulation is at odds with the practical results of its implementation.

Australian businesses (those publicly listed) were obliged to move towards the new international standards by the end of June, 2006, giving ESL several years in which to rearrange itself. Yet the decision to move to the new standards was notified in the 2001 Financial Report.

In many of our conversations, this matter of the devaluation has come up in relation to the viability of the company. Fauna was valued at 4 million dollars in a company worth a total of 35 million. It was not necessarily a death-blow financially, although it wiped off more than ten percent of the company's worth overnight and I came to understand that it represented something much more than a change in the economic picture.

'They told me,' John says, 'that by law I couldn't value the wildlife, and that wasn't true. I learned later but that's what they told me. I didn't believe it was true. I still don't believe it was true, but *I just wore out.*'

The pressures of an unrelenting work schedule had accumulated until John had no more energy left to fight what was becoming a hostile board. John and Proo together had ten times the shareholding of any other member, yet they were subject to the decisions of the board and a CEO.

I asked Proo about the devaluing, because I wanted to know if the UN convention had to be interpreted the way it was.

'We could have pushed through until somebody questioned it, but we were always on the edge. I mean, you could imagine the Greens, in parliament, working that out and screwing us. So it was wise to be pragmatic on that.'

But she has another take on the technicalities of the decision.

'I don't think that the self-generating assets were disallowed just because of C.I.T.E.S. I think the international law on self-generating assets (SGARAS) is different enough for it to have mattered.

'Once that happened (the international standards) it was clear. That was it. Bang. Because I remember we let go two staff from Warrawong . . .because of the international standards we could no longer have on our books people whose job it was to just work the environment.'

On the restructure: 'There was a bit of navel-gazing and we dropped our staff at Earth Sanctuaries. Don Stammer and the CEO stood down, leaving us with our original board.'

Valuing animals was about more than money. 'If you have shares in the company,' John said, 'you own those animals, you saved them; they're yours. The idea is to give people ownership. It's a feeling. You get across this feeling of ownership. It's a company. You own a share of it. You have a vote, you can direct it. You can have your say. You can come and look at it. We can show you what we're doing and so the whole thing is aimed at giving people ownership of the job of saving our biodiversity.'

Statements about this time reflect increasing negativity:

'What made it the hardest was that with all these difficulties I faced over the years, and there was a lot, there was no assistance from anyone to solve them. I had to work out how to solve them, but it built up to this massive thing that I could see where there was no way out. And I know in hindsight that I shouldn't have gone east. Scotia should have been as far as I went. But there was a problem because without the other sanctuaries I probably couldn't have raised the money. *I needed money to get one of them up and making money.'*

This last, somewhat cryptic, statement reflects the unique problem ESL faced. Not only was there insufficient money for the development of the larger reserves like Scotia, but there was, in the end, insufficient money to build the smaller, 'cash-cow' enterprises which were supposed to generate the needed cash flow.

But underlying it all was a very personal consideration. John was ever a crusader as much as a businessman. He put his name on the line for the methods he believed in and the devaluation decision was interpreted, rightly or wrongly, as a personal attack.

'The stopping of the valuing of the animals was *an attack on my integrity* more than anything else. It basically said, "What you're doing is bullshit." And once I had to agree that what I was doing was bullshit then there wasn't much point me trying to tell people how valuable it was saving wildlife. It undercut me and made me of no value.

'*My word was of no value, so therefore I was finished*. And they knew that. That's what it was done for. *To take away my integrity*. It worked very well.' Conspiracy again.

Valuing wildlife was what John had taken to the public and was the basis for asking them to invest in his company. It was the foundation on which the company was built and is, by John's own admission, his life's purpose.

In a more self-evaluating mood, John described the events a little differently, perhaps exaggerating his own isolationist tendencies.

'I'm not a good people manager, you see? I don't like people. That might be the reason. I only did it all to get away from people, but I kept getting thrust back. You have to go in a board room and discuss with them and convince them all. That was hell for me. I hate it. It just gets too hard. You feel yourself going mad. I'd learnt that if I pushed myself too hard I'd just have a breakdown and I could see that happening. I resigned from there. I didn't see I had a choice, really. And I can't blame anyone for that. It's me. I wasn't tough enough. *If I'd have been a Murdoch I could have handled it.*'

Publicly, the shock move scarcely rated acknowledgement. The shareholder newsletters, normally a rich source of information on everything associated with ESL from the top to the ground, held little to indicate exactly what initiated the changes. The words, 'Dr John Wamsley has resigned . . .' were the sum total of information surrounding John's self-removal, although it coincided with a major restructure.

The newsletter labelled 'Summer 2001-2002', was the last to contain an article by the CEO. The tone sounds subdued, although still containing a note of anticipation, if not hope.

'On behalf of the ESL Board of Directors, I encourage shareholders to consider our new Share Purchase Plan for Earth Sanctuaries Ltd . . . You have all been very supportive in the past and we are calling on you again to consider this offer . . . Regrettably our share price has continued to fall. Institutional investors have been selling and given the unusually small trade of our shares, a large parcel of shares on the market leads to a drop in the share price.

'The good news is that the revenue from our operational sanctuaries for the September quarter is up 10% on last year, and 6 mainland mala (Lagorchestes hirsutus hirsutus) at Scotia are doing well.

Warrawong has won two more awards . . . the Hon. Alexander Downer MP launched the new Wetlands Rainforest Walk . . . We have received a few questions about the future of Buckaringa Sanctuary in the Flinders ranges. Buckaringa is not for sale. However, ESL's highest priority is the east coast and development of Buckaringa will be well down the track.

'2002 is the International Year of Ecotourism and the Year of the Outback in Australia. ESL has interests in both so we have a great marketing opportunity ahead of us . . .'

What most of us have forgotten from those years was the effect of the introduction into Australia of the Goods and Services Tax. This tax is now so entrenched that no one gives it much thought anymore. While the financial report noted, 'Trading activities were disappointing during the year as ecotourism income struggled *in the post-GST environment.*

Nevertheless around 50,000 people had an experience at an Earth Sanctuary during the year.'

The phrase 'The beginning of the end' is an odd one, but perhaps not so ably expressed in any other language. Although the company continued its operations for another two years, something critical went missing once John stepped away. The greatest 'intangible' on the company's books was not the little animals which couldn't be legally traded, but the energy of an idea. John embodied that idea physically and metaphysically. It followed him around like a self-generating light source and illuminated the dry economic corporate entity which was ESL.

'If there was one thing that brought Earth Sanctuaries down, it was my realisation *that it was a waste of time.* So I don't think I achieved anything, in the end. I showed people how to do it and that it *could* be done, but if people don't want to do it then it's not going to happen.

'What does that prove? Probably that was the thing that was the end of it all. The realisation that *it can't be done.* We're going to lose it all. We're going to lose it all very quickly. In a hundred years Australia will have nothing.'

This is John at his most pessimistic, yet it never gets in the way for long and he would later come back to the company for a final hands-on task, the kind he always loved.

The first newsletter to appear after the CEO's departure was edited by Proo, who became managing director, stepping into the vacuum left by John's abdication and the changes wrought within the company structure.

Of Proo's involvement as manager of the company, John said, 'I thought that at least I owed her that, to let her do it if she wants to do it. I had my chance and I stuffed up. So that's the way I felt about that. That she deserved the opportunity if she wanted it.'

John's affection and respect for Proo is very obvious. When I asked if the trauma within the company affected his relationship with her, he said, 'No. I made sure it didn't. That's one of the reasons I never discussed it with her.'

The priority for John became to preserve his sanity and Wirrapunga (from the aboriginal words for the 'goddess of small things') was the means to do that.

For a couple of years after moving from Warrawong (which became a commercial venture rather than a home) John and Proo lived in a house at Stirling (also in the Adelaide hills) where the landscape, though heavily wooded, is about 99% exotics. This didn't suit John very well at all.

'The original house (at Warrawong) was a mud house and I built an extension on it. As Warrawong expanded it took over more and more of the house and we ended up, Shane and Proo and I, in one room. Proo inherited a house in Stirling from her parents so we moved in there but I didn't like it. It was comfortable as a house but there wasn't a native plant in the yard. Why would you want to have a yard like that? You could go into the house without going into the yard. It was built on the road. So I never went into the yard and after a couple of years Proo got the message.

'She asked me to come home when I was over in Victoria doing Little River. She asked me to be home on Saturday because there was a house for auction and she wanted to buy it. She wanted me to okay it. I walked up the drive and half way up the drive there was a bearded orchid. I said, "Yeah, this will do." Because the house didn't matter. All houses are houses as far as I'm concerned. It's what's out there that's important.'

Unwittingly, Proo found a life-saver for John, ready for when he would need it badly and whether by intent or chance, Wirrapunga is across the road from Warrawong.

The style of 'editorial' comment in the newsletters changed under Proo, whose writing could be called 'gentler' than what we saw from John, though no less passionate when talking about the mission to save wildlife. She doesn't shy away from presenting the uncomfortable reality of ESL's precarious situation.

'ESL listed on the Australian stock exchange in 2000 because we believed it would allow us to raise the necessary funds to achieve our vision for saving Australia's wildlife. Since listing, despite acting on independent financial advice, we have been unable to generate sufficient funds to get Little River Earth Sanctuary operating. We have attempted to get placements from institutional investors. We have attempted to borrow from banks. We have attempted to get government assistance. We have attempted to raise money from shareholders. Although partially successful, especially the last, we have been unable to raise sufficient funds to enable us to move forward. We now realise that it is unlikely we will be able to find support in the foreseeable future to the degree that we had hoped.

'Our low share price has also confirmed that some shareholders would appreciate a return of their capital. On the other hand, the continuing support of many shareholders demonstrates the demand for a successful and transparent conservation program.

'As advised to the Australian stock Exchange on the 14th January, the board and senior management have therefore decided to take the necessary action to restructure the company and return capital to those shareholders who request it.

'Since we have the responsibility of the fate of thousands of rare animals, we will be immediately calling for expressions of interest in all or part of our assets with the hope there is someone (or some people) out there with sufficient expertise and funds to carry on with the vision to save our wildlife in full or in part.

'We must stress that all operating sanctuaries are continuing to trade and that ESL is not bankrupt, insolvent or anything like it. *It owns properties valued at over $12 million that have no mortgages.* However it is running out of cash and will eventually get into trouble if your directors allow the current position to continue indefinitely.

'We thank you all for your fantastic support, it has been very reassuring that there are 6,800 people out there committed to the conservation of our wildlife.'

When John absented himself from management, Little River prepared for opening, but with a limited amount of its land fenced. Marulan and Blue Mountains were, of course, already abandoned. Scotia was well set up, though only a percentage of its vast area was fenced. Populations of animals thrived in Warrawong, Yookamurra and Scotia.

Tiparra, Dakalanta and Buckaringa (this last with its yellow footed rock wallaby population intact) remained undeveloped parcels of land.

Of the ESL 'stable' of properties, Proo said, 'All these balls were in the air and occasionally one came back into the hand but mostly they went "splat".

'It was very hard. The board pulled us in different directions and I think probably we should have stayed in Scotia, Buckaringa, Yookamurra country. Eastern Australia was a new minefield for us.'

The aim of the restructure was to reduce the ESL venture down to Warrawong and Little River, while also retaining the arrangement at

Hanson Bay on Kangaroo Island. The rest, including extra land purchased to expand Yookamurra and Little River, was to be sold off.

In a country like Australia, with a limited population and so few people with wildlife expertise and money combined, ideal buyers were limited.

Animals remained the focus throughout all of the difficulties of the restructure. After her fashion, Proo included articles about three different animals in the newsletter. The southern brown bandicoot success story is one of the best conservation outcomes from the work of Warrawong.

'In 1988 the status of the southern brown bandicoot was "common in some parts of its range". However, in November 2001 the southern brown bandicoot was declared nationally endangered. The collapse of this species during the nineties shows a need for reform of current management practices.

'A female bandicoot usually has two young at a time. The young are very tiny when they leave the pouch. So small, they fit easily through the inch and a half netting of the feral proof fence. All around Warrawong there is an ever-moving number of bandicoots repopulating the district. Our neighbours stop me in the street to ask, "What are these creatures?" and I delight in explaining how the bandicoots move through the fence, how important they are to the environment, and for people to be happy that endangered animals live on their land.'

Also reported, notice of the discovery of at least two baby mala at Scotia and the translocating of a mallee-fowl from the Little Desert Lodge in Victoria to Yookamurra.

Kevin Lynch, a long serving Director of the company, became the new Chairman and several team members either resigned or were laid off.

In a subsequent newsletter, an explanation of John's removal from active involvement, thus: 'Dr John Wamsley also resigned from the board because he felt that as the founder and largest shareholder he needed to remain aloof from the internal issues.' This sounds like a way of giving some plausible explanation to the shareholders.

John believed all of the company's assets ought to have been sold and the money returned to shareholders in order to maximise the returns on their investments, thereby winding up the company at that point. He further believed one of the bidders intended to purchase all of the assets, but that at the end they 'cherry picked' the best of the deal.

The final transactions were described this way: 'The responses to the calling of expressions of interest gained an initial 68 enquiries, 25 of whom put in a formal expression of interest. When the bids closed, the board had a number of options to consider.

'Paramount in these considerations was the interests of ESL shareholders and the preservation and continuation of our conservation projects.

'The board has made the following decisions: Tiparra has been sold to the Indigenous Land Corporation, and Murrawoollan has been sold to the Winten Property Group. Each group has indicated their intention to look after the environmental assets of each block.

'The Western Australian group, the Australian Wildlife Conservancy (AWC) has bid for the 4 main conservation blocks: Buckaringa, Dakalanta, Yookamurra and Scotia. They have indicated their desire to continue with the conservation already established at Yookamurra and Scotia.

'Dr Don Stammer (the former Chairman) has kindly offered to purchase Blue Mountains Sanctuary.'

In a letter from AWC CEO Atticus Fleming to Greg Follent (who represented ESL in negotiations) AWC's intentions were spelled out:

'AWC will rigorously maintain the integrity of the existing fences at Scotia and Yookamurra.

'AWC plans to substantially expand the area which is enclosed by feral-proof fencing at both Scotia and Yookamurra. i.e. we will increase the fenced area at Scotia to substantially more than 8,000 hectares and at Yookamurra to substantially more than 1,100 hectares. The extent to which we will expand the fenced areas and the timetable for such expansion will depend inter alia on the financial resources available to AWC.'

An Extraordinary General Meeting (EGM) convened at Warrawong on 4th July 2002. All of the sales as well as a share buy-back gained approval from the shareholders. John's voice alone expressed dissent as he wanted the company wound up entirely.

'I was sledging the board (at the meeting). They gave me the shits. I let them know very clearly that I didn't appreciate what they were doing.'

Despite all the upheaval, the tone of the newsletters stayed almost upbeat, with a great deal of news and information for shareholders. It even featured a message from John, who loved to write and found the wherewithal to do it even when upset and barely coping. Ethics dictated that he let the shareholders know he wasn't in any way upset with them.

*'Because of the dire straits Australia's wildlife was in, we had to travel faster than we could sustain. We've taken a tumble but I wish to make sure you understand, we didn't waste shareholder funds. We, and that means you, the shareholders of ESL, have turned around Australia's record in wildlife management. When we commenced we were alone in trying to save our wildlife. It was ESL who introduced Australians to their wildlife. Now the AWC proposes to take our big conservation projects off our hands . . .'*

Every effort aimed to make the transition workable and among the many public activities advertised were some jointly held with AWC. But AWC were keen to make a complete break from the old culture, as evidenced by their turning down of an offer of help from the Earth Sanctuaries Foundation.

I asked why AWC wouldn't welcome that help and John answered, 'They had to expunge me totally from it all. I can't remember how it all happened but I had to go. I wasn't a suitable person to be part of the new world.' Perhaps a case of throwing out the baby with the bath water.

'They were insular as a group,' says Proo. 'They didn't want the Foundation, they didn't want anything to do with us and there are several reports of various managers and staff mouthing off about us and saying what dreadful people we were. So they were keen to see a new broom sweep clean and there was no acknowledgement that this was a project started by Earth Sanctuaries or John Wamsley or anything like that. Now, I think it might have changed a little bit. I think they might be a bit kinder. Every now and then you hear something that might be a little bit kinder but they are very insular and very much cut their own path.'

Around this time the foundation applied for a grant of $2 million from the Natural Heritage Trust money (derived from the privatisation of Telstra). It was the intention of the foundation to buy Scotia Sanctuary, but the government said they could only have it if they worked in collaboration with AWC. It lends credibility to the idea that John and Proo were completely out of favour with the government.

*Interestingly, this very large amount of money was handed over to AWC after the sale.*

In spite of some differences in approach, Earth Sanctuaries Foundation Board agreed to support conservation projects at all the sanctuaries established by ESL because it was recognised that the members had strong loyalties to sanctuaries they supported in the past.

An anecdote told by Proo serves to illustrate a point. 'When AWC visited Scotia, Atticus Fleming, who was the CEO, looked at our vehicles, which had been running around in the bush for a long time, and he said, "What do you drive Fords for? Why don't you drive Toyotas?" And John sort of answered it quite sweetly by saying he couldn't fit into a Toyota, he was tall and the Ford gave him room. But if you look at the price of a Toyota Landcruiser versus whatever we were driving there's about a thirty thousand dollar difference. But that was where they came from. They could afford those things.'

AWC are doing wonderful work, and this cannot be gainsaid, only it is not fulfilling John's greater vision. There may be no place in the realities of this space-time continuum for that vision. His ideas are perhaps best seen as a kind of ambit claim upon our sincerity.

Proo echoed her husband's sentiments from those years when the dream was being dissolved. 'Whether we like it or not, there is a continuing belief that the private sector should not be involved in serious conservation. Probably the most disappointing part was the refusal of the Federal Government to help us. Although we received some small temporary assistance, in the end we had to repay every cent of assistance we received from the Federal Government.'

One novel bright spot was the filming of a major motion picture at Little River.

'A filming contract was recently signed to utilise an area of the Little River property for the production of Ned Kelly. This is a major motion picture starring Heath Ledger, Geoffrey Rush and Rachel Griffiths. All environmental concerns have been taken into account and this project will provide some welcome finance to aid in the development of Little River. It will also provide considerable publicity for the area and the property.'

Strangely, alongside the financial struggle, there continued to be support and success. During the upheaval of the restructure, ESL gained *a further 1000 shareholders*. Visitor levels increased at Warrawong to *50,000 per year*.

'Warrawong continues its traditional role of being the showcase of what we are all about. Film crews, families, tourism industry functions, VIP's and visitors from SA, interstate and all over the world continue to come and join the Warrawong experience.

'The koala walk at Hanson Bay becomes more and more popular with upward of *20 buses visiting each week.* Hanson Bay is now recognised as one of the best places to view koalas in the wild.'

On top of all this, 'Yookamurra earth sanctuary has just won the *Barossa Tourism Award for a Significant Tourism Attraction.*'

John's work featured in a book, 'The New Economy of Nature' by Gretchen Daily, one of the world's leading ecologists and Katherine Ellison, a Pulitzer Prize-winning journalist.

Shareholder approval of the ethical and professional conduct of the company restructure appeared in print: 'Wow. What an effort! Satisfied all parties in the best possible way . . .' and, 'The management were alert and responsible enough to recognise and admit to the issues before doom was complete. Top marks for honesty, integrity and dedication to the cause . . .'

It must have made the necessary sell-off that much harder to take, given that the tide of goodwill was still in flood.

Remarkably, Proo's vision remained crystal clear. 'I am determined to rebuild the company into a profitable conservation company *to prove that conservation can be a self-sustaining business* and to continue to offer the wildlife of Australia a voice.'

In light of subsequent events it reads like a sad illusion, but Proo simply could not give up. I suspect there was a direct connection between her heart and all of the animals she had hand-reared, translocated or spoken to every day.

The sale of assets raised five million dollars and with this money the push for a profitable business in the East continued unabated.

CHAPTER NINETEEN

# LAST HOPES

WIRRAPUNGA, WHERE JOHN SECRETED HIMSELF, is only 1.2 hectares in area. A very different kind of challenge and plants rather than animals were the focus.

The new situation was strange for John and to a lesser extent, for Proo. With Warrawong right next door, Proo went to the office each day trying to grow the business while John stayed on the home property, throwing himself into the world of small things and hidden relationships. Maybe it became mathematics again, or the need to prove it was possible to restore something which had been degraded. After all, if the earth cannot be restored, then we have already lost everything.

'Wirrapunga kept me sane,' John says. 'This was a place where I didn't know if it could be restored or not. I look at the place where we have morning tea at Almanda (in Scott Creek). It's a grassy area which is all weeds and I ask the question, "Can this be restored?"

'I didn't know whether I could achieve anything here (at Wirrapunga) or if I was just wasting my time. I knew I could turn a hectare of bush into a conventional garden, *but can you turn a conventional garden back into bushland*? I think that if we're going to save ourselves, if we're going to save the world, we've got to understand how to do that.

'I don't think it's just here (in Australia). I think the structure that you live on has to be a natural system or it's desert. You've got two choices.

Either you can have desert or you can have bush. You might change the bush a lot. You might change patches of bush but everywhere in the world there's a basic structure holding the environment together, which is to do with what evolved in that area. And I think what we're doing by destroying it all is bad. It's destruction of species. We're making bits of it into desert. Gradually making bigger and bigger deserts.

'How many bricks can you knock out of a brick house before it collapses? That's what biodiversity is all about. We're building a desert. I think that's all you can call a paddock of weeds or a paddock of vineyards or a paddock of pine trees. It's just a desert by another name. It's a monoculture and a desert's a monoculture except it's a monoculture of sand. It's the same sort of concept. It's this basic community of living organisms that we destroy. I don't know whether we can keep doing it or not.

'We think we can *exist* independently (of natural systems) but whether we can *live* independently is another thing.'

Somewhere in a discussion about the *method* of restoration there is a place for consideration of how our ethics may come into conflict with what is necessary to that restoration. It has never been more relevant than in our present-day society, where public sentiment, based on completely understandable feelings about the need to be kind to animals, can get in the way of culling. Even when culling will prevent a more protracted (and inevitable) death from starvation.

As John expresses it, the idea of applying our ethics to other species is absurd. '*There are no ethics in conservation.*'

John is innately philosophical and reflective, but with the ability to think things through and form conclusions. *Mathematics* again. And the conclusions lead to simple methods, even if the end result is to restore something highly complex. Nature will do the hard part if we just do *our* part.

At Niagara Park, as a child, he merely wandered out in his back yard and then as later it provided a refuge from unbearable stress.

The methods of restoration of the home block John called Wirrapunga were, and remain, simple. It is a matter of getting rid of unwanted plants and encouraging the desired species.

Against the popular custom of 'cleaning up' in fire-prone areas, organic litter is left where it occurs. 'Clean' equates with 'sterile' in a garden.

Larger pieces are broken up in the hand and put back to decompose more readily. Places where herbaceous plants like orchids and lilies appear are marked with small sticks so those areas can be left undisturbed for the next flowering season.

Patience in the extreme is required for the weeding, especially where it concerns small bulbous plants like native orchids which are easily disturbed or destroyed.

One patch was infiltrated by small weeds called 'smooth cat's ears'. They were easy to simply flick out of the ground with a small stick without interfering with the orchids. John was removing these weeds one day when a snake suddenly landed at his feet. It had mistaken the weeds, as they sailed through the air, for prey, probably thinking they were frogs. It launched itself at the 'frog' only to find there was nothing edible there. John says it had a rather startled look on its face! He knew not to move, and soon the snake went on its way.

Absolutely everything John does in the bush is done methodically. The weeding is no exception.

'Since seeds can remain dormant and viable in the soil for over fifty years, it would be helpful to know what grew on that one square metre over the last 50 years to know what seeds were in the soil. These seeds are waiting for the right conditions to tell them to germinate. If they do not find the right conditions they gradually become unviable.

'If we assume that about 20% become unviable each year and if there is no replenishment, then if there were 10,000 seeds of a certain species in our one square metre one year then there would only be one left after 40 years. We could assume that after 50 years all seeds of that species were gone.'

This thorough way of working through the logic is extended to the weeding process to explain how ultimately we are left with only the desirable species.

John is opposed to the 'Bradley' method, in use for a long time, believing it leads to species impoverishment. For every task in bush care John will have his own unique take on the methods, and the results speak for themselves, especially at Wirrapunga where, to the casual observer, the land is untrammelled bush.

It must have been a curious thing for someone accustomed to travelling around Australia supervising major conservation projects to be spending his days in one place, peacefully engaged in weeding and nurturing a bush garden. But the respite was to last about a year before he was asked to contribute his expertise once again to ESL

Proo took over at a time of looming uncertainty.

Kevin Lynch, as chairman of ESL, delivered an honest and straightforward annual report:

'A year of mixed fortune for Earth Sanctuaries Ltd. It started with the sadness associated with the final disposal of the Yookamurra, Scotia and Buckaringa sanctuaries, as well as the Dakalanta property, the details of which were included in our last report.

'Both Warrawong and Little River returned disappointing trade results and senior management has worked very hard to address these problems.'

Even the core, iconic Warrawong Sanctuary fell behind, affecting the cash flow for other projects. The reasons for this are not clear, but it was an ominous sign.

'ESL's share price has continued to lag well below asset value and there is little prospect of paying any dividend for some years.'

These kind of pronouncements had potential to deter new investors, but telling the truth about the company's position was the ethical and legal thing to do. One has to agree with the shareholder who praised ESL's openness and integrity. It is to be expected that a company which is motivated by idealism, rather than money alone, would never seek to be dishonest in its dealings. Of course, it is also a reflection upon John and Proo, whose honour no one who meets them could ever question.

Kevin Lynch tempered his report with good news and among that news was an announcement whose timing couldn't have been better to lift John's spirits, although it was at odds with the downturn in his company's fortunes.

'ESL's founder, Dr John Wamsley, was named by the Prime Minister (John Howard) as *Australian Environmentalist of the Year* and we extend our heartiest congratulations to John. It was a timely recognition of over thirty years' work in saving Australian wildlife.'

*The Australian Environmentalist of the Year Award*

In one of his most cynical moments during our interviews, John said of the award that the government must have thought, "What could we give John Wamsley so that he wouldn't go completely bonkers?" It was thus interpreted as almost an ironic slap in the face after all the bureaucratic obstruction ESL experienced.

Such an award, however, represents the highest honour Australia can give to a person working in this field. The ABC reported it on 1ˢᵗ June 2003:

'The Federal Environment Minister, David Kemp, says Dr Wamsley has campaigned tirelessly for 30 years on behalf of threatened species and helped raise public awareness of the devastation caused by feral animals.

'He is especially noted for his dislike of the domestic cat (sic), demonstrated by his wearing cat skin hats in public.

'In the 1980's Dr Wamsley established Earth Sanctuaries.

'He is now developing methods to reintroduce native grasses to bushland and to manage woody weeds.'

The award draws an important distinction between John's aspirational influence and the fortunes of the company designed to implement his ideas. It represents the pinnacle of national recognition even as it came about after the downsizing of John's company and John's own removal from direct control.

The final piece of good news concerned the continuing efforts of the downsized board, with Proo as Managing Director, to establish a sanctuary near Sydney. The fact that a brand new venture was in the pipeline is testament that some within the board still had faith in the wisdom of going east.

'We were all excited at the opportunity to acquire the lease from the NSW government of the Waratah Park property at Terrey Hills, on Sydney's outskirts.

'The interest shown in that venture, associated as it is with the television show "Skippy, the bush kangaroo", has created a great deal of interest, in Sydney in particular.'

This time belonged to Proo.

CHAPTER TWENTY

# PROO AND THE
# LEGACY OF SKIPPY

THE NOTION OF A 'SEA World' or 'Theme Park' mentality was stronger than ever. This was a proven money-spinner on the east coast but it was anathema to John's concept of animals in a wild situation. The two concepts sat uneasily with one another because theme parks rely on their assets being 'in your face' and interactive, backed up by purely commercial entertainments. A wildlife sanctuary in John's model was something more subtle, combining the quiet chance of animal encounters with education and an 'immersive' experience of the natural world.

Waratah Park had one big advantage and that was its already existing profile as a tourist drawcard for a generation which still remembered the famous television series.

'Projected attendance figures indicate that the income derived from this property will, within a few years, bring ESL to a cash neutral or break even situation. It is a sad fact of life that the operations of any company on the stock exchange involves significant overhead expense, which in our case, must be met from visitor entrance fees.'

The company was not broke and it owned its assets outright. Kevin Lynch repeated assurances for the shareholders.

'ESL's properties are not mortgaged. It has sufficient capital to carry on for some considerable time yet but your board is committed to ensuring that the value of the company is not completely eroded by the continual dilution of its capital to cover day-to-day running costs.'

Finally, it represented a foreshadowing of things to come, a pragmatic approach hinting at the dichotomy between the remains of the vision and what could realistically hope to be achieved.

'If the projections at Waratah Park are not met and trading losses continue, the directors will review the whole future of the company. *If the Australian public is not prepared to visit our properties in sufficient numbers to make the sanctuaries commercially viable, the whole future of the company as a listed sanctuary developer, in its present form, will need to be reviewed and changed.*'

In this extraordinary time, with different currents moving within the company, Proo was carried along because her own dedication to the dream she had inherited from John would not let her give up. She felt side-lined by the board during the preceding couple of years and then had to cope without the support of John. I questioned her about it all.

Question: 'I find it hard to believe that after all this trouble you would have wanted to keep going. It must have been so stressful. I would have thought you would try to wind it all up and finish it. But somehow you kept going.'

'Ah, you see, the problem is *the gift of the gab.*'

Question: Who's gab?

'You see, it's John's philosophy. *When you live with John, you live with his philosophy.* And so from my perspective I guess I'm a different genetic make-up and you can't walk out on that. John said, a number of times, I should have sold off all the other titles. No way, at any point of my life, would I ever have considered that.

'To me, conservation land has to grow and we learnt the hard way, you can't do conservation on small areas, so the idea of just selling it off, once it is inside the fence . . . I understood that if it wasn't already fenced you could get rid of it. Not if it was fenced.'

She referred to the *living* part of ESL's assets, that is, the animals.

Somehow, Proo's will, in this matter, turned out to be stronger than her husband's although it wasn't just a matter of *will* but of *survival*.

As John says, 'I just decided in my own mind that I couldn't afford to get involved or I would have been in trouble mentally. I couldn't handle it and I didn't want to think about it. I didn't want to do anything about it. I had to separate myself from it, that's all.'

It would take a royal commission to untangle the complexities of this time in the company's story. Motivations and objectives were no longer focused together and the east coast proved to be ever a difficult target to hit.

Publicly, in the 2003 annual report, Proo projected a strong and confident line.

'This year has been a year of expansion under my management. Our wildlife assets have continued to thrive, demonstrating the methods put in place by the Founder, Dr John Wamsley, prove that all our wildlife really needs is a piece of feral-free Australia.

'The purchase of Waratah Park and its conversion into an Earth Sanctuary is creating a great sense of excitement and refocusing for the Earth Sanctuaries team. Once again we are building fences, eradicating ferals and reintroducing species back into their former range.

'The entire Waratah Park Project has received enormous goodwill from everyone. Shareholders, Volunteers, staff and I are very grateful that the founder, Dr John Wamsley, *returned to ESL to become the Project Manager for Waratah Park.*

'Be assured, Senior Management is working very hard to address all issues affecting the business and looking at new ways to improve profitability and conservation outcomes.'

In reality, the situation was fraught and awkward, both for personal and for practical reasons. Her reflections on that time tell a story of frustration and stress.

'When we did Waratah Park, the kind of tribal-ness or village mentality that Sydney is based around is very strong, so if you say you've got a business at Duffy's Forest, well some people don't go to Duffy's Forest. It's not quite like Adelaide. Adelaide is a much more inclusive area, really. And trying to understand that market, to get a sanctuary to work, was actually hellishingly hard and it was the same in Melbourne. They're isolated from what goes on in SA, for a start, so you can't say, "Look, there's this earth-shattering thing that's happening in SA and it's happening here now. They just don't think like that. And they have their own experts in conservation.

So it was very hard to get a toe-hold with any of them. But we had started Little River and we got it to the point where we were running walks.'

With profound honesty, Proo adds, 'My job was just to wind it (the company) up. I didn't understand that, to be quite honest, until closer to the end.'

Question: 'Did you really believe you could keep it going?'

'In a way, I did. It was very hard, though, because John *disposed of himself* out of the debate and we had always worked very much as a team. He said very clearly he didn't want me bringing my troubles home. He wasn't ever speaking to the board ever again. So he didn't want to know what the board was saying. He didn't know what was going on. He didn't want to know.

'So if you like, I knew the talk, but I had to be prepared to do the walk and I had no profile. John had profile. So we staggered, I suppose. It was a very difficult time. I used to do my morning walk simply saying, over and over again, "*They don't shoot people in Australia, they don't shoot people in Australia.*"

'Because it was so hard on me to try and find a way through all of this. And I remember there was one hell of a barny because Greg Follett, who was hired to source potential investments, found Waratah Park. He said it might be a good deal, so we moved ahead and bought it and John took over the job of doing it. He did a brilliant job. *But the board were furious. Absolutely furious.* They had to approve the purchase, there was nothing wrong with that, but *they didn't want John in the system.*'

Question: 'So there'd been a real falling out?'

'Well, when you have a public company or when you have a business of any kind, if it's the sort of business that's meant to survive, and ours was meant to, then it's got to have both a business plan that's successful and it's got to be able to grow from the founder. And there are thousands of companies that have brilliant founders but then can't go from there to the next step of finding someone from the ordinary world to come in and make that work. And in many cases they stay on good terms with the founder, for the founder to just step back and demonstrate how things are done.

'Companies set up by entrepreneurs always have to grow from the initial management and board structure to a more conventional and stable framework. But as is often the way, Founding Directors can be a hard act to follow. This was the case for ESL. The fire and the commitment in John's unique style of leadership was replaced with a more conventional style and within a short time the company foundered.

'We had a number of flaws in our system, most of which were covered by the SGARA's, the self-generating assets, but once we lost the ability to account for that in our books, we really couldn't go forward successfully.'

The sense of alienation from the board had its origins some time before.

'I firmly believe that both John Stammer and the CEO understood, for right or for wrong, that John and Proo had to go. I don't know how John survived that particular couple of years, but for me, I was just squeezed. I had my finger in everything, I watched everything that was going on. I was up on the front till, I'd be still doing walks, I was occasionally still cooking breakfast for the dawn walks. I was into everything and I was head of the management team and *I was immediately squeezed out of everything.* I remember saying to a work compatriot, *Do you want to go and talk to her? (meaning the CEO) I'm just sitting here.*'

John, although quite removed from the board, contributed an article to the annual report and put on a brave face, in spite of the angst surely underlying his words.

'There is no doubt that Earth sanctuaries is the world's most successful conservation group. *Six species of mammal have been taken off the endangered list because of Earth Sanctuaries' work.* This year I was named 'Prime Minister's Environmentalist of the Year.' I accepted that award on behalf of the members of Earth Sanctuaries.

'The problems encountered are, like most problems, just imaginary. Earth Sanctuaries has performed better than anyone, including Proo and I, ever imagined. There are, however, perceptions that something is wrong . . .'

John then makes a comparison between charities and businesses (as he had done before) which concludes with what must surely be one of his best satirical lines, alluding to the business of ESL.

'*It should be interested in making a profit. It shouldn't be mucking around trying to save the world.*'

Of course, the truth is that it needed to do both.

He ends on a bravely upbeat note. 'Nevertheless, Earth Sanctuaries can boast success after success. I believe the model we have developed is the best possible given the constraints we have to work under. I thank all our members for their continued support and look forward to more successes in the future.'

Around this time there would be yet another honour for John and Proo with an award of 'Centenary Medals' for their services to conservation. John Howard wrote the letter of congratulations.

'This distinctive Australian commemorative medal marks the achievements at the commencement of a new century of a broad cross-section of the Australian community including your contribution to Australian society. Australia is proud that it has many outstanding people who have helped make our country and the wider world a better place.'

Like the other award bestowed by the Prime Minister, it sat strangely with the ever-diminishing profile of the company behind the environmental work.

Waratah Park waited to be developed and tried in the marketplace. The site, unique in its background history, had as a shop-front the well maintained 'Park Ranger Headquarters' building which formed part of the film set for the 'Skippy' series.

Existing infrastructure like this made the development viable, in the way it would have done at the ill-fated Canyon site.

Visible from the site was the beautifully wooded and hilly terrain of Kuringai Chase National Park. The people of Sydney regularly visited the area to see the film set and to ride on a miniature train. Budding 'Skippys' were on view in enclosures.

Once again John wrote articles for 'Earth News' and now he wasn't afraid to wear his heart on his sleeve. Perhaps there was nothing left to lose. Waratah Park served as a place to reintroduce the animal from his childhood, the red necked pademelon, back to NSW. Some of the details we have already touched on, but the article tells the pademelon story very clearly and is some of John's best writing.

'I was ten years old and sitting quietly on the forest edge watching a small group of wallabies grazing. It was in sandstone country north of Sydney. My family had bought a bush block and cleared some of it for a citrus orchard. I used to get up before dawn, sit in the forest and watch the magic of dawn unfold. Later I learned that the wallabies I had been watching that morning were red-necked pademelons. But! They were very special red-necked pademelons. They had a white hip-stripe as the early paintings of Sydney pademelons showed. I also learned that today, red-necked pademelons no longer have white hip-stripes because the Sydney sub-species were gone. Or so I thought.

'It was thirty-two years later. We had completed Warrawong earth sanctuary and were collecting animals to reintroduce there. Proo and I were at a closing down sale of a backyard zoo at Peterborough in South Australia's mid-north. I was looking at ghosts from my past, a pen of red-necked pademelons, with white hip-stripes. What were these beautiful animals, which should be living on the fringe of a rainforest, doing here in South Australia's dry north? I was told that their ancestors had been purchased at the Twin Street Pet Shop, in Adelaide, twenty years before.

'Of course, Warrawong wasn't their rightful home, but then, neither was Peterborough. We bought as many as we could afford and I made them a promise. *One day I would take them home.*

'The small colony of white-striped red-necked pademelons has thrived at Warrawong. There are now over fifty individuals in the colony. However, my attempts to take them home have, so far, proved fruitless. There was Canyon Sanctuary, The Brick Pit, Murrawoollan and Blue Mountains. For various reasons they failed. Waratah Park is my fifth attempt to return these beautiful animals to their rightful home. *Although I am bruised and bleeding from my previous attempts, I am not yet beaten.*'

Another part of the article reads almost like an apology for walking away and a plea for a last chance. It is quite moving. 'Before Christmas I plan to return the white-striped red-necked pademelon to their home. But there is much to be done and I plead for your help. Please! This time make it work. For whether it succeeds or fails is really up to you. It is your decision. *I promise to do more than my share*, but I need your help . . .'

In the last personal part, John restates his message for Australia. '. . . the reason for the horrific loss of our wildlife is not a shortage of money, or expertise, or knowledge, or anything logical. *It is simply because we do not care enough.*'

Proo may have inadvertently handed John exactly what he needed at the time, a chance to throw himself into another project, doing what he did best, getting dirt under his fingernails and seeing animals released into a new home.

The hard physical work of fence-building proved therapeutic for John, with no need to be concerned about the business side of Waratah Park. In a straightforward contract arrangement he agreed to build a sanctuary up to operating standard. His respect for Proo was again on show, for he only agreed to do it because she asked it of him. Proo needed John to be involved and this was a way to make that happen without the pressures John could no longer wear. But one condition he placed upon the deal, namely, there had to be clear and unequivocal approval from the relevant authorities, in this case the local Warringah Council.

Such approval was duly obtained, but when the work was already underway and in a repeat of the kind of frustrations which had always dogged sanctuary development, someone successfully lobbied the council to rescind the approval.

Rather than being crushed, John took this as a red flag to a bull, firming his resolve that a sanctuary be built. Centrelink provided workers and John's son, Shane, took a year off to help as part of the team.

Somehow, John defied authority and kept building, after an absurd restriction meant he could not use machinery on the site. *The fence was built by hand.* Surely John's final act of stubborn defiance. This kind of hands-on work remained John's brilliant forte, not just for his organisational skills and experience, but also for his seemingly limitless capacity to engage in hard physical work.

'It was bloody hard work, I can tell you, because they did their damnedest to stop me. They didn't know I'd done it until after I'd done it.'

This showed the *fait accompli* principle at work again. A 'done deal' is hard to gainsay, and in Proo's scarcely disguised dig at the opposition, she wrote, 'Even the Warringah Council has bent over backwards to accommodate our needs, although *sending 15 inspectors to the site in 4 weeks is probably a bit much!*'

Extraordinary volunteer input figured large, as people rallied to John's call. Proo paid tribute to all who worked on the project.

'Dr John Wamsley, who came out of retirement to oversee the conversion, has worked with tremendous energy and focus to achieve the conversion in the time frame demanded.

'The staff working with John, namely Bob, Robert, Rodney, Jake, Cara, Merinda, Shane, Steve and Ben have all worked many long hours on the fence line, the clean-up and the landscaping in rough and ready conditions. *All have also put in many long hours as volunteers* to make sure the project is "on time and under budget". No one could ask for a more committed group of workers.'

In the end, it seems the residents of Duffy's Forest simply didn't like machines operating in their backyard but there were no insurmountable objections to the development.

Animals came next. Proo described a 'gruelling 17 hour non-stop drive from Warrawong to Waratah Park with 53 long-nosed potoroos and rufous bettongs for release.'

Skippy, the film star, was an eastern grey kangaroo (or rather, a series of them) and it was always intended that Waratah Park should have these animals on view to tie in with the film heritage. Easier said than done, for kangaroos do what kangaroos do best, which is to hop. They were simply not around when they were needed. What John did about this is a case study in his lateral method of problem-solving and native wildlife 'wrangling'. As simple as the solutions were, it is unlikely that anyone but John would have thought of them. They involved *observation*, not book learning.

'One of the biggest challenges was to have the big kangaroos, the Eastern greys, where they could be seen. When Waratah Park closed down last year (i.e. the previous business) the RSPCA took most of the animals. Six Eastern Greys went to Macquarie University. About ten jumped the fence and were not captured.

'This small mob of Greys became well known throughout Duffys Forest over the next six months or so while the fence was being constructed. They were "well chased" by the local dogs and were quite spooked by the time the fence was completed. During this time they spent the days down near Cowan Creek to the West of Waratah Park and the nights grazing in the "horse paddocks" of Duffys Forest to the east. Of course they crossed through Waratah Park each evening and morning.

'When the fence was completed, this small mob of Skippies were not fussed at all by the 1.8 metre high vermin proof fence. They simply jumped it. When the six returned from Macquarie University, they joined the other mob and jumped it with them.

'So! We had two problems. Firstly, the small band of Skippies were only temporarily within Waratah Park each day. Secondly, they weren't there when we needed them to show off to our evening visitors who had come, after all, to see Skippy.

'Since we knew this would happen, we had spent a lot of effort developing "their" habitat to make them feel welcome. This is what we did:

'On studying this small band of escapees, it was clear they needed a few things. They needed to be safe from the local dogs who were intent on making their lives exciting. This was achieved with our fence.

'However, we noticed that they always headed for a bit of high ground where they could view their surroundings and assure themselves they were safe. We had some excess materials that had built up in the park over the years, so we built them a viewing mound in the middle of their old paddock to the south of the visitor walkway.

'Finally, we studied what they ate when they visited the local horse paddocks. Their favourite grasses were buffalo and kikuyu. So we gave them a nice kikuyu lawn on the northern side of the walkway. We also planted the edges of the "native otter habitat" with a buffalo grass lawn.

'So now the big Eastern greys appear on their mound about dusk. After convincing themselves that the area is free of dogs, they move across the visitor pathway to munch on their favourite grasses. They now have no reason to jump the fence and the visitors are assured of seeing these magnificent animals living in the wild as they should.'

Southern brown bandicoots, promised for Waratah Park and sourced from the adjoining National Park, never arrived. John expressed the frustration very well. 'Someone was doing a PHD on the extinction of the southern brown bandicoot in that area and interfering with the status quo would have upset their research!'

*This is true. It actually happened.*

If John had been allowed to give the animals a safe breeding area, the young would have moved through the fence to populate the surrounding area, thereby messing up the research project. The cats and foxes had to be allowed to do their work. *There are no southern brown bandicoots left in NSW today.*

More from Proo: 'When the Conservation properties were sold to AWC, it put five million dollars in the coffers. So then the question was "Where do we want to go?" We still had Little River, which we went on developing. Greg Follett found Waratah Park because there was the thought that we could continue.

'We never had a serious marketing budget for Little River or Waratah Park. *We started to run out of money.* Waratah Park wasn't performing well. Warrawong was tracking along in its usual fashion, just under profitability all the time. Little River was not profitable but we'd had the film "Ned Kelly" shot there so for half a year we'd made a profit. And then we had to make another decision about what we were doing and so *the decision was to wind up.*'

John completed his contracted job months ahead of schedule and Waratah Park opened to the Sydney public, though it never got the numbers hoped for and in the end it was only another prize for the made-up corporation who took what was left of the assets and the dignity of Earth Sanctuaries Limited.

CHAPTER TWENTY-ONE

# A CIRCLING OF VULTURES

MYLOR IN THE ADELAIDE HILLS is today still a very small town, no doubt fortuitously kept that way by rules which limit development in the reservoir catchment surrounding it.

Bushland to the west bears a sign announcing it is part of 'The Valley of the Bandicoots.' This is a five kilometre corridor of reserves and cooperating private landholdings with the aim of providing a continuous area of habitat for wildlife, especially the southern brown bandicoot. Part of the initiative involves educating people about 'responsible cat ownership,' the new term for dealing with the problem of straying cats.

Many thousands of native species have been planted to help with cover for the bandicoots.

I can't help but be reminded of a film I saw in the nineteen eighties called 'The man Who Planted Trees'. It concerned a shepherd who, single-handed, planted a forest and thereby gave the gift of life to a region which had been laid bare. In the version of this film I saw, the shepherd returned to a village which had been abandoned when the land became denuded, and the people who were enjoying the rejuvenation of life thought he was merely an old vagrant and drove him from the village, unaware they owed him everything.

Along Stock Road in Mylor you can still see the fence John built decades ago and the trees he planted, sometimes indistinguishable from original bushland. Young bandicoots escape through the mesh of the fence to repopulate surrounding land. Feral plants and animals are recognised for what they are and their removal is part of law, even if we have a long way to go before sufficient funds and energy are given to the problem.

John's legacy is palpable everywhere in the hills. The 'Valley of the Bandicoots' owes much of its substance to him, though the youngest members of our society may be unaware to whom they owe their inheritance.

The 'nature corridor' idea is a long way from Stirling Council's old policy, changed by John during his term as councillor, in which roadsides were to be cleared and levelled, then planted with exotic trees.

When John began his one-man crusade, we were infants in our understanding of the natural world and of what we had allowed to happen to it. During the two decades of the business that was Warrawong and its off-shoots, the world grew a little in understanding of its own fragile and beautiful complexity, meaning there was, at least, scope for others to take on the drowning aspirations of conservation as espoused by ESL.

The buyers of ESL's assets were imperfect custodians, for they lacked the grand picture, the penchant for reckless experimentation and the means of raising large amounts of private capital but they preserved enough of the dream to inspire and embolden later people involved in privately owned nature conservation.

AWC still operates the sanctuaries they purchased, although their efforts could never measure up to John's exacting standards. The good work being done is a long way from John's plan of fully fenced and expanding reserves. In the real world, it is the best that can currently be achieved, but as the great big wheel turns, we are now witnessing a proliferation of feral-fenced reserves across Australia.

Curious about what remains of John and Proo's wildlife introductions at the sanctuaries, I asked John if there were still numbats at Yookamurra. The thought of these beautiful and unique little animals complementing the mallee is somehow comforting.

John replied, 'I don't know. Would it help me knowing? *I can pretend that they are, can't I?*'

Other questions I have directed at him about the fate of the sanctuaries are met with the same lack of information. It isn't about resentment, but rather that it is simply too painful for him to know what may have become of the animals.

Only recently I discovered that numbats are, in fact, still extant in good numbers at Yookamurra, along with other endangered species introduced there by John and Proo.

All of the labour of love at Waratah Park and all of Proo's heroic efforts to maintain the momentum and the dream only led to the inevitable final wind-up of the company. The $5 million from the first sale of assets went on land purchases and infrastructure development. ESL's board knew what they had to do and sourced a buyer for the remaining assets. That buyer was a company called ES Link.

ES Link seems to have been set up just to take over ESL. The company dissolved itself very quickly afterwards. They bought out the shareholders. Basically, they were developers who had a certain element of 'eco-tourism' in their portfolio of activities and were happy to run something that mimicked doing conservation, giving people "warm fuzzies", but they weren't prepared to actually do anything else.

ES Link held all the cards, because ESL was looking for a quick sale and ES Link knew it. Proo had little bargaining power. She admits to feeling 'shattered and totally demoralised.'

The strength of Proo's emotional response was plain to see as she related the details of ESL's final days. As she had previously said, '*When you live with John you live with his philosophy,*' and after all her struggles to maintain the company based on that philosophy, she was obliged by the indisputable reality of the financial situation to bargain with people whose motivation paid only lip-service to serious conservation.

'I was naïve. There was no way in the world I wanted ES Link. They horrified me. I did go and do my research. We went to Lake St Clair (in Tasmania) and had a look at their accommodation (they managed an eco-lodge). They had a plan. Once they were talking to the board about it . . . after that I was not in a position to change things around. I know I felt more hamstrung . . . it was also to do with decisions being made at Waratah Park. John had left by then. We had a manager there. He always wanted to have what I refer to as "koalas on sticks". I said we wouldn't do that. We would not have animals in cages. Somehow along the way he got his "koalas on sticks". There were various decisions that were being made and I couldn't do anything about them.'

But not all of it was grim. 'Their spokesperson (ES Link's spokesperson) was quite nice. He ended up buying Little River and developed it privately. He actually believed in conservation.'

ES Link took over Earth Sanctuaries for a payment of 4.2 million dollars and sold it on to their development company for fifteen million dollars. What conclusions can one draw?

A condition came with the ES Link deal. From Proo: 'Our contract was just appalling. Our contract was we could never say anything about anything ever again full stop. So the only thing you could do was to totally withdraw, and the one thing I'd have to say about John was that he was very good at finding life beyond Earth Sanctuaries.'

Proo remained in the thick of it during the difficult final months.

'For me, well, the model we got left with was very hard to deal with. I don't know, *it's very hard retrospectively to think of anything other than the fact that we failed.* And all these things dovetailed in at the time. You've got to be able to handle it. I used to walk around the block saying, well, I've got to accept that we're no longer a conservation group. *The purity of the plan was always so good and the fact that we couldn't make it work was a really bitter blow.*

'I was in charge for five minutes but once ES Link came to the table and the board were considering it, with much to-ing and fro-ing, there might have been six or seven months during which they curtailed me from making any more decisions. And because ES Link were pulling the strings from behind, for the last nine months I played an awful lot of solitaire. We had an annual general meeting in November and then an extraordinary general meeting on the 17th March 2005. After that I was finished. ES Link were then in complete control legally. *Nobody wanted to know us.*'

ES Link owned a resort at Lake St Clair in Tasmania (not exactly to do with conservation) and had various contracts with the Department of Environment. They had permission to be inside National Parks. It could be that ES Link were afraid they would lose their government contracts if anyone knew they were connected with John and Proo.

A former employee commented that ES Link appeared terrified of John. 'Perhaps they knew they had feet of straw, I don't know, but they were terrified that he would come out with some blast or another and sort of sink them or be at odds with them.'

John wanted to buy Warrawong, but he was told the asking price was

$5 million. Way beyond his scope. The board then sold it to ES Link for $1million.

On Development (John): 'One of the people we were negotiating with at the time explained it this way, that you buy for x and then you sell off all of the bits until you've recovered your money and then what you've got left is profit. And that's how developers work. Now if you imagine for one minute that you're involved in conservation, then acquiring more land is way more important than reducing your land. So it was a very difficult time but we knew exactly what was going on.'

On the remaining wildlife: 'The advertising was done extremely privately to make sure we didn't make a fuss and National Parks or law enforcement people never came in. There was no intent, for instance that the Foundation could have put management agreements over the wildlife or they could have pulled everyone together to look after the wildlife. There was nothing. Because the blocks were all revegetated there was no consideration under the native vegetation laws either.'

I personally find it almost obscene that the wildlife were given so little consideration in the transactions at that time. The fate of the animals seems to have been the last thing that anyone considered in the process of the sale. Parcels of land were sold off in a feeding frenzy, making many millions for those who had grabbed them in the name of conservation.

But there is always a new dawning. 'I think the saving grace was really Idaway (the name given to a newly purchased property in the Southern Flinders Ranges of SA). We found that the weekend before the 17th March. It was all clear from about mid 2004 what was going to happen. It just took time for everyone to finish gouging out and strategizing and everything else. And John had said, very wisely, "Let's look forward to 30 years of happy, healthy retirement. Let's plan for that." He overtly seems to be able to walk away from things a bit better than me. I can get a bit caught up in things. A bit emotional. I'm a girl, let's face it!

'In buying Idaway we had something to focus on, and you just need to focus elsewhere when you're faced with shit like that, and so with that in our eyesight it took a lot of the immediate grit out of it. At the same time we went across and visited John's family. We hadn't done much of that over the years. We sort of moved on and started doing what we wanted at Idaway. That year we had very late rains. The rains didn't come until June,

I think, and I remember sitting out here on our brown chairs an awful lot of the time. Because there's another thing that happens and that is that you can actually have a rest. Because, before, whether I wanted it or not I had to go to work and a lot of the time I was watching things happen that I didn't want to happen. Watching the surveyors come and surveying off the various bits that ES Link sold off. Watching all of this stuff go on and not being able to do anything about it, keeping faith with the staff, keeping faith with what was going on. So it was very nice, in a way, to not have that. You needed something to look forward to and Idaway probably picked us up out of that. But it does take months to heal.'

John and Proo were nothing less than fallen stars, but the loss is ours because nothing else shone so brightly in the conservation firmament and today we have nothing comparable to the momentum they generated.

*Proo and John*

## CHAPTER TWENTY-TWO

# PEOPLE BELIEVE IN FAIRIES

I BROACHED THE SUBJECT OF SNAKES to John when we were in the thick of the bush one day and told him how I considered black snakes to be more aggressive than some other snakes because of their habit of lifting the front part of their body off the ground.

John has been a snake-handler from his childhood and knows what he's talking about when it comes to these reptiles. He quickly set me straight on the habits of snakes.

'It wasn't being aggressive. It was raising its body up to get a better idea of what you were. Snakes don't have especially good eyesight. They rely on their sense of smell and their tongue is the principle organ for this. The tongue is forked to give it directional smell in the way we have two eyes for binocular vision or two ears for directional hearing.

'By lifting its body and flicking the forked tongue it is only trying to ascertain what is in front of it. Is it prey or is it a threat?'

I have now a new understanding and respect for black snakes, which I always admired for their beauty. Even the forked tongue was explained. My previous 'understanding' was merely a belief. *But it was a belief I had held for at least thirty years.*

A small thing, but it illustrates a point.

Quite early on in our association, John spoke about the difficulty he had when dealing with people because they 'believed in fairies'. People are guided by their beliefs. He used to expect people to understand what he was trying to get across and become flabbergasted when they reacted irrationally, but he finally realised the problem was one of entrenched belief, without the need for any rational basis to underpin it. 'Once I worked this out, I got on much better with people because I understood where they were coming from. *People believe in fairies.* This is just how they are.'

John is a patient teacher when it comes to the public at large. He can present information in an interesting and often humorous way, winning people over with his manner, breaking down the beliefs in a gentle way. His voice is a deep bass which is quite relaxing to listen to. His written words, however, can create a different kind of impression.

With senior government people he has been markedly less patient than with the general population and this has led to very public battles. Proo once said that in dealing with people she was the carrot and John was the stick. People reacted to her in a very different way. Her own writings carry an entirely different tone and aura. Together they succeeded, but not in every fight.

John has the problem original thinkers often face. They are so far removed from conventional sensibilities it is hard for them to accept that others do not share their views.

The tragedy for conservation of the natural world is that by the time enough people understand what you are saying and by the time laws follow public opinion it is usually far too late to save the things you are talking about.

Wirrapunga, into which John retreated for the sake of his sanity, started not with a belief but with an idea in search of a proof and it taught him that he needed extra information. Hard information of the kind only obtained at a university. John enrolled to study second-year Botany for a term at Adelaide University. The aim was to understand something about the structure and development of the amazing life-forms he worked with. He claims that Botany was harder than mathematics, but then, mathematics came as easily as breathing to him. Quite obviously, the new knowledge opened windows in his perceptions.

'I'm happy now I understand basically the way that a community (of living organisms) works, how it got there and how important it is.

'You've got this incredible concept. Plants are trying to do things. They've got an aim in life. A tree tries to grow. If you took any bit of land anywhere in the world and you put a bubble over it, something would happen in there. Things would start to grow.

'You've got this dynamic situation, the bush. I'm interested in the Australian bush but this happens everywhere in the world. Every bit of surface on earth went through this process over billions of years, developing a community of living things. Whether it be the Antarctic or the Arctic or anywhere in-between.

'So you've got the bush wanting to do something and then you've got all the factors that stop it from doing those things. And this all together gives you the dynamics or the management plan that creates what you've got.

'There are places where grazers and crops evolved together. The grass grew to be the best thing that can grow well while it's being grazed. So there are grazers that need grass and grass that needs grazers. It made the American prairie, the African veldt and the Eurasian steppes.

'I realised there was a lot I didn't understand about communities. I wanted to understand more about this concept of the community of living organisms, which I decided was what the guts of the matter was all about. And I realised I'd have to learn a little about what made life tick because there were things I didn't understand.

'You've got this wonderful thing called life which everybody should understand and maybe all those days when I should have been paying attention in school, *maybe I should've been listening.*'

Throughout all the years of mathematics lecturing followed by the years of trying to get his message of conservation across, John remained intrinsically a teacher. In mathematics he wanted his students to grasp what underlies the formulas they used and in conservation he wanted the public to know how extraordinary the animals were because only then would they want to save them.

The drive to educate others is very strong in John. Likewise the tendency to push an idea just as far as it can go and the capacity I have remarked on before to arrive at novel, lateral ways of rendering those ideas.

In an article for 'Garden' magazine in February 2012, John outlines the basic approach to restoration of his block and the techniques used:

'So when I retired from Earth Sanctuaries Ltd I returned to my other love, the management and understanding of our local bush. Wirrapunga consists of 1.4 hectares. We use 0.2 hectares for living, including the house and vegetable garden and my current passion has been to return the other 1.2 hectares into what it was 200 years ago, a grassy woodland ecosystem.

'Although defined as a 'Grassy Woodland Community', the grassy woodlands of the Aldgate Valley contain only 10% grass species. However, a further 70% of species are less than one metre tall. Orchid species make up 10% of that mix.

'The return and ongoing management of these many small species has required much experimentation, interference and the employment of many common gardening techniques so that the seed bank stored in the soil (sometimes for up to 50 years) can germinate.

'These techniques include reducing unnecessary competition, stopping the medium and tall shrub layers from becoming too dense, controlling woody weeds, hand weeding of all non-native species and creating events such as mowing to emulate heavy grazing or fire to create renewal. Not allowing any nutrients other than the natural breakdown of litter so healthy mycorrhizae can develop and be maintained.

'The results speak for themselves, with over 200 species returned of their own accord. This far exceeded my best expectations, and as feral species have been slowly brought under control, I have been able to source and physically return a further 150 species, and to demonstrate that remnant bush can be managed as a garden. Unobtrusive "wallaby tracks" wind around mature stringybarks, banks of acacias, showy Epacris, Epilobiums, native grasses and over 50 species of orchids and lilies. A bog garden provides water for birds and butterflies plus habitat for frogs. Nest boxes for birds, possums, native bees and wintering ladybirds all add to the rich diversity.

'Mulch from the weeding program goes to sustaining a large vegetable garden producing an all year round supply of fresh fruit and vegetables.'

Here is another first. In 2011 Wirrapunga became the first ever indigenous garden to be included in the Australian Open Gardens Scheme. No one before John had thought to submit such a 'garden' to this scheme, even though the scheme had been in operation for 24 years. *This is what I mean by lateral thinking.*

John likes to recount how a tradesman visiting his home commented, 'I take it you're not a gardener, then?' All the visitor saw was native bushland. A 'garden' is something made up of introduced plants and constructed features. In his sweeping way, John disparagingly talks of these traditional (and mostly European-style) gardens as 'a kind of pornography' and still laments the destruction of the last old-growth stringybark forest in SA to make way for the establishment of the Mount Lofty Botanical Garden.

Temperate and Mediterranean gardens of introduced species have long been part of South Australian culture and this style persists in spite of the 'grow native' sentiments which began in the seventies and the water shortages of successive droughts. Most people accept the juxtaposition of traditional and indigenous styles throughout SA but for John it is totally unacceptable. This is understandable when you connect, as he does, the exotic cultural expressions with the ravages perpetrated upon our remaining bushland.

John used to like going for walks around Mylor but now finds it too depressing when he sees what has happened to the roadside vegetation and in the private yards where once it might have been possible to find orchids, native grasses and all manner of small or large native plants.

The proliferation of introduced species is very easy to see, especially in Spring, when plants like Erica and broom are in flower. Much of it is on government land, yet the regulations pertaining to declared plants are not enforced. Wirrapunga is truly an oasis.

John the educator was hard at work with Wirrapunga. It isn't enough to do something for your own satisfaction; it must reach others to do some good in the world.

'I'm an optimist,' John says, 'that's the problem. I've got this strong belief that if you show someone, then they'll do it, but it doesn't work, does it? So I thought, okay, I'd turned this fairly degraded hectare of land into something that's pretty good. What do I do with it to help the bigger picture?

'I saw an advertisement for the "sustainable garden" competition and I thought, "Bloody hell, that's what I've been doing for the last several years, developing a sustainable garden." So I entered the competition. They said they couldn't give us the top award because it's not really "gardening", but they gave us the silver award, not the gold award. I came out of left field. They weren't ready for me. Proo does very good submissions and they came and it blew their mind. They couldn't believe that anything like this could be done. They'd already decided who the winner would be. It was a native garden but not an indigenous garden. It had to be a sustainable garden. The winning garden was more sustainable than a rose garden, I had to agree with that.

'So then I entered the next year and took out the gold award. They recommended us to the "Open Garden" scheme, so we became part of that.

The judges for the award commented, *'An extraordinary garden, a rare example of properly managed bushcare, flora restoration and conservation of local native plants. An interesting highlight was the successful pollination of native orchids. The passion and commitment of the owners to the project over a long period of time is an inspiration and example to all who are lucky enough to visit and learn by instruction and example.'*

'I did that (the Open Garden) for 6 years until I thought I'd pushed it as far as I could. Proo entered me in the ABC "Gardener of the Year" award and they sent a note saying they thought there should be a documentary made on it, but they couldn't give me the award.

'I couldn't get on "Gardening Australia" because they're a little bit afraid of me. I'm so far to the left that even the left wing don't want to know me!'

Oddly enough, on one occasion, even something as innocuous as Wirrapunga attracted comment designed to undermine it.

'When I had one of the Wirrapunga open days, I put on my web-page that people would be able to see this weekend, Thelymitra irregularis, which is the spotted pink sun orchid. According to the book I quoted from, this species is extraordinarily rare, with only nine accepted sightings in SA since settlement. That was a quote straight out of the book.

'This bloke puts something up on my web-page saying that he's a member of the Orchid Society of SA. He says, "These aren't that rare, we see one at least every decade."

'I answer with, "Thanks, here am I trying to raise money for conservation and you stuff it up."

He replied, "Sorry about that, I didn't realise where you were coming from."

'If he had said, "We only see one of these every ten years. This is an extraordinary opportunity, you should all go along and see this." But he didn't. He had to be derogatory. Why?'

If John errs on the side of finding 'Reds under the bed', maybe he's on to something. Australians are supposed to be notorious for tearing down their own high achievers.

John's land is now the only place within a wide area where the original system of plants is on display, including the beautiful tussocks of Mount Lofty Ranges mat-rush, the so-called 'native grass' which remains green through most of the summer (and doesn't burn like the introduced grasses which dry up completely). Right down to the edge of the road, the weeds have been painstakingly removed to give the indigenous plants a chance. The adjoining verges are all carpeted with exotic species.

'The miracle of life is so incredible.' John says. 'How all these things fit together. Then you understand that evolution did it all. The rules of evolution are so simple. Of course there's life on other planets around the universe. Whether or not there's stupid life like what we've got here I don't know!

'We've only had a very short time and we'll probably only last a very short time. There will be an extinction and we'll start again, I suppose. The rules of evolution say that life just has to start in a very primitive form. The offspring tend to take after their parents. There's a variance in species and a selection process. The whole thing's unbelievable and yet it's so simple. It gave us what's out there over a few billion years.'

How john has managed to immerse himself in the smaller world of his own block of land is best explained by these words, 'So I learnt I didn't have to go all over the world to find incredible things happening. I just had to wander out in my back yard.'

## CHAPTER TWENTY-THREE

# IDAWAY

SOMEHOW, WHETHER BY SHEER UNCONSCIOUS chance or by virtue of a reputation which precedes him, John manages to attract difficulties which he must overcome in order to live in peace.

Idaway was purchased as a haven from the stresses and disappointments of the ESL years. A final refuge where John and Proo could sojourn with the nature they so loved.

The record of obstruction to their plans reads like a repeat of the past, even though the intent was not to build an earth sanctuary but to create a simple getaway. What comes through in the events is the same maverick determination on display in all of John's dealings with life at large.

He has chronicled the events thus:

'After retiring from Earth Sanctuaries Limited we decided we needed somewhere to relax and recuperate. Both of us were literally worn out. It goes without saying we loved the Australian bush. In her book, 'Seven Australian Youngsters', my younger sister said I always 'wanted to be a hermit and live in the bush' and since Proo grew up at Wirrabara we headed for the Flinders Ranges. We purchased 500 hectares of bushland in Beetaloo Valley in the southern Flinders Ranges east of Port Pirie. This was in May, 2005.

'Before the purchase we checked the Port Pirie Council Development Plan to ascertain that we would be able to build a cabin on the land. If we weren't able to build we wouldn't have made the purchase. The idea was to relax away from the hustle and bustle of suburbia. We called this paradise Idaway.

'The latest Development Plan for the region, dated 10th March 2005, had just been published. Our block was in the 'Ranges Zone'. The Ranges Zone was divided into two sub-zones – Policy Area 17 named the 'Conservation Policy Area' and the Policy Area18 named the 'Agriculture Policy Area'. For us the important bit was under **Principles of Development Control.**

'Paragraph 9 stated, 'Tourism development comprising small scale, low impact farm stay, farmhouse, bed and breakfast hikers hut, cottage or bunkhouse style accommodation in a working farm eco-style atmosphere is encouraged.' On reading this we assumed it meant that a *hikers hut* would be *encouraged*. So! Naively we purchased the block thinking that we would be able to build a Hikers Hut of some form. We learned this was not to be the case.

'Access to Idaway is difficult. The property consists of three blocks of land which are referred to as the eastern block, the western block and the southern block. Once upon a time there was public road access to each of these blocks. The Roads (opening and closing) Act sets out very clearly when and how a public road may be closed. However, when the Morgan-Whyalla water pipeline was built the road to the western block was lawfully closed. When SAWater took over the Beetaloo Reservoir they closed (I suspect unlawfully) the public access road to the eastern block. This meant the only remaining public access to Idaway was via a public road leading off Mills Road, Beetaloo Valley, traversing land owned by a farmer called Bill Fradd, and then forming part of the boundary to Idaway.

*Unlawful locked gate across public road, Beetaloo Valley*

Beetaloo Valley is an interesting place, sort of 'past the end of the road'. Left behind as the rest of the world moved on. It would be surprising to find anyone living there who wasn't born there and the few that do, including Proo and I, would find they were not welcome. Even the police were reticent to go into the Beetaloo Valley. But that will come later.

'I signed a contract to purchase a cabin kit and applied to Port Pirie Council to build a "Hikers Hut". Three neighbours objected. One argued that the power lines would be a fire hazard. A second argued that they were not able to build anything on their block so neither should I. The third argued that he didn't want masses of tourists travelling across his land. The Council argued it should not be built as it was Council policy that no development whatsoever was allowed on that block of land.

'It turned out that nobody in the Port Pirie Council had read their Development Act under which our cabin was a desired development. An Act of the SA Parliament has precedent over Council Policies and so we gained approval for our cabin.

'There was never any intention to have power connected to the cabin, given that the cost of connecting to the grid was $60,000 versus $2,000 to go solar. Nor did we intend to develop the block as a tourist attraction. Our whole reason for purchasing the block was to *get over* the tourism endeavours.

'Probably the rarest plant in South Australia and maybe even in Australia is the spiny daisy, *Acanthocladium dockeri*. The Foundation for Australia's Most Endangered (FAME), the foundation I started to help save Australia's biodiversity, were funding the recovery plan for this species. Since the species was indigenous to the Beetaloo Valley I decided to plant a patch of them at Idaway.

'The residents of Beetaloo Valley did not understand why someone would buy 500 hectares of bushland and do nothing with it. Clearly there was something going on they didn't understand. Now I had fenced off about a hectare of land and planted mysterious plants in it. Surely he was up to no good. The police contacted me and told me they suspected drugs were being grown on the property and they wished to investigate. After I gave them permission I heard no more.

'My son Shane and his partner Alison had two daughters and they loved visiting Idaway, but it was a bit cramped in a cabin built for two. To take some pressure off the cabin I decided to build a 'shed' which they could use as a base when visiting. So! Back to the Development Act. In 2009 it had been amended. Paragraph 9 now stated, 'Tourist accommodation should be confined to existing dwellings in the nature of a farm stay or bed and breakfast accommodation, be located within the Mount Remarkable National Park or, if outside the National Park be sited within 100 metres of the Heysen Trail.' Basically, no development whatsoever was allowed on the Idaway block. This was going to be harder than I thought.

'After reading the Development Act one must go on and read the Development Regulations. After the Development Regulations comes the Schedules and then Schedule 1A deals with Development that does not require development plan consent. Bingo! I applied to Council to build a shed. They said, 'No development whatsoever is allowed on your block'. So I supply them with a copy of Schedule 1A of the Development Regulations 2008. Council gives me approval to build a shed.

'After building the shed I received a letter from the Port Pirie Council dated 28 March 2014. It read, 'Re: unlawful development – Sections 314, 315 and 373 Hundreds of Napperby, Warnertown'. Apparently a second cabin had been built. Has someone built something somewhere on the 500 hectares of bush that I don't know about? No! A neighbour is upset that someone has built a shed when he has been told he cannot. If only he'd asked me, I would have happily told him how to build a shed. Anyway, a Council officer inspected the site and I received a second letter stating, 'The Officer found no evidence to suggest the site had a second cabin. On this basis, there is no breach of the Development Act 1993 and therefore investigation into this site has discontinued.'

'I applied to build another shed and got approval.

'In February 2014, Proo and I were asleep in our cabin at Idaway. At about 1am Proo's smart phone received a message. It read, 'Fire emergency – evacuate immediately.' Having lived most of my life in areas of high fire danger I wasn't greatly moved but Proo insisted that we go out on the verandah and look. It was an amazing sight. It looked like the sun was rising in the north. The Sky was red. It was clear that behind the hill immediately to our north there was a real fire. The problem was that the only track out was to the north. It was certainly eerie driving towards a massive fire not knowing whether you were going to make it or not. But! John and Proo are still here.

'The fire burnt out the whole escarpment. It burnt out the whole 500 hectares except for a couple of hectares where the cabin and sheds were built. There was a reason for this. I had selected the area for the cabin very carefully. It was next to a water trough. This meant the kangaroos spent a lot of time there so there was no undergrowth on the small clearing the cabin and sheds were built on. From my point of view this meant the fire caused us no damage. The bush would get over it. The escarpment had been totally burnt out 60 years ago and, no doubt, it would be burnt out again in another 60 years. Unfortunately we (as a society) have never bothered to try to understand our bush.

'I thought no more about it until I received a call from a neighbour informing me that he wanted me to pay for the boundary fence to be replaced. Idaway had lost about 15 kilometres of fence. If all the neighbours wanted me to pay half then I was up for quite a sum. Accordingly, I made a claim on my insurance. The insurer appointed someone to handle the matter and I told him I didn't want anything, but asked him to sort it out with the other neighbours. This he agreed to do.

'Natural disasters are very interesting events. When the disaster actually happens everyone helps everyone else. It is good to see society functioning. It makes one think that society isn't too bad after all. Then the bucket of money is put on the table and greed takes over. It is no wonder I tend to opt out.

'Being fascinated with all species of life I learned, at an early age, the concept of predation. I understood the ideas of high order predation versus lower order predation. The concept of predation in the case of *Homo Sapien,* our own species, is a bit harder to understand. We are, after all the highest order predator of all, but we tend to hide it. We personally don't do the killing except in some case such as going fishing. Normally we buy our dead animals already quartered and dissected.

'However, there are other forms of predation. When we occupy land and don't allow the life forms that lived there before, we are predating. When we destroy insects that annoy us, we are predating. When we steal from others, we are predating. When we are corrupt, we are predating on our fellow species by taking what rightfully belongs to others. As such we are one of those species who predate on their own.

'The bullying and abuse I received at boarding school and the corruption I encountered among public officers were clear examples of this. The first police officers at Newcastle I had to deal with were corrupt. The Newcastle building inspector was corrupt, as was the Newcastle government rent officer and, more recently, Stirling Council plus various government officials. You may say this was in the past and things have changed but let us fast forward to the present. The only public access to Idaway was via a public road from the Beetaloo Valley.

'After the fire burnt out most of Idaway, BlazeAid came and rebuilt fences including two across the public road accessing Idaway. No longer was there any public access to my land. My neighbours had taken the opportunity to steal my land and fence me out.

'My first reaction was to ask the landholder involved if a gate could be placed in the fence to give access. The neighbour replied no, that he neither needed nor wanted a gate in his new fence. He reinforced his argument by ploughing up the road and planting a crop on it so that even if a gate was inserted in the fence it wouldn't give access. He then issued me with a fencing notice claiming that I should pay him $5,771 for boundary fencing, including the fence across the public road built by BlazeAid. I complained to BlazeAid but they weren't interested.

'Next I complained to the Northern Areas Council, who replied saying they would look into it. And so the argument went on and on. The Port Pirie Police acted very strangely. For some reason they didn't want anything to do with the Beetaloo Valley. *I spent three years trying to gain public access to my block.*

'The neighbour's action was listed to be heard in the Port Pirie Magistrates Court on the 7th April 2016. A notice on 3rd March said I had to 'file and serve a list of all documents that are relevant to any issue in the proceedings'. However, it didn't tell me what I was defending. Therefore I had no idea what to lodge. A woman at Port Pirie Magistrates Court said she was surprised the documents didn't give me this information and she advised me to get legal advice.

'Wandering down the street I saw a sign that said, 'Boylan Lawyers', so I went in. After a long wait and much discussion I was shown into an office and introduced to Ms Shelley Anderson. I gave Shelley Anderson the Notice of Directions Hearing together with all documents filed with it. She said she had no idea what it was about. I told her that was why I was there. She said either she or I would have to go to Port Pirie Magistrate's Court and find out what it was about. Of course I had already attempted that and she would have to do it. She said she would do it and then advise me on what to do. The day before I had to lodge my response with the Magistrates Court I still hadn't heard from Shelley so I rang her. She said she had looked at it but that she thought it would cost too much to read it all, so she hadn't. Therefore she couldn't advise and I would just have to do the best I could.

'Having no idea what my neighbour was on about I decided to lodge whatever I wanted. So I submitted the documentation I had on the fence that had been built across the road, denying me access.

'I attended court. The magistrate disqualified himself saying he had done some work for me in the past. The case was adjourned to 10th November 2016. I received an account from Boylan Lawyers. I refused to pay and after a while they accepted that.

'I sought publicity over the incredible state of affairs that existed. I owned this wonderful paradise but couldn't enjoy it because someone had unlawfully closed the only public access road. Most said they didn't believe me. They said that this just couldn't happen in Australia. One journalist published the story online but it quickly disappeared from the web after complaints from the Northern Areas Council staff.

'I saw a number of other lawyers. Their advice was all the same. Something like. Look! This is not happening. It cannot happen in this country. You have absolute right of access. If you pay me a large sum of money I will sort it for you. I complained to the local Member of Parliament, Geoff Brock. What a waste of time he was.

'I complained to the ombudsman. The ombudsman then telephoned and said that in her opinion I had access (since the Northern Areas Council *said* I had access) and the case was closed. So! Here I am still with no public access to my block. The only hope was the Magistrates Court. The second magistrate adjourned the case saying it was too complex for him and that he would appoint an appraisal expert.

'The expert reported back to the magistrate pointing out that there seemed to be some confusion about which block was which and basically stated to the magistrate the facts as they actually were rather than what everyone assumed they were. The Magistrate ordered the landholder to give me access and further I should pay my neighbour nothing. After three years, public access to my land had been returned.

'I sit in my favourite chair on the verandah at Idaway, watching the many birds and animals come in to drink and bathe at the water trough, surrounded by bushland. It takes me back to when, at just ten years old, I told my younger sister that all I wanted to do with my life was to be a hermit and live in the bush. I got it pretty right. Why would anyone want to do anything else in this crazy world?

The last three years had been pretty tough. If the Bangor fire hadn't happened. If my neighbour hadn't wanted to steal my land. If BlazeAid had been a bit more responsible. If I had walked into the office of a competent lawyer. If the police did their job. If the local council had been a bit more competent. If my local member of parliament had done his job. If the ombudsman had done her job. *If.*

## CHAPTER TWENTY-FOUR

# TODAY

JOHN'S HOUSE IS ONLY A short drive from the Mount Bold reservoir catchment, so it was natural he spent time wandering around that area, the more so after his duties with ESL ended.

'As part of doing Wirrapunga I was interested in what does exist out there in our bush, so it started when I used to walk in the SA Water land but they told me I wasn't allowed in there anymore. So I went over the road into the Scott Creek Conservation Park. I used to wander around in there. Basically trying to get a handle on how things worked. That's where I decided what you need to do to get orchids established. I wanted to know how the bush looked after itself.

'One day I was walking through and there was a car parked there with a sign saying "volunteer" on the side. There was no one around but when I came back one of the 'Friends' of Scott Creek was there.

'I was interested in the fact that the park was being looked after better than, say, Mylor Conservation Park. I could see the difference. It wasn't degrading quite as fast. So I sat down next to him and had a chat. I asked him a few questions and I thought it would be interesting to be part of it. So I joined the group.

'I was happy to go along with what they were doing. I didn't want to stick my nose in. I didn't go there with the intention of changing their concepts or anything. I got to go into all sorts of places within the park

I hadn't seen before. Tom (the late Tom Hands, who ran the group) was very good. He showed me which plants were which. He was a wonderful bloke. But I used to constantly question him on why he was doing what he was doing. He said it was no good giving people jobs to do that would only make them give up. He gave them things to do that they would like going to.'

'I was constantly distressed with the creek systems there. They were deteriorating and I didn't like that. At Almanda creek I said to Tom, "Why don't we do this creek? It's the only permanent creek in the park and it's full of blackberries." I knew Fox Bog (a formerly permanent wet area) was in trouble. It was drying out and something had to be done if we were going to save those plants. He told me the resources weren't there.

'So I asked if I could do it and I started doing that in my spare time as well as going to the working bees.

'Then we had a day when we went down to another part of the park and were working on a hillside. Except for the occasional boneseed daisy the bush was pretty good. And I was thinking to myself, "The creek at the bottom of this is going to be fantastic." And when we got to the creek it was full of blackberry. Tom had got there at about the same time and I said to Tom, "What the fucking hell is this?"

'He said, "It's blackberry."

'I said, "I know it's blackberry! But why is it here?"

And his answer was the same as before, namely, "We don't have the resources to do it."

'If we go back a bit. When the government started Scott Creek Conservation Park in the seventies, a ranger lived on site and the budget for a ranger would have been in excess of two hundred thousand dollars. The budget gradually reduced and in 2013-2014 it was zero. It was the first year they got zero. Nothing. Not one cent did that park get in that year. It sort of shocked me because I'd assumed they were still getting *some* money and it shows you why we're losing our biodiversity. The government isn't willing to do conservation. It was interesting how about that time Alan Holmes, who was the head of the department of environment was retiring and he made a speech one day and he said, "There will be no more money for conservation in SA and if the community wants their conservation parks looked after, then the community will have to look after them."

'So all this was happening at the same time and I said to Tom, "How much money do you need to look after this park?" And he gave me a figure. It was $20,000 per year for ten years. I said I would raise the money on a couple of conditions. The work had to be done properly, a botanist was to audit what we were doing and an annual report had to be compiled to show what we were doing each year. Tom said okay to that.

'It came out in conversation that Tom had just put in an incredible effort making an application for funds. I got him to email it to me so I could "jazz" it up a bit and make it acceptable to the public, because it was written for public servants. That's where it started.'

Tom's grant application, written in partnership with Tim Drury, morphed into the 'Almanda Report', because John was fascinated by the name, Almanda. Following the zero budget allocation of 2013-2014, the amount of money available in 2014-2015 for conservation work at Scott Creek was over *$50,000*. The disciplined approach, detailing the group's objectives, paid huge dividends.

'That chuffed Tom no end. He couldn't believe it.'

The government funding continued to come for bush care projects at Scott Creek, perhaps because of the accountability inherent in the 'Almanda Project' approach, where our work was quantified and put on an evidence-based footing.

'I showed that if people were serious about conservation they could raise the money.'

With a grin, John says, 'I don't know what will happen now because I'm sort of worn out. I don't want responsibility anymore. I figure I'm getting close to eighty (years) and I couldn't be bothered being responsible.'

Part of John's efforts involved crowd funding. 'One of the things that interested me and sort of showed me the impossibility of doing anything was that I sent an email to basically every politician that had anything to do with SA. All the senators from SA in the federal government, all the members of the SA parliament and the Prime Minister and Deputy Prime Minister. Anyone who might be interested. I sent a letter to all of them setting out what we were doing and asking for a two dollar donation. Out of two hundred people *only three of them sent a donation*. Those people are Penny Wright, Michelle Lensink and Anne McEwen. This demonstrates that political allegiance is irrelevant (a Green, a Liberal and a Labor).

Barnaby Joyce couldn't see his way clear to give us two dollars. The Prime Minister couldn't see his way clear to give us two dollars. None of our local members around us could see their way clear to give us two dollars. The Premier couldn't see his way clear to give us two dollars. And I thought, "Why the fucking hell do I try if these bastards whose job it is to look after this country couldn't give a stuff?" So it sort of let me down a lot on that.

'The other one that let me down and made me decide I didn't want responsibility anymore was there is a group in Australia who are there to administer grants. A registered group made up of people who give grants to charities. And I sent them a thing on it setting out exactly what we do and they have as their members literally hundreds of groups, including every conservation group in Australia. All of them got a request for funds for the Almanda Project and not one of them gave a cent. Not one cent. So I thought it's just mad, the whole conservation thing in Australia is stupid. Just stupid.'

Hand-in-hand with this fund-raising is the story of the plant which John has called 'Almanda Blue'. Unique things seem drawn to John and Almanda Blue is truly unique.

'What happened was that when I started doing the Almanda Creek, Tom said, "There's some interesting plants down here. A Pratia (now called Lobelia) grows here. So we battled through the blackberries and ended up in the creek. He reckoned that was where it grew and we looked and looked but there was no Pratia, there was nothing. He came up with this pinch of mud and he said, "Here's one," and he put it in my hand. There was nothing in it. I'm sure he was bull-shitting. I don't know.

'I brought that home and I planted it out there in the garden, in a little bog garden I built to save riparian plants. And this plant came up but it was a water cress (a weed) so I pulled it out and threw it away. I sort of lost interest and then I looked one day and there's a plant growing there in the little stream. But I figured it wasn't happy in that stream so I moved it out of the stream, just onto the bank, and it grew. It grew these bloody long runners. And I thought that was strange.

'So I potted up some of them and that was Almanda Blue. I tried to find out what it was and nobody could tell me. You assume that government departments are there to help you and to do their job but they're not. They're just there because they get paid to be there, that's all. And if you take a plant down to the SA Herbarium to get it identified and it's an unknown plant, they won't tell you it's an unknown plant because you're not a botanist. You're not allowed to have unknown plants. They've got a default position in case they don't know what something is. So it came back that it was Pratia pedunculata. I know what Pratia pedunculata looks like and it wasn't that.

'So I fiddled with it and I looked things up and one of the things I discovered was that you can register these plants, if you've got a new variety. So I registered it. And they came and looked at it and I had to do trials and the experts came and looked at it and I had to write it all up. Then I got this phone call from them. They asked if I knew what the parent plant was and I told them it was Lobelia (formerly Pratia) pedunculata. They told me it *wasn't* Lobelia pedunculata. And I said, "I'm sorry, but if you take it down to the herbarium in Adelaide and ask them what it is they'll tell you it's Lobelia pedunculata. That's all I can tell you. I'm not going to argue with someone who has a degree in Botany." So they said I'd have to send it to an expert in Canberra, which I did. And it came back that it looks like it's a new species. An undescribed species. And until it is described it could be called Lobelia pedunculata.

'In the first year we had it I grew quite a lot of them and sold them. We raised four or five thousand dollars for the Almanda project. I don't know what I'm going to do with it. I've taken out a US patent and an Australian patent.'

The new species is a peculiar plant. It grows runners which bear a mass of blue flowers, but these runners die back after about a year or so and no more flowering runners appear. Thus it is possible to get a beautiful display of tiny, cascading flowers from a hanging pot but only in the first year. To get a plant with flowering runners again requires that a new plant be propagated from the runners. Nurseries may not know what to make of this plant, unless it is marketed as a kind of annual.

With his inventor's ingenuity, John devised a watering system specifically for Almanda Blue, because, being a riparian species, the plant likes to keep its feet wet. The system involved an elevated dish attached to a water supply with a float-operated valve.

Almanda Blue is still under investigation to determine its suitability as a commercial species. One day it may proudly take its place as a nursery plant, propagated in its thousands and all derived from the fistful of mud Tom Hands lifted from the Almanda Creek. It's John's idea that its sale will raise ongoing funds for conservation work at Scott Creek.

In line with his habit of constantly pushing the envelope of possibility, John's next idea is to get Open Garden Scheme recognition for the Friends of Scott Creek open day walk along a section of the Almanda creek and through the Almanda swamp. This is asking a lot of the Open Garden organisers, because a piece of bushland within a public park has not been recognised as a 'garden' before. Wirrapunga was a long way from the traditional ideal of a garden, but restored public bushland takes it to another level.

The Almanda Creek work has become a significant, separate project in its own right.

Such are the changes which have occurred along the creek it is impossible to picture the scene as it was just a few years ago.

The regenerative powers built into the fabric of the natural world have stunned us all with their elegance.

Blackberry, which once blanketed the entire length of the creek, has been reduced to occasional seedlings or small shoots from the few tough rhizomes remaining.

On the elevated banks above the creek, fast growing colonisers like native Geranium and Senecio have taken advantage of the light and space. Native orchids have returned, even in places where the mat of introduced grasses would seem to make it impossible for them to grow.

Many indigenous grasses have also managed to survive in spite of incursions by vigorous, unwanted species. New arrivals of species are regularly noted. Native lillies, buttercups and violets, Acacia seedlings and ferns among many other species jostle for room with the beautiful grasses.

In lower places, alongside the permanent, flowing waters, riparian species have all but pushed out the usually ubiquitous, invasive plants. A wealth of sedges, rushes and ferns line the pools where native fish are thriving.

The creek is a hot spot for uncommon or rare species, including the dominant Manna Gum Silky Teatree Woodland Community itself.

The various sections represent an interesting progression from a 'battle zone', immediately after slashing and poisoning of blackberry, to a recovering community where the indigenous species can help repress the exotics.

The lesson to be taken from this work is that a very small number of people can facilitate the processes of the natural world so that the earth itself does most of the work.

John calls it 'gardening' rather than bushcare and one day 'gardening' may be synonymous with this kind of work, rather than being an activity in pursuit of maintaining an exotic ecosystem.

Lastly, John believes we need to be clear about what we are doing. It is not enough to simply remove weeds. That is not an end in itself. We are motivated by our values and the value we espouse is the preservation and enhancement of biodiversity. It has never been possible to argue the practical worth of such a pursuit, but it is lately becoming clear the earth may be at a tipping point as we lose species whose interrelationships we have not even begun to understand.

## CHAPTER TWENTY-FIVE

# FINAL THOUGHTS

JOHN SAYS, 'NOBODY'S EVER SAT down and said, "What do we want the world to look like in 200 years' time?" Nobody would think of saying that.'

Completely true.

Happiness is surely everyone's goal, yet we all have a different vision of what it would mean to be happy and for many, or even most people it has little or nothing to do with the natural world. Indeed, most of the world's people can't afford the luxury of contemplating the natural world at all, except in so far as they need to exploit it to keep from starving.

Herein lies another part of the problem in conservation. We cannot expect people to share our concerns about saving species while those same people barely subsist and by the time we manage to give everyone within an irrationally expanding population a reasonable standard of living, it may be too late to save anything.

John shared a little of his inner thoughts about the future of the world and while it reveals a definite trend towards pessimism, this is alongside his undying commitment to hands-on nature conservation and perhaps this is the true measure of all who work for the earth, that they do so in spite of the odds.

'*Once we destroy ourselves,*' he says, 'the earth will evolve. The earth won't think very badly of us having been and gone. It will get on with itself, doing what it knows best, which is evolution. And I guess it doesn't matter. I don't know. This is where I have great difficulty because *nothing matters very much and very little matters at all*. "Nothing is good or bad but thinking makes it so" (Shakespeare). It's true in a way. But I don't know. Isn't there fundamental good? I don't know. It seems to me there is something that's fundamental about good things.

'Our duty is to give the next generation a choice. If it's gone, then they haven't got a choice.'

Choice is the key. It can be validly argued that modern man is a 'natural' agent of management in the same way that indigenous man was such an agent. Indigenous peoples have no doubt brought about enormous changes to the landscape of most continents, but without mechanisation and because of a need to preserve species for food, their alterations to the ecosystem allowed for great diversity.

We have sophisticated technology, machines and mechanised farming. It is within our power to produce a landscape filled with just a handful of adaptable species. Again, it is down to choice. We can *choose* to lose most of our animals, plants, insects and the microorganisms which support them, or we can maintain such diversity as still remains.

Scientists recently announced that more than fifty percent of all the earth's wild animals have disappeared in the last forty years. This is a terrifying statistic, yet it scarcely rated a mention in the media.

Likewise the revelation that not only are all the world's oceans, from pole to pole, polluted with micro-particles of plastic, with ramifications we don't even yet understand. Now we learn that most of the world's fresh water is similarly polluted. Again, it rates only a tiny, fleeting mention in the news media, along with the disgraceful fact that Queensland has the second highest rate of land clearance on the planet behind Brazil.

Sometimes I feel that civilisation is sleeping, and that one day it will wake up and realise what it has done, but that will be far too late.

John said, 'My life has been about running into problems and solving them or running into opportunities and trying to take advantage of them. There are moments in your life when you have to decide what you're going to do.

'I think I always knew that life doesn't have a meaning. I never cared what others thought of me. The only thing which worries me is what *I* think of me. So I think that's what makes me do what I do more than anything else. I don't think helping Homo sapiens is of any benefit to anything. There's an oversupply of them in the world.

'The only thing that ever matters to me is t*hese wonderful communities that evolution gave us.* Communities of living organisms which we're happily destroying as quickly as we can.'

I asked him why the communities of living things were important to him.

'I don't know. It's the only thing I can look at and say, "There's something that's a miracle," if you like. There's something that's somehow absolutely worthwhile.

'There's certainly not a meaning to life that I can understand. There's a meaning to *how* you live. It's not a meaning, I suppose it's something to do with being able to sleep at night. I've got very strong convictions on how we should treat other living things as well as Homo sapiens.'

John reiterated his concerns about corruption in society, the concerns that arose way back in his time as a property manager.

'I've got very strong anti-corruption beliefs. I think corruption is the biggest problem the world faces. When it's all boiled down, that's what's wrong with Homo sapiens. They have nearly a necessity to be corrupt. Life's about problems and opportunities. There aren't many people, it would appear, who can bypass the opportunity to be corrupt, if it pays to be.

'Should we be happy because our politicians aren't quite as corrupt as politicians in some other countries?'

On the environmental 'debate': 'People make up their mind and then they look for things to win their debate. *We shouldn't be winning debates, we should be trying to save our environment.*

'We've got to start with what we know and what we know is that there is a way of saving Australia's wildlife in the short term with fences, so we have to get on with it and do it.

*'And if some time in the future you work out a better way to do it, it wouldn't be hard to put holes in the fences.*

'Scotia was really the demonstration that it could be done. The bridled nail-tail wallaby was presumed extinct for forty years. A small colony was found in Queensland. Scotia has 90% of the world's population of this species. I suppose just for that it makes it all worthwhile, even without the other stuff.'

Species were taken off the endangered list while Earth Sanctuaries was in operation and perhaps directly as a result of it. This is a stunning achievement, yet I doubt that it is publicly recognised and applauded. The astonishing thing, to my mind, is that the *way* to save these animals was, physically, such a simple thing. It came down to providing a safe place for them to breed. But this didn't mean confining them in cages, where artificial pressures make it hard for them to behave the way nature intended.

The Australian bush is exquisitely suited to proliferation of the animals which evolved alongside it. *The animals made the bush and the bush made the animals.* All John really did was to remove the elements which weren't part of the original evolved system.

The most monumental principles derived by science are often capable of simple expression.

The final sell-off, after the ES Link merger, showed little respect for John's legacy in the original sanctuary of Warrawong. The birthplace of true wildlife conservation in Australia was treated as a cash cow.

'ES Link started selling off its blocks. I understand they sold Little River for something like $6 million. They offered the Warrawong blocks at about half a million each and sold five of them. So they bought the company for $4 million and sold it for $10 million.

'*Nobody gave a stuff about the animals.* Least of all the Department of the Environment. The last of the Sydney species of the red-necked pademelon, what happened to them?

'The 'core' part of Warrawong was three titles, ostensibly purchased for conservation purposes at a cost of $1 million, but after a while two of the blocks were sold for half a million each and the other block was sold for $1 million. The zoo then leased it.

'So Warrawong was ultimately sold for $6 million and I wasn't allowed to buy any of it.'

The commercial carve-up of Warrawong is difficult to accept in itself, but worse than the profit-driven sale of blocks is the disdain shown for the wildlife so lovingly nurtured by John and Proo. To this day the fate of the animals is unclear. John was correct. *If we value something at zero then no one will bother saving it.* Not even the government.

The silence surrounding the fate of platypus at Warrawong is the most baffling aspect of this end-game. Platypus are, arguably, the most extraordinary living creatures on the face of the planet. We were privileged, here in SA, to have them reintroduced, via John, to the mainland. Yet there is neither concern nor any legal protection for them.

The Adelaide zoo had care of them but the zoo ultimately couldn't make a commercial success of Warrawong.

'Fancy owning the only platypus display in SA. When you look at what they're doing with pandas and what they weren't willing to do with platypus, it shows basically the problem the zoo has.

'That's the story of our government departments, they don't give a stuff about anything.'

I must confess to being perplexed by the way that a huge amount of money, presumably from government revenue, was spent to set up a panda enclosure, yet we have not even chosen to remember that there is a rare platypus population on our doorstep.

John says, 'Each year one or two baby platypus escape though the fence at Warrawong and are eaten by foxes. These animals, if protected, could bring in millions of dollars to help save our endangered wildlife.'

The logic is inescapable.

John has the advantage now of hindsight to analyse what happened to his dream.

'It's alright to say you should be happy with little things. If I was just doing it from the point of view of giving Proo and I a happy life and we had just stuck with Warrawong it would have been fine. It would have given us a very good retirement and a very interesting life.'

Remember that at its peak Warrawong attracted 50,000 visitors in a year. This figure would have grown over time and as more infrastructure became added to the sanctuary. It had the potential to be the biggest tourist drawcard in SA, rivalling Tasmania's Mona for its unique status and cultural importance.

'I thought at first that just having Warrawong would demonstrate what *could* be done and that others would do it, but they didn't. So I thought, well, I have to do it, and I believe very strongly in the fact that if you find yourself in a position where you *can* do something that needs doing, then you have an obligation to do it.

'And so I did it, the best I could. But it wasn't good enough and I accept that and you could say, maybe it's not possible to be good enough. I don't know that anybody *could* do it. I don't know, because you're talking about a lot of money and people who have a lot of money didn't get it by being conservationists. They got it by destroying everything they ran into, basically. So it's not a simple matter.'

John's reflections vary from one interview to another, depending on how fatalistic he is feeling. I asked him if he felt that he had let anyone down when the company folded.

'No. No. I'd given it a pretty good shot. None of the shareholders have complained. When I see them they're all still proud of the fact that they were shareholders. They all tell me with pride, "I used to be a shareholder." I've never had anyone say, "I'm one of those people you took down."

'It was good to do it. I enjoyed myself thoroughly doing it.'

There are still regular shareholder get-togethers with John and Proo and John is rarely out of the local paper for long, being sought after for his opinion on everything from possible platypus sightings in the Sturt Gorge to possible (and highly improbable) Tasmanian devil sightings or new developments at the old Warrawong site.

Warrawong finally has genuine conservationists as its new owners. David Cobbold and Narelle MacPherson, who hail from Western Australia, where they operated Peel Zoo near Perth. There has been a lot of media and community interest in the reopening of the sanctuary. The public response to a volunteer clean-up day at Warrawong was overwhelming, with a large crowd of people turning up. Few things are so South Australian or generate such pride as Warrawong, yet as with the bad old days of early private involvement in conservation, there are people who still seek to oppose it.

A crowd funding campaign to raise money to buy back the land with the main platypus dam was going well, having raised thousands of dollars, when a couple of people used facebook to undermine the funding drive, effectively bringing it to a halt. The sentiments expressed sought to cast doubt on the viability of the new endeavour by linking it to the demise of the original. Fortunately, the owners are not deterred, but it shows how some entrenched, misguided and puzzling ideas can still manage to surface in spite of the passage of one and a half decades.

John was shocked to find that David and Narelle thought he would not want to see them and this impression was, again, the result of false information on social media. But the wheel is turning.

The local paper has been very supportive. A recent article put Warrawong on the front page with a large colour photograph of the owners, employees and volunteers. The article read:

'Distance is no barrier for Warrawong. Let the animals come to you in their new mobile wildlife sanctuary.

'In anticipation of Warrawong's re-opening, owners David and Narelle will bring "edutainment" to schools, workplaces and events throughout Adelaide.

'Warrawong 2U is about providing everyone with the opportunity to interact with and learn about Australian wildlife.

"It's about developing an appreciation for Australian wildlife." David said. "We're brought up on a diet of foreign animals. We know about lions and elephants but we don't know much about Australian animals and it's a real shame.

". . . At the moment we're working with several species such as ring tail possums, squirrel gliders, kookaburras and rufous bettongs. New animals will be introduced to the program on a continual basis."

'Warrawong also welcomed on board its first full-time employee.'

The property containing the large platypus dam has now been repurchased and the reticulation system John built to circulate water through the dams and wetlands was restarted by John at an official ceremony. John's involvement in Warrawong is once again significant. In a similar reversal he was recently invited to speak at Yookamurra's anniversary celebrations.

There is a kind of duality in what John thinks about the current state of affairs in nature conservation and his ongoing involvement. On the global scale, this is what he has to say:

'It's quite bizarre, what's been happening. *People don't even know what conservation means anymore.*

'Maybe I'm just old-fashioned. The guts of it all is that if you go back 10,000 years before Homo sapiens decided to take over like they have, every bit of the world evolved as a special community of living organisms. It gave us incredible biodiversity all over the world. And now to say that we as Homo sapiens are trashing all these communities, one at a time, down they go, and we're going to continue trashing them until not one of these communities is left intact. To me it's an absolute disaster and I couldn't allow it to happen if I thought I could do something but now I accept that I've got to allow it to happen because I can't stop it and nobody else is going to stop it from happening. And so that's it.

'I still do the best that I can with the little resources I've got and I'll continue to do that, not because I expect to get anywhere but I wouldn't be able to sleep at night if I didn't. That's all.'

And everything John did was about 'problem solving and discovering things'. He jokes that this memoir could be called 'My Life as a Scientist'. He is adamant that it wasn't *for himself*. First came mathematics problems, followed by saving Australia's wildlife from extinction, the restoration work at Wirrapunga, restoration at Scott Creek and finally the ongoing fate of the land at Idaway. In each instance he pushed as far as he could before moving on to something else.

And this: 'You don't teach science, you help people discover it.' Like Proo, John is a natural educator.

'And when I'm dead,' he says, 'all that will be left is this memoir.'

On the extinction of species, John is adamant that it doesn't happen for no reason. He has invented a new English word, *extincted*, to denote that *we* are bringing about the disappearances.

'We, Homo sapiens, have *extincted* these species. It's got to be known that *we* are doing it. It's not some natural means.'

This word gives us ownership of our actions. *We* have extincted the toolache wallaby, the desert bandicoot, Gould's mouse etc etc. All of the 30 species of mammal that have disappeared from the face of the earth since European settlement.

'We have examples where language is built in such a fashion as to make a political statement. "Extinct" is an adjective. We say a species has "*gone extinct*". There is no verb. We cannot say, "We have extincted the species." No! That may mean we (*Homo sapiens*) did it.'

A current article in the Guardian newspaper deals with the very indifference which John has always railed against.

'The environment and energy department's annual report for 2016-17 shows that of *1,885 listed threatened entities* (i.e. animals and plants) in Australia, just 712, or 38%, were covered by recovery plans that are in force.

'Many recovery plans are just fantasy documents because they're not implemented.'

'A further 176 species and ecological communities were identified as requiring recovery plans but didn't have them.

'Species without a recovery plan are now expected to have what is known as a *conservation advice*, which is typically a shorter document, sometimes fewer than five pages including references. *It has no legal power to compel Australian governments to protect a species*, they only have to *consider* it when making approvals under the EPBC act.'

An Adelaide paper very recently contained a two-page spread, with colour photos of the 'Top twenty endangered species in Australia.' I will say that again. *The top twenty endangered species in Australia.* Enough said.

I sought a way to finish this account of John Wamsley and I was determined to end with a note of hope. Such hope lay in one of John's legacies, the foundation he created and now going by the name of F.A.M.E.

Already to its credit, among numerous other ventures, is the project to reintroduce the western quoll to the Ikara Flinders Ranges National Park. These animals have not been seen in the region for 130 years. In conjunction with the SA government, this represented *the first public-private partnership for conservation in SA.*

But the latest and most ambitious scheme muted by the government involves the 're-wilding' of the southern part of South Australia's Yorke Peninsula. 'Re-wilding' is a new buzz-phrase coined to describe the re-introduction of animal species into areas from which they have been historically excluded (both within Australia and overseas).

The idea is to build a feral-proof fence across the narrow bottom part of the peninsula and introduce locally extinct species back into the wild. Re-introduction is not just for esoteric purposes but as a means of benefitting farmers through creating a better balance of wildlife in which, for example, native carnivores can reduce the impact of mouse and rabbit populations on crops.

This 250,000 hectare proposal would create *the largest feral-fenced area in Australia*. It is eerily redolent of John's vision.

But what appeals to me most is the extreme but fortuitous irony inherent in the government's appeal to the private sector for help.

John spent his energies battling to get government help for his wide-reaching ideas at a time when the government didn't want private people involved in conservation.

We have moved through 180 degrees, so that now the government is courting private, not-for-profit organisations like F.A.M.E, *which John created*, in order to implement its plans.

Whether John accepts it or not, there is an enduring legacy from his time with Earth Sanctuaries. It is true that no one has yet come up with a means of combining profit-making private enterprise with pure conservation, but it is now common to see private initiatives in this work, albeit as charities. The bulk of wildlife conservation efforts in this country now come from private bodies. These are now the norm in the conservation landscape.

John's feral fencing has become the standard way of protecting wildlife. An Australian Geographic article gave late recognition to John's revolutionary thinking, naming him one of their 30 conservation heroes, to mark the magazine's 30 years of publication.

**30 YEARS OF** AUSTRALIAN GEOGRAPHIC

# John Wamsley

He was the prime minister's 2003 Environmentalist of the Year, but this controversial conservationist is probably best known for his feral cat skin hats. Regardless of whether or not you agree with his methods, John made Australia sit up and take notice with regard to the nation's appalling mammal extinction record (the world's worst); 30 species and subspecies, mostly marsupials, have become extinct since Europeans arrived. Many of these extinctions are linked to cats and other feral species. John was instrumental in getting the law changed so that people wouldn't be prosecuted for shooting feral cats. He was the first property manager in Australia to fence off feral-free enclosures to protect wild-living native animals, such as bilbies, from feral predators.

*Part of the Australian Geographic article. John with the last Yookamurra fox (now stuffed).*

If you can inspire and motivate people, so that they emulate what you have done, then you have not failed. If you can change a culture, you have not failed. And if you have saved even one species of animal from extinction, you deserve a spot in history.

Private involvement is now entrenched within our psyche and this owes its beginnings to what John and Proo did. I cannot think of any other people or ideas which have had such an impact on conservation awareness in Australia.

If you want a list it is easy to make one, starting with gimmicky protests and ending with a dream: Feral plant awareness, feral animal awareness, feral proof fencing, rabbit eradication, numerous successful reintroductions, platypus bred in captivity and reintroduced to mainland South Australia where they had been extinct for decades, nocturnal wildlife tours, the Earth Sanctuaries Foundation, the first (and only) publicly listed company in the world with wildlife conservation as its core business, the beginning of private conservation in this country, the opening up of an awareness about the interaction of living organisms within a community and the first natural bushland to be accepted under the Open Gardens Scheme.

Just how far ahead of his time John's actions were is neatly illustrated in a letter of support written to the Adelaide Hills local paper nearly thirty years ago:

> *How unfortunate that Dr Wamsley remains a voice in the wilderness. If his words were to fall on some influential ears perhaps we would create a more favourable environment, not only for the animals but for ourselves, with less severe droughts and dust storms. In view of some of the latest predictions for this planet, any scheme which offers an end to the current spate of destruction of the earth's resources has to be worthy of serious consideration and urgent action.*

It is sobering to think this kind of public debate existed before terms like 'Climate Change' were in vogue.

Feral-proof fencing is once again in the spotlight as the Australian Wildlife Conservancy expand John's concept into larger areas. What is not generally known is that John built AWC's first sanctuary, Karakamia, in Western Australia and AWC owe their existence to his work.

Finally, I accompanied John on a walk through Warrawong as it currently stands. I expected it to be a rather haunted and nostalgic experience, but I was not prepared for the apparently 'wild' beauty I found, as John's plantings have assumed the guise of natural, temperate forest, albeit with many eastern species. The fallen timber and towering trunks assumed a character only time can instil.

But the best was to come, as we stood at the dam after hearing a disturbance in the water on the other side.

Right on time, like an apparition or a messenger, a platypus appeared at the surface, floating, fully exposed and still, while we drew our breath in wonder. I had waited all my life for such a sight. The outline of this animal allowed no other interpretation, so well did it match the numerous photographic images which were all I previously possessed.

John is once again involved with Warrawong in its new incarnation.

'Perhaps at eighty years of age,' he says, 'I can now enjoy my bush.'